WASATCH
Summer

To Marilyn & Jim

a novel

ANOLA PICKETT

Anola Pickett

BONNEVILLE BOOKS
SPRINGVILLE, UTAH

ISBN 13: 978-1-59955-481-5

Published by Bonneville Books, an imprint of Cedar Fort, Inc., 2373 W. 700 S., Springville, UT 84663

Distributed by Cedar Fort, Inc., www.cedarfort.com

LIBRARY OF CONGRESS CATALOGING-IN-PUBLICATION DATA

Pickett, Anola.
 Wasatch summer / Anola Pickett.
   p. cm.
  ISBN 978-1-59955-481-5
1. Mormon pioneers--Fiction. 2. Cache Valley (Utah and Idaho)--Fiction. 3. Child labor--Cache Valley (Utah and Idaho)--Fiction. 4. Historical fiction, American. 5. Bildungsromans, American. I. Title.
 PS3616.I285H36 2010
 813'.6--dc22

                          2010035657

Cover design by Jen Boss
Cover design © 2011 by Lyle Mortimer
Edited and typeset by Melissa J. Caldwell

Printed in the United States of America

10 9 8 7 6 5 4 3 2 1

Printed on acid-free paper

Wasatch Summer is for my great-great-grandmother Naomi, an American Indian whose native identity is unknown. Wherever she grew up, I hope that she and someone like Hannah became friends.

ACKNOWLEDGMENTS

I owe a tremendous debt of gratitude to several people who helped Hannah's story come to life:

When I visited the Mormon Visitor Center in Independence, Missouri, Stacy Jorgensen Bevan greeted me at the door. A native of Cache Valley, Stacy gave me verbal descriptions of the area and shared a Jorgensen family story about one way to chase off a bear. Hannah uses their method in the story.

Utah sheep rancher Charlie Young patiently and cheerfully answered all my questions about summer grazing.

Darnell and Smokey Rides At The Door provided information about aspects of Blackfeet life that I hadn't even thought of, helped me with phonetic pronunciation of Blackfeet words, and encouraged me to finish the book. I'm especially grateful to Darnell for reading the finished manuscript and pointing out changes to make my portrayal of the Blackfeet more authentic.

To the men and women who care for the Pioneer museums in Utah and Idaho. They preserve artifacts, written records and oral family histories of the pioneers who settled the area. Guelda Clayson, Richmond DUP Museum; Joan Woodward Bennett, Franklin Relic Hall; Virginia Park, Cache Museum; Patricia Record, Logan Library; and many other Cache Valley folks generously shared their knowledge of the valley's history.

My Wednesday critique group walked with me chapter by chapter through Hannah's story. Their warm support and helpful criticism guided my journey with Hannah. I'm grateful to Judy Hyde, Barbara Stuber, Sue Gallion, Judy Schuler, Laura Manivong, Victoria Dixon, Lisha Cauthen, and Tessa Elwood, who were with me from the first word to the last.

My son Gerry and husband, Peter, are always there for me. They share my love of the written word and encouraged me to bring Hannah's story to life. Thanks, guys!

And, finally, to Heavenly Father and the Creator for a sustaining inspiration and guidance.

One

"Contemptible. C-o-n-t-e-m-p-t-i-b-u-l. Contempt-ible." That word sucked all the breath out of me.

"Incorrect," Miss Taylor announced.

Fiddlesticks!

Matthew Colton flashed me a grin of victory. We were the last two standing in the Friday spelling bee. I seldom made it that far. I could spell any old word on paper, but when my tongue went to say letters out loud, it jumped way ahead of my brain and tripped into some careless mistake.

Suddenly the schoolhouse door banged open, and Uncle John's tall frame filled the doorway. His grim look pushed my mind from spelling over to worry. He spoke quietly to my teacher.

Miss Taylor frowned. "Hannah, gather your things and go with your uncle."

I hurried to the cloakroom, pulled on my coat and

scarf, snatched my dinner pail, and rushed to the doorway. Something was bad wrong.

My classmates watched in silence.

Outside, Uncle John untied Zeke and climbed into the saddle. Without a word, he pulled me up behind him so quickly I thought my arm would snap off.

"What's wrong, Uncle?" My cheek pressed against the scratchy wool of his coat.

No answer. Zeke broke into a full gallop, and we tore through the cold, gray morning. The mountains edging our valley blurred into snow-topped walls.

I thought about our family's trials the past year. Crops had failed. My brother Caleb left to work in Montana. Papa died in January, and we sent word to Caleb. He didn't come home or write. It was near time for him to take the sheep to the mountains for summer grazing.

Sure that some new sorrow waited at home, I shouted into the wind, "What's wrong?" I'd about had enough of misery.

His sharp words cut through the freezing air. "Your ma's got birthin' pains."

This news shivered through me. Mama's babies did poorly at first. Four of my sisters died before they were weaned. They were buried on the hill with Papa.

Uncle John's voice cut my shivers short. "Aunt Margaret needs your help."

I sat straighter. When my sister Catherine was born

two years before, the women had rushed me away to wait in the kitchen with Papa. Now I could help!

Minutes later, I ran into our house and rushed past the parlor to Mama's room.

She lay huddled on the bed, eyes closed, forehead knotted with pain. Catherine fussed in her crib nearby. I bent to kiss Mama's cheek, but she didn't seem to notice. Why was the room so gloomy? Mama loved sunshine. I went to open the curtains.

"Hannah!" Aunt Margaret caught my hand. "Your mother needs dark and quiet."

"But Mama likes her room bright," I protested.

"Child, you don't know a thing! Take Catherine to the kitchen and bring some towels. John's gone to fetch Sarah Colton. When she gets here, she'll heat the kettle."

I brought the towels, settled Catherine in her crib near the warm stove, and then stepped back into Mama's room. My aunt nudged me to the door.

"But I want to help!"

Aunt Margaret clucked her tongue. "You'd just be in the way. Birthin' is work for women. You tend to Catherine. Soon as he's finished feeding our stock, John'll come look after the two of you."

This miffed me considerable. I didn't feel the need to be "looked after" like my two-year-old sister, but there was no arguing with Aunt Margaret. When she declared the way a thing should be, that was that.

I moped by Catherine's crib until Sarah arrived. Ever since Papa died, Sarah had worked with the Relief Society to make sure we had enough to survive the winter. She'd even seen to it we had livestock feed. Without her help, we might have lost our sheep.

Shortly, my aunt appeared in the doorway. "Hannah, come here!"

I jumped up. Now I could be of some use!

"Go finish your ma's chores. Bundle up Catherine and keep her with you until your uncle comes back."

I stepped outside to the sound of my aunt's nagging. "Make sure the ewes are sheltered, and don't drop the eggs again!"

The day before, I'd skipped to the house with my basket of eggs. I forgot the shaded spots where sunshine hadn't yet melted the winter ice. My boot slid into a slippery patch and tumbled me to the ground. Three eggs cracked open under me. Mama was set to use those eggs for corn pudding. That night she had made me write *Look before you leap* fifty times.

Now I called back, "I'll be careful, Aunt."

I scuffed at the snow as I trudged toward the barn. Catherine toddled behind me.

"No, Hannah, you can't help. This is women's work!" I mimicked Aunt Margaret's nasal singsong. "Take Catherine. Do the chores. Don't drop the eggs!" As I kicked a frozen clod of manure, heavy steps thundered behind me.

"What're you muttering about?" Uncle John said.

"N-nothing." Had he heard me imitating his wife?

"I'll take Catherine inside. Hurry and get your work done." He scooped up my sister and perched her on his shoulder.

I straggled on to my chores, followed by three barn cats yowling for food. "Go catch yourself some mice," I hissed.

When I got back to our warm kitchen, Uncle John sat by the window, playing horsie-ride with Catherine. She giggled as he bounced her on his foot.

My uncle looked up as I sat at the table. "I've an appetite for biscuits, Hannah. Reckon you can mix up some?"

"Soon as I can, Uncle." Mama tried hard to teach me her recipes, but I'd never done biscuits on my own. I wished I'd paid more attention.

Flour . . . lard . . . salt . . . sugar . . . milk. I measured best as I could remember and slid the pan into the oven.

While he waited, Uncle John went outside to fix a loose porch railing. I settled with the Aesop's fable book Grandma had given me for Christmas. I'd about finished "Androcles and the Lion" when Aunt Margaret shouted, "Glory! What's burning?"

I'd forgotten my baking! I pulled a pan of flat, charred biscuits from the oven. I scraped the black away and smeared butter to cover the damage.

Uncle John wrinkled his nose when he came in.

"Hannah, you 'bout burned the place down right while your ma's birthin' a baby!"

The biscuits tightened my jaw and puckered my lips. *Fiddlesticks!* I'd left out baking powder and added an extra dose of salt. I braced for my uncle's complaints, but he gobbled up my awful baking without a word. Only a few dark crumbs decorated his plate. Mama claimed if a man was hungry enough, he'd eat most anything. I reckoned Uncle John was hungry enough that morning!

"I'm leaving now," he said. "Got a broken wagon wheel to fix."

I played with Catherine while the women bustled in and out, fetching towels, heating water, and making sage tea. No matter how I begged, Aunt Margaret wouldn't let me see my mother.

I ran to my room upstairs and pulled my charm string from under the pillow. On the way back to the kitchen, I slipped it into my apron pocket. Mama said I'd meet my true love when I'd strung one thousand buttons and charms. For now, having my chain close was a comfort. I went back downstairs to wait for the baby to come.

Whenever Mama let out a heavy moan that near tore my heart, I patted a button and asked Heavenly Father to help her. Morning dragged to afternoon. The winter sun sat low in the sky when Mama's moaning turned to quick, heavy groans. She gave one mighty scream, and a baby's cry burst from the bedroom.

"It's a girl, Elizabeth!" Sarah announced. "With a fine head of black curls!"

Catherine and the new baby had Papa's dark hair. Mama and I were blondes. Matthew Colton called me "strawhead," but Papa said Mama and I wore crowns of sunshine. Remembering his words made my eyes fill.

"Come, Hannah," Mama called.

Blinking back tears, I walked to her bedside. She lay flushed and smiling, her hair spread across the pillow. She held a tiny bundle.

"We'll call your new sister Alice for Grandmother Turner."

Mama held my hand as we thanked Heavenly Father. "Please bless our new baby and keep her healthy."

Then I ran to the hillside graves to tell Papa and my sisters the happy news.

Two

One Monday morning in April, Miss Taylor made an announcement. "We've been asked to sing at the Centennial Day celebration."

Everyone talked at once, their words tripping over each other. Girls right off chattered about what they'd wear. Boys mostly wanted to know if there'd be good treats. It was an honor to be in the program. April 30 marked the 100th anniversary of George Washington becoming president of the United States. Utah wasn't yet an official state, but *The Logan Herald* reported there would be celebrations all over the territory.

"I've chosen Hannah Turner to sing the solo."

Everyone turned to look at me, and I wanted to slip through the floor crack by my desk. I heard Matthew Colton guffaw.

"Pardon?" I asked. Surely I'd not heard my teacher right.

"You will perform the solo."

I squirmed. How could I sing alone in a hall crowded with grown-ups? It took all my courage to stand in the Friday spelling bee. If I mixed up spelling letters, what awful blunder would I make with the words of a song?

At noontime my best friend Molly Tuttle and I sat under the oak tree at the edge of the schoolyard. Molly chattered away as we opened our dinner pails.

"I hope Ma makes me something new for the celebration. My Sunday dress is way too tight across here." She pointed to her chest. Molly was near thirteen, more than a year older than me.

I was still flat as Mama's griddle. I seemed to grow *up* but not *out*. Mama would probably let down the last growth stripe in my one good dress. "If you're getting a new dress, *you* should sing the solo," I told Molly.

She giggled. "Me? I draw pretty pictures, but I can't sing one note right!" She nudged my arm. "You're the one blessed with a heavenly voice."

I frowned. "Matthew Colton doesn't think so. Did you hear him snort when Miss Taylor said I'd do the solo?"

Molly's hand fluttered like she was swatting at a fly. "Matthew's just having fun."

"He's hurtful," I insisted.

Molly smiled. "My brother Aaron used to act ignorant around girls, 'specially girls he liked. Now he's right mannerly. Maybe Matthew's sweet on you."

My face heated up. "Take that back!"

That afternoon, I was still so fussed at Molly thinking Matthew liked me special that I walked home alone across the fields. By the time I reached our front porch, I decided being mad about a silly boy wasn't worth losing my best friend.

Molly and I hugged our way back to friendship the next day and traded buttons to seal our harmony. I gave Molly one made of scrimshaw ivory, and she handed me a pretty cameo button.

I spent every minute of April fretting over my solo. I made no claim to the Turner gift for music. God had blessed my parents with musical talent. Papa could play any number of instruments and Mama charmed heavenly music from our parlor organ. They both sang like angels. My fingers struck false keys. My voice cracked on low notes. How could I sing alone before a crowd?

Mama wound my snarled hair around woolen rag strips the night before my ordeal. "You'll have a halo of long, golden ringlets."

Looking pretty wouldn't make up for sounding awful! "If I forget the words or hit a sour note, everyone will laugh."

Mama jerked a rag hard enough to shake my brain. "It's an honor to be chosen. If you ask Heavenly Father for help, you'll have nothing to fear. Facing a challenge you're not ready for will help with the next challenge sent your way."

I tried to puzzle out what Mama meant and hoped Heavenly Father remembered to help me.

The next evening, we rode to town in Uncle John's buckboard and arrived just in time. My throat clenched as we climbed the steps to the Sego Springs Church Hall. The place was so crowded that some folks had to stand along the back. My classmates were lined up along one wall.

"Mrs. Turner, sit here." Aaron Tuttle gave his seat to Mama and baby Alice. Molly was right about him turning polite.

We stood through two long orations and Brother Johansen's prayer. I was one big fidget by the time Mrs. Lewiston finished her fancy violin piece. Then it was our turn.

Miss Taylor led us to the stage. When we'd finished "Come, Come Ye Saints," the class went back to stand along the wall. I trudged to the front of the stage on legs so wobbly I thought I'd pitch right over into the audience. Miss Taylor played the opening notes. My throat closed up. I couldn't squeeze out one sound.

My teacher smiled and played the notes again.

Somehow I began. "Mine eyes have seen the glory of the coming of the Lord . . ." I caught sight of Matthew pinching his nose like he smelled something rotten. My innards knotted up, but I managed to finish the song. On the last note, I ran behind the stage, crying with relief.

The damp night air promised rain as we rode home. My family's praise mixed with the sound of horse hooves clopping along the dirt road.

"I didn't think folks would ever stop cheering for you," Uncle John said.

"Your Papa would have been so pleased, Hannah!" Aunt Margaret exclaimed.

Mama squeezed me tight against her. "You did us proud," she whispered.

But all I could think of was Matthew Colton's ugly gesture. How could he be so mean? Latter-day Saints were supposed to be kind.

Three

A week later, school was out for spring planting, and Uncle John laid in seed for our fields. The ewes had lambed, and our small herd now numbered forty-one. Catherine loved seeing the "wambs" feed from their mothers. Soon someone would take our sheep to the mountains for the summer so that our crops could be safe from their hungry mouths. Until then, I tended the herd. This chore mainly took care of itself, thanks to our dogs, Rosie and Shep.

Tending the chickens was a different matter. They had their own minds. I knew I should love all God's creatures, but those birds sorely tried my patience. Near every day, a hen ran off to lay her eggs and sit on them in secret. We needed every single egg to sell or eat, so I had to search bushes and barn corners for hideaway eggs.

All through May, something worrying hung in the air. Nothing seemed to please Mama. She even snapped at baby Alice. My mother and Uncle John took to talking every evening after supper. When I'd come near, they'd fall quiet.

I was walking back from the barn one evening when I heard my uncle talking loudly inside the house. "Elizabeth, there's no other way."

Mama's voice cracked. "This'll end with me losing another part of my family!"

I ran to my tree swing and pushed myself through the warm breeze. What did Mama mean about losing part of her family? Was Catherine sick? Baby Alice?

Mama's call interrupted my questions. "Hannah, come inside. Your uncle and I want to talk to you. Hurry, now."

I dragged my foot against the hard ground to stop the swing, dreading whatever waited for me. Life without Papa and Caleb left a hole that had filled up with sadness and extra work. Was there room for one more misery?

"What are you doing out there?" Mama's voice snapped my mind to attention.

"I'm coming." I trudged toward the house, but then I spotted a little green lizard I'd seen yesterday by the pump. It skittered across the ground and disappeared under a thistle plant. I poked the leaves with a stick, trying to coax it out again.

"Hannah Turner, stop your lollygagging!" Mama's voice sounded plumb worn out.

The air inside our farmhouse hung heavy and serious. Mama's mouth thinned into a tight line, and her long fingers picked at her apron. Uncle John looked straight ahead, his face stern and set.

My heart lurched. "What's wrong?" I sank into my rocker and stared at the pink roses trailing across the wallpaper.

"You tell her, John," Mama said.

Every part of me, teeth to toes, clenched into knots.

Uncle John frowned. "It's near time to take the sheep up to the summer range, and Caleb's still away."

I nodded. I'd been wondering who'd take his place with the sheep.

"Your uncle will work our fields along with his own," Mama said, "plant our crops, and care for the livestock. We need extra help from you, Hannah."

I already did the milking and washing up. I fed our animals and gathered eggs. Helped with the cooking and tended to my sisters. Emptied the chamber pots every morning. What else could I do? "I'll weed the vegetable garden, Mama," I said. I swallowed hard and added a chore that I sorely disliked. "I'll even beat the carpets."

My uncle shook his head. "We need you to do more."

I studied the wallpaper roses. What more could I do?

Mama's voice sounded hoarse, like she had a bad cold. "There's no other way. You'll take the sheep up for summer grazing."

I gasped. Tend the herd? Alone with the dogs and sheep? Instead of a summer at home, I'd have months of loneliness in the mountains above Cache Valley.

It was too much.

"I can't manage that by myself," I protested.

"There's no one else," Mama said. "We can't lose our sheep. We need them for our livelihood." Her voice was thin as sewing thread. "Tending them in the high country will be the same as down here."

"But it *won't* be the same," I said. "I won't have family in the mountains. You'll be down here. If something goes wrong, you can't help me." I'd never been away from Sego Springs, except to visit Grandma Swenson's farm a few miles away. Now I faced a whole summer with no friends . . . no sweet little sisters. Worst of all, I'd be without Mama. "I'll be alone."

"You're never alone. Heavenly Father is always with you." Mama's gaze stayed on her hands, and her voice was whispery soft.

I considered her words. If I asked Heavenly Father to be with me in those mountains, would He really keep me company? He couldn't play games with me like Molly or tell me stories like Mama. I kept those thoughts to myself.

"'Sides," Uncle John said. "Rosie and Shep will keep you safe, and they'll be good company. Shep's worked the summer grazing since he was a pup. He'll let you know if you do something wrong. I'll take you up to the sheep camp and bring fresh supplies every week. The days'll speed along. In a blink of an eye, you'll bring the flock down to clean the fields after harvest."

An eyeblink? A whole summer was enough time for serious mistakes. Papa told me over and over that I rushed into things without thinking. "Look before you leap," he'd say. I shuddered. What if I forgot to look first up there?

I turned to my mother. "Mama, I want to stay here with you. Please."

Last fall, Mama made me a promise: "Come summer, I'll teach you to spin and dye the yarn. Then we'll weave it into cloth."

I reminded her of that promise.

"I'm sorry." Mama studied her hands. "You're the only one we can spare for the summer grazing." She stood up quickly and stepped outside.

My uncle cleared his throat. "Listen to me, Hannah."

The roses blurred as I blinked back tears.

"Things are bad enough without your family losing more. The sheep need to summer in the mountains so the crops can grow. You know how important this is."

I nodded. It'd do me no good to disagree.

I fell asleep that night clutching my charm chain. I rubbed the tortoiseshell button to let out its dead fish smell. The awful odor reminded me of the summer ahead.

Four

The next day I was washing up at the pump when I saw Sarah Colton walking toward our house. Matthew lagged behind her, toting a gunnysack. The way he struggled along, you'd think Matthew was pulling two hundred pounds. With a loud grunt, he dropped the sack on our porch.

Mama came to the door. "Morning, Sarah. What a welcome surprise. My little ones are asleep, and I just put some bread to rise. I was fixin' to brew some peppermint tea."

"A fine idea, Elizabeth," Sarah said. "Could you use these potatoes? We had such a big crop last year, I just couldn't use them all up, and it's planting time again."

"Thank you, Sarah." Mama lifted the sack so easy, it might have been full of feathers. "They'll be put to good use."

For sure, we'd have fried-up potatoes for supper. Sarah had brought us a share of her family's food. She knew we faced hard times, and she was helping us the Latter-day Saint way.

As soon as the two women stepped inside, Matthew pinched my arm. "Come on. I'll show you how to swing proper."

I pulled away. "Race you to the tree!" Even though Matthew was some older than me, I could outrun him. I reached the swing first. Planting myself on the wooden plank, I pushed off. By the time Matthew caught up, I was soaring. "Here's how to swing proper!" I shouted as the breeze pressed against my skirt.

Matthew grabbed one rope and yanked it back and forth. The swing jerked around like a wobbly top. I tried to hold on as best I could, but my fingers slid down the rope. My hands burned something fierce as I slipped off onto hard ground. A rock scraped against my left elbow.

"Thought you could swing proper!" Matthew bent over double, laughing at me.

I blinked back tears. "I can do something more important," I snapped. "I'm taking our sheep up for summer grazing."

"You?" Matthew laughed harder. "You're just a girl. A scaredy one, at that. You think you're like that gal in New York who wants to be a prizefighter?"

Miss Taylor had read us an article from the *Logan Herald* about this. "Shameful!" our teacher had declared. "Boxing is not a fit sport for young women."

Matthew listed more failings. "You can't even thread a worm on a fishing hook without getting all squirmy. You screamed like a baby when Billy Smithson jumped out from the school privy in a ghost get-up. Anyways, girls can't tend sheep. They're supposed to cook and sew and—

"Do whatever needs doing!" Sarah had come up from the barn with Mama. She knuckled Matthew's head. "Hannah's a good, strong girl who helps her family."

"Yes, ma'am," Matthew mumbled. "Sorry." Red-faced, he stared at the ground.

When our mothers were out of earshot, Matthew said, "You really taking the sheep to the mountains?"

"That's right." For a minute, I forgot my fear of being alone, about keeping the flock safe, or forgetting to look before I leap. I felt proud that my family had given me such an important job.

"Ain't you afraid Indians'll sneak up at night and steal your sheep?" he asked. "They might even steal *you*."

"Our dogs will protect me."

"Hunh! They're herding dogs. Shep's so old, he can't hardly walk. What if there's bad weather? Sometimes it snows up there in the summer. You thought about coyotes? Or mountain lions? Wolves? Snakes? There's a mean bunch of bears up there. You gonna take your pa's rifle?"

"I-I'll be fine," I stammered. "Papa taught me to shoot." That was true, but I hadn't fired a single shot since he died.

Matthew guffawed. "Shoot what? Fence posts? Your pa's old hat? That ain't the same as wild animals charging you or Indians on the warpath. If that happens, you'd shake too hard to pull the trigger."

"I'm a steady shot," I insisted, though I'd never really hit a moving target. "You just aim to scare me."

"What if you get the tissick?"

"Tissick!" I snorted. "I know enough to cure a cough!" Did he think I was ignorant?

He stuck his face so close that I could see an egg smear on his chin. Why couldn't he bother to wash himself proper? "The Bear Lake monster could get loose and mosey on up to your camp!"

Ever since I could remember, I'd heard stories about that monster. I wasn't pleased to be reminded of it, but I wasn't about to let Matthew know that. "How could it climb a mountain? It's a water creature." My trembly voice revealed the lie to those brave words.

"You can't never be sure what a monster'll do. 'Sides, don't you know bad luck comes in threes? You already had two. I reckon number three's waitin' in the mountains."

"And just what are those two?" I demanded.

"One, your pa's passing. Two, ruining the President's Day celebration."

I shook my finger in Matthew's face. "You should be ashamed, talking about Papa's dying like it's just some piece of bad luck!"

Before I could say more, Sarah called that it was time to leave.

As soon as the Coltons left, I ran inside to ask Mama about the rifle.

She sat in the parlor, nursing Alice. Mama hummed one of her made-up tunes and stared out the window. The afternoon sunlight turned her hair gold.

I sank to my knees next to her. "Mama, when I take the sheep up, will I need a rifle?" Maybe she hadn't thought of the perils that might require a weapon. Surely my question would change her mind about sending me into the mountains alone.

Mama nodded. "You'll need it for protection, what with all the wild critters roaming the hills. It's good your pa taught you to shoot."

My hopes flew away like leaves in an autumn wind. I moved through afternoon chores without thinking. I was cross with Catherine. Supper had no taste. I sat on the porch until dark, staring at nothing.

Worry about the months ahead kept me awake all night.

Five

For the next week, we spent every spare minute getting me ready. Mama made a new bed tick and stuffed it with strips of dried corn husks that Sarah had collected from our neighbors. I'd sleep on a summer bed softer than my old straw tick.

I'd need no church clothes this summer, so I mended my two everyday dresses. I patched the oldest one with bits from Mama's scrap bag. As I stitched a torn hem, I frowned at my old doll, Liza Lou. "No use taking you. A sheep camp's no place for a doll. 'Sides, I've got to be all grown up now."

Uncle John made a sturdy cage for the two laying hens I'd have for the summer. I'd start out with a few eggs packed in cornmeal. The cool mountain air would keep them fresh until the hens started laying again.

The night before I left, we loaded the camp wagon with dishes, a skillet, and some kettles, along with blankets and my rocker. Tins of salt, baking powder, and flour filled the storage boxes, along with bags of potatoes and beans. I made sure I had a good supply of raisins and dried apples and brought along a jug of Aunt Margaret's honey. Mama hung a broom, washboard, and tub next to the door. She handed me a coil of rope. "For a clothesline."

My uncle tethered firewood bundles to the camp. "This'll do you for a week. Use the ax if you run out."

I stared at the wood. This summer I'd cook my own meals. There'd be no one to tell me I'd stoked up too much heat for stew or not enough for biscuits.

Mama piled sheets and blankets on top of my new tick. "In the morning, bring your feather pillow and Grandma Swenson's quilt. You'll welcome the extra cover. More often than not, a mountain night can feel like winter." She had already packed my overcoat and an old pair of Caleb's leather work gloves. Mama reached in her apron pocket. "You can't share my hairbrush this summer, and you'll need something to tame those snarls. Here's your pa's old brush."

I held the unexpected gift to my cheek. How many mornings had I watched Papa use it to smooth his hair? The bristles still held a few dark strands.

Before going to bed, I added my sewing basket, Bible, and Aesop's fables, along with two of Molly's animal drawings to decorate the wall above my bunk. I was sore tempted to take Liza Lou, but it seemed childish to need a doll for company.

We finished loading the camp as the last light dipped behind the mountains along the valley's western edge.

Clean worn out from packing, I climbed into bed for my last night at home. I curled up with Liza Lou in Grandma Swenson's quilt. Memories of happy times playing in the sheep camp flooded my mind.

When Caleb brought the sheep down and cleaned the camp, we stored it in the barn. Till the air grew too cold, Molly and I played house in the wagon. It was right cozy, with a sleeping bunk fitted into the back end under a window and a woodstove along one side. Sometimes we pretended to cook supper and eat at the drop-down table. The canvas roof reminded us of the covered wagons that some Saints drove across the mountains.

Last fall, Rosie birthed her puppies in the camp wagon. Five black-and-white fur balls huddled together in the bunk's far corner.

I wanted happy memories to help me drift to sleep, but Matthew's ugly warnings crept in. No matter which way I turned my summer, dangers stared back at me like the streak of light in my cat's eye button.

I got up well before dawn, holding Liza Lou tight. "I'm taking you with me!" I tucked her in the pillowcase along with my charm string and tiptoed downstairs. No one was about. I lit a lantern and stepped into the gray-blue morning. After I left my bundle in the camp, I hurried to the chicken shed.

The two hens I chose squawked as I loaded them into their summer coop. "I understand why you're complaining, but we're bound to go to the mountains today. You'd best be quiet."

They paid me no mind.

Before I went back in the house, I ran up to our hillside burying place to tell my father good-bye. "I promise to do a good job, Papa, but I'm scared clear through." I swiped tears away with my jacket sleeve.

At breakfast the coal-oil lamp made eerie shadows on the wall. Our meal was silent. Before I finished my oatmeal, Mama left to pack some salt pork and a round of cheese inside the camp.

Papa's wide-brimmed hat still hung from its peg by the door. I snatched it up and put it on. Its smell of sun and sweat would remind me to look before I leaped in the days ahead.

Outside, Catherine pulled on my skirt. I bent to kiss her. "You'll soon be running, Cathy. I'll teach you how to skip when I come back." I held Alice close. "I love you, little one," I whispered.

Our oldest cat, Turnip, slunk from under the porch. Purring mightily, she rubbed against my leg. Caleb had named her. "She's a turnip for sure," he'd said. "No matter what's going on, she'll 'turn up'."

"Mama, can I take Turnip with me?"

"No. We need her here. She's our best hunter." Mama went inside.

I bent to rub Turnip's gray fur. "I'll see you when the crops are in."

My mother called from the porch. "Hannah, your pa would want you to have this." She handed me his guitar.

My sadness exploded into tears. "I miss Papa!"

"I know." Mama stroked my head. "Crying won't help."

I clung to her waist. "I'm scared, Mama. I don't want to go! Please don't make me."

"If there was any other way, I'd keep you right here." Mama hugged me tight. "Remember that Heavenly Father will be with you every minute." Her voice trembled. "Just ask Him for help."

We walked to the camp, and I tucked the guitar into Grandma's quilt.

Mama pressed a small bundle into my hands. "Here's a linen piece and thread for a sampler. Working your stitches will be something to do in the evening."

Uncle John hitched Zeke and Lucky to the camp, and the dogs gathered the sheep. Nervous at being moved toward the road, the herd bleated loudly. The woolly stink of dirt and manure filled the morning air as they passed.

Mama held me. "Heavenly Father, bless my daughter and her work. Bring her home safe."

I sat on Lucky, and Uncle John walked alongside the camp. We turned toward the mountains.

We traveled down the road past the Tuttle place. Molly was visiting her grandmother in Logan. She had no idea I'd be gone when she got home. As we rode past the darkened house, I blinked back tears.

The horses plodded east across the valley toward the mountains, where the sun was spreading its first rosy light. Ahead of us, the dogs ran back and forth, keeping the sheep together. The ride was bumpy and slow.

This was my first trip above Cache Valley. I had always seen the mountains at a distance, silent giants rising from the fields, snowy in winter and covered with grasses and wildflowers in summer.

Each year Caleb brought Mama mountain wildflowers to use for dye. I offered to gather flowers while I was at the sheep camp. Mama promised to make a list, but she'd forgotten in the commotion of getting me ready.

When we began to climb the mountains, I felt dizzy to leave flat ground. Surely we'd topple onto a sharp boulder. Would that be Matthew's third piece of bad luck? I clutched Lucky's mane so tight, my fingers turned numb.

Late in the morning, we paused to rest and ate the chicken and biscuits Mama had packed. The sheep *baae*d as they nibbled early mountain flowers. A pair of mourning doves watched from a distance.

"Reckon they're waiting for our crumbs," Uncle John said.

The doves cooed in agreement.

I tried to spy our farm, but it had blurred into the valley's patchwork of crop fields and pastures. I couldn't keep my fears quiet. "Matthew Colton said Indians up here might steal me away." I didn't go into the rest of Matthew's danger list.

"True enough. Some Indian families summer in the mountains," Uncle John said, "but Matthew's wrong about them stealing you. If you're peaceable, they'll be the same. They're looking to survive, just like us."

"But Matthew was sure—"

"A person can be sure about something without having all the facts. Remember how folks in Franklin were certain they lived in Utah Territory? Turned out they'd been on Idaho land the whole time."

I nodded. Every Latter-day Saint knew that story, but it didn't offer me any comfort. "Being wrong about where you live isn't the same as paying danger no mind."

Uncle John nodded. "True."

"Why would Matthew tell me such a thing?"

Uncle John chuckled. "Sometimes a boy doesn't rightly know how to talk with a girl, Hannah. More so if he likes her special. He ends up talking sassy to cover up his soft feelings."

My face burned at that thought.

The sheep wanted to keep eating, but our dogs got them moving, and we continued our rugged journey. The sun was straight above when we came upon a shallow, sloping canyon. A thick pine grove offered the herd restful shade, and quaking aspens blanketed the hillsides. "The sheep will find plentiful grasses under those quakeys," Uncle John said, using his favorite name for the aspen trees that seemed to shiver in the wind.

The canyon floor had a level spot to settle the camp. Uncle John backed the wagon to the sloping canyon wall, leaving room for me to go in and out the door. A huge rock, flat as a tabletop, lay nearby. Across the canyon, a stream rushed down to the Logan River. I was pleased to have water close by.

"Be mindful of the stream," my uncle warned. "It's near to overflowing from snow melt. One good rain could flood it. Take the herd upstream to drink, where it's calmer. Sheep don't like stirred-up water."

Seemed I'd have to keep watch over more than the herd.

We moved the sheep to feast on undergrowth. Shep prodded wandering ewes, while Rosie eagerly worked the edges of the herd. The dogs barked out sharp commands, and the sheep obeyed.

Uncle John dug a fire pit near the tabletop rock, checked the cook stove, and filled my lanterns with coal oil. He hauled water and emptied it into the storage barrel.

I toted a bucket inside for cooking and washing up.

After we tied a clothesline from one tree to another, we sat to enjoy a dipperful of cold water.

Uncle John pointed to a nearby quakey. "See that rotted-out hole? It looks 'bout right for a chickadee home. They'll gather bits of sheep wool snagged on tree bark and bushes. Use 'em for their nest."

The prospect of a nearby chickadee home cheered me some.

My uncle stood. "You'll be right cozy. I put on a fresh canvas cover to keep you warm and dry in any weather— even a snowstorm." The sun's glow was slowly dipping toward the west. "Time to head home. Chores can't wait much longer. See you in a week." As he saddled up Zeke, he reached in his jacket. "Glory! I almost forgot." He handed me a packet of writing paper. "Your aunt thought you might like to write letters. I'll deliver them for you."

As I watched him ride away, I longed for him to leave Zeke or Lucky for extra company . . . and a way to leave if need be. I said nothing. Our horses were needed at home.

Uncle John disappeared around a turn in the rocky path.

I wouldn't see another person for seven days. Somewhere above me, a woodpecker beat out his steady rhythm on a hollow tree.

It seemed the loneliest sound I'd ever heard.

Six

Travel and unpacking left me bone tired. After the dogs and I moved the sheep to their overnight spot, I ate the last of Mama's chicken. I settled near the flat rock, planning to read from my Bible, but I couldn't find it anywhere. Surely I'd packed it. Had it fallen out along the way?

Thoughts of falling recalled the deep trenches my uncle dug to hold the camp wheels in place. He'd swung the shovel with a grin. "Now you won't roll down the hill!" Fresh worries. What if the wheels shook loose while I slept and smashed the camp against a boulder?

Stop thinking of danger! Instead, I listened to the sheep. They *baa*ed deep like my father's bass, and their tinkling bells reminded me of Mama's sweet soprano. I sighed and took up the guitar to try Papa's favorite hymn, "Come, Come Ye Saints." Papa believed mastering one song would unlock other melodies. So far, I hadn't learned a single tune.

I soon gave up. It was time to tether Rosie for the night. If I left her free, she'd badger the sheep like a schoolyard bully. Shep knew to leave the herd alone until sunrise, when the sheep were ready for a fresh grazing spot.

As I straightened up, a heavy growl rumbled from above. Goose bumps ran over my arms. I'd never heard such an awful sound. Was it a wolf? A mountain lion? Matthew's warnings came back to shake my mind.

I scrambled into the wagon and grabbed Papa's rifle. I crept to the farthest corner of the bunk and reached inside the pillowcase. My charm string was gone! Where could it be? I was too frightened to look outside. Instead, I wrapped blankets around me and Liza Lou and prayed I wouldn't need the rifle.

Sometime after the moon's light began to fade, I finally slept.

Still gripping Liza Lou and the rifle, I woke to barking dogs. Fussing hens and hungry sheep added to the ruckus. I untied Rosie, and the two dogs raced away to their work. I followed. When the sun grew hot, we'd move the herd again to the pine grove shade to rest and drink from the stream.

Fee-bee-yee. A chickadee flew by, carrying a bit of fuzz, and landed in the quakey hole. Quick as a glowworm's flash, the little bird fluttered out again. I smiled a welcome to my new neighbor.

While the cook stove heated up, I searched for my charm chain. Five years ago Grandma gave me a black button from an old coat for a touch button to start my string. I'd added thirty-eight more. Now the string was gone. My stomach churned at the loss.

After breakfast, I began a letter:

> *Dear Molly,*
> *It's so lonely up here. I feel like the only person in the whole world. I wish you were here.*

An idea came to me: why couldn't Molly visit for a week? She could come up with Uncle John and go home the following Saturday.

> *Ask your mother if you can—*

The dogs barked an angry warning that sent a shiver down my neck. I heard a horse neigh and looked toward the sound. My heart jumped. On a ridge directly above my campsite, two Indian men sat ramrod-straight on their horses. Silent and unsmiling, they fixed their eyes on me.

I had no place safe to hide. I'd left the rifle in the camp. Matthew's words about Indian dangers made my skin tingle.

I bowed my head. *Help me, Heavenly Father. Please!* If the Lord answered, I was shaking too hard to hear Him. Head down, I shuffled backward toward the camp. *One step . . . two . . . three . . . almost there.* A rock caught my heel and tumbled me hard onto my backside. I scrambled to the camp door and reached for Papa's rifle. Clutching the cold metal, I looked back to the ridge.

The men were gone.

I blinked. No Indians watched from above. Were they riding to my camp? I listened for the sound of horse hooves pounding down the mountainside. The stream gushed over its rocky bed. Wind rustled through the trees. I heard the chickadee's song and the sheep's complaints, but no sound of hoofbeats.

Miss Taylor's lesson about mirages came to my mind. People crossing a desert sometimes think they see water ahead. When they come closer, the sight of water disappears.

Had I seen a mirage of Indians?

No! Two men had watched me from the ridge. My heart pounded as I wondered why they'd left. Maybe they'd gone for help to steal the sheep. What would my family do then?

I looked again. The ridge stood empty.

After I prayed for help, the men were gone. Mama said every asking prayer needs a thanking prayer. I closed my eyes. *Thank you, Lord. Please keep me free from harm.*

I opened my eyes again and spotted a ewe wandering out of sight. "Shep! Get that stray!"

Shep stared hard at the ewe until she hurried back to the herd.

After a while, I stopped fretting about Indians. I

washed up in the stream and gathered sticks for kindling. Now what? If I had a bit of time at home, Molly might visit. We'd tie a rope to the porch railing and take turns skipping while Catherine watched.

Thoughts of Molly sent me back to my letter.

> *This morning, I thought I saw two Indians watching me. I reckon I imagined it. Remember my make-believe friend Josie?*

When I was four, my twin sisters were born small and sickly. Mama spent all her time caring for them, so I made up a play friend to keep me company.

I went on:

> *I have some musical neighbors. Chickadees are building a nest nearby. I hope they start a family.*

I put the letter away. The sun was overhead, and the sheep willingly followed the dogs' commands to shade and water. Soon their bleating stopped, and they slept.

After adding water to the beans I'd soaked overnight, I set out food for Rosie and Shep. They paid their dinner no mind. Instead, both dogs set up a fierce noise. Barked. Growled. Bared their teeth. Shep's fur stood in a sharp ridge down his back.

I turned to get Papa's rifle and saw the reason for their ruckus.

A group of Indians moved toward the camp.

Seven

Heavenly Father, please keep me safe!
The group seemed to float over the rocky ground.
Two women rode horses. One had a cradleboard hanging
from her saddle. Four small children walked close to the
women, along with a girl who looked to be about my age.
They moved slowly toward me.

I sank onto the rock and let my food tumble to the
ground. My insides wobbled like a bowl of Mama's pudding, not set firm. There was nowhere safe to hide from
these strangers. The canvas camp offered no protection,
and I'd left the rifle inside.

I sat paralyzed. Even my heart felt crippled. The group
stopped near the chickadees' tree. They made no sound as
they looked at me. *Why had they come?*

I stared at the ground, and my throat squeezed shut.
*Heavenly Father, protect me. Watch over the dogs and our
sheep. Keep us safe. And please show me what to do.*

Mama taught me that if I quieted myself, I could hear
God's voice. How could I listen to Him when I was shaking so?

Then something changed. The dogs stopped barking.

I looked up. Rosie and Shep sat quietly by the rock, watching the strangers.

I stole a look at the girl. She watched me, her dark eyes serious but not unfriendly.

Our gaze held for what seemed an eternity. No one spoke, but some understanding took place between us.

I had been brought up to welcome strangers. Mama always invited visitors into our house and served them peppermint tea. But Mama was a grown woman and had a proper parlor for guests. I was just a girl with two dogs and a sheep camp. I took a deep breath.

"Welcome." My voice wobbled.

The Indians nodded, and the two women dismounted. Their sleek black hair shone in the sunlight. The woman with the cradleboard was tall and lean. Her companion walked with a slight limp and seemed somewhat older. They gathered the children into a loose circle around my rock. The girl stood directly across from me.

The older woman patted Rosie's head, and a little boy scratched Shep behind the ears. The dogs seemed thoroughly happy with this attention.

It seemed as if we might make new friends.

The tall woman spoke. "We are Ams-kap-bee-pea-gun-knee."

I frowned at this strange word. Were they Shoshone Indians? Many Shoshone lived in the Cache Valley area, but

I had never spoken with them. Some were Latter-day Saints.

The woman swept her arm toward the valley. "Your people call us Blackfeet."

Oh. Not Shoshone. I nodded to show I understood.

"We camp close." She waved her hand toward the ridge where I had seen the two men that morning.

"Welcome," I said again.

The woman said, "I am Deer Woman."

"My name is Hannah."

"Hannah. Hannah." In solemn whispers, the young Blackfeet echoed my name around the circle.

The older woman stood close to the girl and said, "I am Raven Feather."

She explained that they had learned some English from an injured trader who lived with them one winter.

I smiled at the girl. "What is your name?"

Her voice was soft. "Always Singing." Her wide eyes were shining black. An upward line, like a little apostrophe, marked each corner of her mouth. Smooth black braids hung over her shoulders.

"You are alone?" asked Deer Woman.

"Yes." Somehow I felt safe telling them.

Deer Woman spoke to the others in her language. A soft murmur drifted through the group. "We came to keep you safe," she said. "We will come again."

My smile stretched full. "I'm happy to know that. You will be welcome." If only Matthew Colton could see me talking with the people he'd warned me against!

Deer Woman and Raven Feather moved toward their horses, and the group gathered to leave. As silently as they'd come, the Blackfeet disappeared around a curve of mountain rock. The dogs and I were alone again. I felt even lonelier than the day before when Uncle John left. It was like someone had given me a bag of lemon drops and snatched it away after I'd had just one piece.

❄ ❄ ❄

Fee-bee-yee! Baa! Chickadees and sheep serenaded me as I enjoyed my bean dish along with Mama's bread. After washing up and settling the dogs, I lit the coal oil lamp and took out my sampler. I pictured Mama sitting by our fireplace after my sisters were asleep. The fire made shadows dance across the floor as Mama ended her day alone. I longed to be sitting by her side.

I sighed and started a border of a bright blue chain stitch. I was planning a corner design of yellow daisies when I heard that awful roar again.

The dogs barked an alarm. The chickadees disappeared into their nest, and the herd's noise grew shrill. I dropped Mama's spotless linen to the rocky ground.

I hoped I would never have to face that angry animal. My heart pounding, I seized Papa's rifle and scrambled into the camp.

Eight

No more roars unsettled the night. I huddled on the bunk, wrapped in Grandma's quilt to ward off fear and the mountain cold. Clutching Liza Lou and the rifle, I drifted off before my prayers were done and slept soundly until a terrible nightmare broke my rest.

I dreamed I stood in our yard back home. Perched high in my swinging tree, Matthew Colton dangled my lost charm chain just out of reach. He pointed behind me at every danger he'd warned about. Snakes, bears, coyotes, and mountain lions charged my way, followed by a band of Indians aiming their arrows straight at me. Scariest of all, the Bear Lake monster oozed up from our well.

A terrible clatter jerked me awake. *What?* Papa's rifle had fallen to the floor. I was pushed against the wall, my legs tangled in a mess of covers and sweaty nightclothes. Damp curls stuck to my face. I'd about crushed Liza Lou flat. I shook so hard I thought the camp would break loose from the rut Uncle John had dug.

How would I endure this long summer if a dream could make me so sore afraid? I was sure I'd never rest again, but after a while I fell back into sleep.

❄ ❄ ❄

The dogs barked at daybreak, and I woke to my third day in the mountains. Time to move the herd. The dogs and I found an old ewe in a tizzy. She rubbed against a tree with all her might, trying to rid her coat of brambles. I helped her coax them out and pushed her along.

After breakfast, I set Liza Lou on my rock while I swept out the camp and gathered more brushwood. The chickadees flew back and forth in a great flurry of action. Bits of wool hung from their beaks. They'd made good use of the ewe's tree rubbing!

Soon after dinner, I saw the Blackfeet coming toward camp. Always Singing led the younger children. Deer Woman and Raven Feather rode behind them. This time I noticed the beaded flower design on the cradleboard.

As the dogs ran to our visitors, I waved. "Hello."

"Oe-keh." They returned my greeting.

I was curious about the little ones. "What is your name?" I asked the tallest boy. He disappeared behind Deer Woman and Raven Feather. The other three followed him and peeked out at me.

Raven Feather smiled. "He is called Wind." She named the other children. "Sits by the Fire, Star, Huckleberry

Eyes." She touched the cradleboard. "Blue Hawk."

I wondered what stories lay behind these unusual names. I repeated each one. Except for the baby, I couldn't be sure what name belonged to which child. The little ones seemed to have taken root behind the women.

Always Singing took something from Raven Feather's saddlebag. She showed me a doll wearing a beaded dress.

"Wait here!" I ran to get Liza Lou.

We held our dolls so that they faced one another, just as Always Singing and I had done the day before.

"Hello," I said in a small, doll-like voice.

Always Singing bent her doll toward mine. "Oe-keh."

Too soon, the women signaled it was time to leave. They gathered the children and slowly walked away.

The scary growl sounded most nights. Every day the dogs and I tended the sheep, chasing after strays and leading them to new grassy banquets. Each afternoon, the Blackfeet came for a short visit.

One day I asked Always Singing about the nighttime growl.

She picked up a stick and drew the outline of a bear in the dirt. "We hear his noise in our camp."

A bear! "It frightens me," I admitted.

Always Singing looked toward the ridge. "Our men watch."

Good! They would know what to do if it came close.

"What is your word for bear?" I asked.

"We do not speak his name. He has strong power." The little lines at the corners of her mouth deepened. "We call him Sticky Mouth. Always dripping berry juice."

"Sticky Mouth?" The bear didn't seem so frightening with this name. I wanted to learn more Blackfeet words. I pointed to Shep. "What do you call dog?"

Always Singing nodded. "Im-ee-taaw."

I repeated the word.

"Dogs help us. They work hard. Pull travois like our horses."

I pointed to Deer Woman's horse.

"Poh-noh-kah-oh-mee-taah."

This was fun! I pointed to my rock.

"Ooh-ko-tock."

I repeated the three Blackfeet words I'd learned.

Our language lesson got me to thinking. What could I share with the Blackfeet?

On my seventh night in the mountains, things changed.

I'd just eaten a thick slice of Johnnycake I'd made that morning when I heard footsteps thumping toward the camp. I slid off my rock and crawled under the camp to hide in the shadows.

"Hallo! Anyone there?" A woman's deep voice

scratched the air. I spied scuffed, worn boots at the edge of the wagon. "I mean no harm."

I crawled out on the opposite side to make it seem I was coming down the hillside. I stumbled and fell. Seemed like whenever I got scared, I turned clumsy.

The stranger rushed around the camp wagon. "You all right? Where's your folks?"

I was afraid to tell her I was alone. "Papa's gone after . . . a lost ewe," I lied. "He'll be back soon." *Heavenly Father, forgive my falsehood.*

She appeared to believe me. "Have you seen a man named David hereabouts? He brought our herd up to graze 'bout two weeks ago."

"No, ma'am," I said. "I—uh, *we*—just been here six days. We've not seen one soul."

"Oh, glory," she moaned. "For certain, something bad's happened. We live up past Franklin. David came down this way 'cause he thought the grazing was better." She sank onto my rock as if she couldn't stand for another second.

I gave her a hard look. Wild red hair poked out from a raggedy wool cap. Her men's pants showed she surely wasn't a Saint. Mormon women wore proper dresses, even when they did men's work.

Mama taught me to always treat visitors kindly. Though she was uninvited, this woman was my guest all the same.

"My name's Hannah," I said.

"I'm called Harriet." She reached out to shake my hand.

"Would you like a piece of Johnnycake?" I had two slices left that I was planning to cover with honey for breakfast.

"I'd be grateful," she said.

As I stepped toward the camp, I heard her footsteps behind me. I turned.

She staggered toward me, tears streaming down her cheeks. "I don't know what to do! I come up with fresh supplies this morning and waited all day for David. He'd not moved the herd. Sheep were wandering, and the dogs hadn't been fed. Something bad's happened. David's a good provider. He'd never go off like that."

Her sad wails near broke my heart.

"Come sit in the camp." I helped her up into the wagon, but I had no idea what to do next.

Still sobbing, she sank onto the bunk.

I offered a dipper of water. Her hands trembled as she lifted it to drink. She gulped as hasty as sheep when they first reach the stream.

"I just baked this today." I handed her my next-to-last slice.

She snatched it. "Thank ye," she mumbled around the mouthful. "Tastes real good."

She reached for my last slice. My heart sank as I saw

tomorrow's breakfast disappear, but I was too afraid of this wild-eyed woman to say anything.

Suddenly Harriet stood and crumbs dropped from her lap. Her eyes burned with a fierce light as she towered over me. "When do you reckon your pa'll be back?"

"I-I don't rightly know." I shrank back against the table 'til my fingers touched Papa's rifle.

"I'd surely like to ask him about David. He say anything 'bout seeing a stranger? David's taller'n me. Black hair. Walks with a sorta limp. Bodaciously kind man. If he met up with your pa, he would'a visited some before moving on."

"No, ma'am," I answered honestly. "Papa hasn't met up with a stranger."

With a loud wail, my visitor flopped onto the bunk. She sobbed quietly for a time and then pulled herself up. "I'd best go."

It was full dark now. I thought of the awful sounds I'd heard at night. Besides losing her way or stumbling in the dark, Harriet might meet up with that bear. Should I ask her to stay? That would be the kind thing to do, and Uncle John would be here in the morning. Surely I'd be safe until then.

"Stay the night," I heard myself say.

"'Twouldn't be fitting. I'm a married woman," Harriet said. "A proper Christian woman. David surely wouldn't like me to share the camp with your pa."

"Please stay. Pa won't be here."

"Land sakes! Did he go off and leave a little bit of a thing like you?"

"No, ma'am. I'm tending our sheep by myself," I explained why.

"Glory, child, that don't seem right."

"My uncle will be here in the morning with fresh supplies," I said.

She patted my knee. "I'll stay the night and fix you a tasty breakfast."

Harriet refused my offer of the bunk. Instead she wrapped herself in a blanket, plucked off her hat for a pillow, and slept as soon as she stretched out on the camp floor. I fidgeted in my quilt and worried whether I'd done the right thing. Harriet began to snore, steady and loud like the old clock in Grandma's parlor. The sound settled me to sleep.

I woke at dawn. Harriet was already at the griddle, cooking flapjacks. Her hotcakes weren't light and fluffy like Mama's, but they were still mighty tasty. While I ate, my visitor splashed water on her face and ran her fingers through that fiery hair.

"I'll go back to our camp. Maybe David's there by now."

I watched her make her way up the mountain and hoped she'd find her husband and that all was well.

Nine

Late the next morning, I heard hooves clopping up the rocky trail. Uncle John soon appeared on Zeke. His pack mule, Flint, plodded behind.

"Mornin', Hannah." He jumped off Zeke and eyed me hard. "Have you been safe?"

"I'm fine." His question put Harriet in my mind. I told my uncle about her visit. "Have you seen her husband? He's tall and walks with a limp." I repeated everything Harriet had told me.

Uncle John looked even more serious by the time I finished. "We'll talk about it later, after we put away your supplies."

Why couldn't he answer me right then? No use making a fuss. I followed him to his pack mule. As we unpacked, I told him about the Blackfeet.

Uncle John smiled. "I'm mighty glad you've company up here. Seems Matthew Colton was wrong."

"He surely was, and I hope you tell him so!"

We sat on my rock to eat Mama's chicken and biscuits. While we ate, I told him my plan to surprise the Blackfeet. "Will you help?"

"One plain board," he repeated. "Simple enough. I'll look through the lumber stack by the barn. If I sand a plank nice and smooth, it should work just fine."

I thanked him. "Another thing—I can't find my Bible. Would you ask Mama if I left it behind?"

"Yes, indeed."

"And I've lost my charm string."

"Useless thing to have up here, but I'll ask her to look," he promised. "Now, how about another biscuit?"

A chickadee fluttered above us.

"Looks like I was right about that quakey hole." Uncle John laughed as the colorful little bird flipped upside down to catch a bug. "That feller could be in the circus!"

While we waited for the Blackfeet, Uncle John asked for Papa's rifle. "Let's get in some shooting practice, Hannah. There's been a grizzly attack up here."

"Oh, no!" Memories tightened my stomach: Matthew's words about troubles coming in threes. Harriet's missing husband. Terrible nighttime roars.

Uncle John handed me the rifle. "I promised your mother I'd make certain you can hit a target."

While he watched me push in a cartridge, he told me what had happened. "A man was cutting firewood for his sheep camp about two miles north of here. Found a near-dead bear cub caught in an old trap. He was trying to free the cub when the mother appeared."

I shuddered. Miss Taylor said that mother bears are fierce about protecting their young.

"Seems she thought the man had harmed her cub. She charged at him and gashed him bad. He managed to stagger off, and the bear stayed with her cub."

All-over chills gripped me.

"Trappers found the man in a gully yesterday morning. Before he died, he told them what happened."

Thoughts of Harriet shook me. "Do you think that was Harriet's husband?"

"Seems likely. We'll pray for him and his family at church."

I might have to face the angry bear that killed Harriet's husband. Sighing, I shoved the rifle against my shoulder.

"Stop!" my uncle shouted.

I dropped the rifle.

"You've not got your mind on this, Hannah! You hold that weapon up against you to fire, you'll break a bone for sure. I know your pa taught you better."

"Yes sir," I mumbled. I rested the rifle on the water barrel.

"Aim for the big knot on that pine tree. Take a breath. Ease back on the trigger."

I gulped in air. My first shot hit wide. The sharp boom cracked loud and echoed across the canyon. I went to reload, but the cartridge slipped through my shaky fingers. It rolled out of sight before I could catch it.

"Steady, Hannah," my uncle said. "You've no use for nerves up here. Hold the rifle firm. Keep your resolve. Remember your job: protect the sheep and the dogs and yourself."

Feeling wrathy at being last on that list, I took aim and fired again. Missed the tree entirely.

Finally I came close to the target and then hit the knot once. Uncle John seemed satisfied that I could shoot well enough to protect the sheep . . . and the dogs . . . and myself. Each shot latched onto the one before until racket and bitter gunpowder smell choked the canyon.

As we finished unpacking the supplies Uncle John had brought, I asked about the nighttime roars. "Do you think the mother bear was crying for her baby?" I expected another lecture on being strong and steady.

He frowned. "I reckon so, Hannah. Bears likely mourn their dead babies same as people do."

Remembering Mama's sadness at losing her babies, I felt sorry for that bear mother.

Uncle John leaned in close. "Bears don't come near camp as a rule. They pretty much steer clear of people. If she's hungry, she may seek a meal in your supplies. Or she might just be curious. Keep your vittles closed firm and shut the camp up tight. You can't ever know what a bear will take a mind to do."

There seemed no sure way to stay safe.

"Heed the dogs," my uncle went on. "They won't bark without good reason."

Scared silent, I said nothing. My skin twitched as I imagined a bear attack.

I thought the Blackfeet would appear soon after my shooting practice, but the afternoon moved on with no sign of them.

"I need to travel home now," Uncle John said, "else Margaret will worry."

"Please stay a bit longer," I begged. "They should be here soon."

But he bent to hug me good-bye. "See you next Saturday. Your ma's depending on you to be a strong girl, Hannah."

I'd been scared mightily by Indians staring down at me, shared my camp with a strange woman, and listened most every night to a mean-sounding animal. I'd faced all this alone.

I was tired of being strong!

Ten

The sun moved to the western side of the valley, leaving purple shadows over the camp. Still no Blackfeet.

A horse neighed, and I looked toward the ridge. Outlined by a ray of sun, two Blackfeet men silently watched me. I waved, but they turned their horses and disappeared. I dropped my hand and climbed into the camp to busy myself with supper. Had I done something to offend my new friends?

They returned the next afternoon. Always Singing pulled a small dog travois. "For Rosie," she said.

Deer Woman explained why they hadn't come the day before. Nodding toward my rifle, she covered her ears. "We heard guns."

When the men had returned from hunting, she had asked them to come make certain I was safe.

"There was a bear attack," I said.

The women nodded.

"White man with sheep." Deer Woman pointed to the mountains beyond my camp. "Our men keep watch."

For several nights after that I heard no roar and prayed that the bear had moved on.

※　※　※

When Uncle John came on Saturday, Flint pulled a travois loaded with supplies, and Rosie ran to meet him. She jumped at Flint's load until I feared the old mule would kick her.

"Here, Rosie. Stop that!" She backed off but kept barking. Her tail wagged double-time.

"She knows I've something for her." Uncle John pulled two shank bones from Flint's pack and tossed one to Rosie, who disappeared under the camp to enjoy her treat. Shuffling along like an old man, Shep waited patiently for Uncle John to offer him a bone.

"Shep seems to be getting more feeble," my uncle said. "I'd best take him home."

"No!" A chill ran through me. Shep had spent his whole life tending our herd. "I depend on him." No dog could stare down a sheep like Shep.

Uncle John nodded. "We'll wait a while. See how he does."

I asked about Harriet's husband. "Was David the one who died?"

My uncle frowned. " 'Fraid so, Hannah. Poor widow's in a terrible state. Neighbor family brought her sheep down last Sunday. Hiram Bushnell helped 'em. Said Harriet was in a bad way."

I remembered Harriet's loving words: "Bodaciously kind man." I shivered at the thought of her loss. "She must surely be sad."

Uncle John patted my shoulder. "Dwelling on it won't change things, Hannah."

I sighed and helped him unload my provisions. When we had stowed everything, Uncle John handed me a bundle wrapped in brown paper. "Your ma couldn't find your Bible, but she sent this. Started it the day you left and been hard at it every evening."

It was a beautiful shawl knit of fine red wool. Last fall, I had watched Mama spin that yarn so thin that a spider would be pleased to weave it into her web. Then she'd boiled up a tub of chokecherries for a lively red dye. "This will fetch us a good price in Logan this spring," she'd said.

Papa's death had changed the normal way of life, and Mama had made no trip to Logan. "I miss Mama so! And Catherine and Baby Alice." I flung myself into my uncle's arms.

He patted my shoulder. "Fussing will do no good. Let's unpack that board you asked for. I have another surprise for you and your friends."

My uncle had brought the makings for a tree swing "This oak tree'll do fine." He tied the swing ropes to a thick limb. Next we worked on my surprise, carefully balancing the board on a flat boulder. I could hardly wait for Always Singing to ride up and down with me.

"This makes a fine ridy-bob!" my uncle said. "You'll all have a dandy time."

Even though Miss Taylor said the proper name for my surprise was "seesaw," I liked "ridy-bob" much better!

When the Blackfeet came, they stopped as soon as Uncle John stepped to my side. "Stand still and wait," I said. I walked to the Blackfeet.

I looked back at my uncle and said the Blackfeet word for uncle. "A-a-ahs."

Always Singing whispered, "Dog face." She frowned.

Dog face? I bristled. Why did Always Singing use such rude words? "My uncle is not a dog!"

"His face has hair like a dog," she said. "Not like Blackfeet men."

Then I remembered that the two men who had watched me had no hair on their faces. No beard. No moustache. My uncle's "dog face" was strange to Blackfeet.

"He is a good man," I said. "He brings me food from home."

Deer Woman nodded. She and Raven Feather dismounted and inched toward my uncle. The little children huddled near the horses. Always Singing waited with them.

"Welcome," Uncle John said.

"Oe-keh," Raven Feather answered.

They slowly moved closer, and I introduced my uncle. "Always Singing is Deer Woman's daughter, but she lives with her aunt, Raven Feather."

The Blackfeet remained quiet. Uncle John did the same.

After a while, I took Always Singing by the hand. "Come see my surprise." In a few minutes, we were gliding up and down on the ridy-bob. It worked just fine.

Wind crept over to watch us, but the other little ones stayed put.

Uncle John sat quietly on a tree stump.

Always Singing and I rode up and down, up and down.

My uncle remained still. When Wind ventured a bit closer, my uncle held out his hand and smiled. Wind turned to his mother, and Deer Woman nodded.

The next time I looked in their direction, I saw that Uncle John had perched Wind on his boot. "Giddy-up, horsie! Go to town!" He gently bounced Wind.

Caleb used to play this game with Catherine. Once again, I wondered about my brother. He left to help our family, but he'd only made things worse.

Uncle John suddenly dropped his foot. "Oops! Little horsie, don't fall down!" Wind giggled so hard at the surprise that he had a hiccoughing fit.

Deer Woman snatched him up. Wind wriggled and stretched his arms toward my uncle. When the little boy whispered to his mother, she handed him back to Uncle John. Soon three small Blackfeet lined up, waiting their turn to ride the horsie to town. Deer Woman and Raven Feather watched from my rock.

Deer Woman gave Uncle John a special title. "You are Horse Ride."

He laughed. "That's a dandy name!"

Before the Blackfeet left, I showed Always Singing my new shawl.

She held it to her cheek. "Chokecherry red. Soft. Warm. Good for nighttime cold."

"My mother made it."

"We will leave in chokecherry time."

Leave? I was just getting to know her! "When?"

"Grandfather will give the sign. He is our leader."

Too soon, my visitors prepared to return to their camp.

"Good-bye," I said. "Please come tomorrow."

Deer Woman nodded. "Tomorrow."

Uncle John started his journey back to the valley. The dogs and I crowded around as he hitched Flint to the travois. "See you in a week." He mounted Zeke and was gone.

I was alone again.

After a week of bright, clear days, the sky turned bluish-gray the next afternoon. The sun set behind cloud banks the color of strawberry whipped cream edged in lavender. I wished Molly was here to paint a picture of the scene.

How I missed her! Molly could always make me smile. She had enough spunk for both of us. I didn't own one bit of spunk. If someone told Molly to take the sheep for summer grazing, she'd march straight up the mountain without a whimper.

The dogs darted back and forth as we nudged the herd to new grazing. Suddenly the sun disappeared, like God had snapped His fingers to call it home. The air hung still and heavy. The sheep broke into a staccato of nervous bleats as the sky darkened to deep gray. I added wood to the fire pit and gathered the hens into their cage.

Fixing to work on my sampler, I hung the lantern and settled on my rock. I hadn't decided what to stitch, but I was set on a Bible verse. Before I could thread my needle, a sharp wind whipped the rich smell of rain across the canyon. Heavy drops pounded the rocky ground and hissed into the fire. The first summer rainstorm.

The dogs raced under the wagon. I tied up Rosie and scrambled inside to burrow under the bedcovers with Liza Lou. Thunder cracks shook the camp and lightning flashes glowed through the canvas roof. Yowling wind rocked the wagon 'til I thought it would go crashing over. *Heavenly Father, please bring us through the storm. Watch over the sheep and my dogs. Amen.*

By morning, the thunder had grown faint. The wind weakened, the rain changed to a patter, and then stopped altogether. *Thank you for keeping us safe.*

I peeked out the camp door. The stink of dirty, wet wool wrinkled my nose. Fallen limbs and torn leaves covered everything. Trees dripped leftover rain, and the overflowing stream churned the ground into mud soup. Storm winds had tossed the ridy-bob off its rock and tangled the swing ropes. Everything in sight was a mess.

I longed to get off this mountain!

Rosie's barking pulled my attention to the sheep. A mass of curly wet fleece, they were so huddled together that it was hard to tell one from the other. Panicky baas filled the air, matched by the hens' crazy clucking. I'd left their cage out in the rain, and they were so fussed I feared they'd run away if I let them out.

Something else was wrong. Rosie barked and pushed against my legs, like I was a sheep that had wandered off.

I realized Shep was gone.

Eleven

"Shep!" I called. "Come on, boy. Time to move the herd."

While I tugged the chicken cage to a sunny spot, Rosie kept nudging me toward the sheep.

"Rosie, stop pushing! We'll go as soon as I find Shep. You're in the wa—"

Up ahead, I saw Shep asleep under a pine. His back was toward me. "Oh, Shep, you're all wet. Why are you sleeping out here? Wake up, boy!"

He didn't move.

Rosie ran to Shep. Sitting on her haunches, she turned to me and whimpered.

I slogged through the mud and saw the reason for Rosie's sad cry. Shep wasn't asleep. He was dead. Something had ripped his throat open. Blood puddled around his head. His body was spattered red. "No!" I howled. I dropped to the muddy ground and buried my face in Shep's fur.

"Why?" I screamed.

Shep was dead, no matter the reason. Some animal had come to steal a sheep, and Shep had fought the thief. The storm had covered up sounds of trouble. What would I have done if I'd heard the two animals struggle? It shamed me to admit it, but I was glad I'd not heard.

I cradled Shep, unmindful of the blood staining my apron. I stayed there until my tears dried, but then I forced my mind back to duty. "Rosie, let's count the sheep." We had started out with forty-one head.

". . . thirty-eight, thirty-nine, forty." I counted a second time. One lamb short. The nighttime killer had killed Shep and taken one of our herd.

Rosie and I went to move the sheep to a new spot. They bleated louder than usual. Mourning the lost lamb. Missing Shep.

As Rosie and I walked back to the camp, I spotted a bloody carcass not far from where Shep had fallen. A turkey vulture circled above the body. I shivered. Matthew would say I'd had my third trouble . . . Shep and a lamb, both dead.

I fetched a blanket to wrap around Shep. Struggling under his weight, I stumbled back to settle him by the camp door. Uncle John had been right. Shep was too old for this work. He should have been enjoying the summer with Mama and my sisters.

Just before noon, I heard Zeke and Flint on the trail. Rosie ran to meet them.

"That was a mighty fierce storm!" Uncle John jumped down from Zeke and scratched Rosie's head. "Near blew the barn away! How did you fare up here? Your ma was plenty concerned for you." He looked around. "Where's Shep?"

I told him what had happened. "It's all my fault," I said, "If I'd let you take him home, Shep would be alive." I sank onto my rock.

Uncle John sat beside me. "Not true, Hannah. It was Shep's time. He died doing what he loved—looking after the herd."

"I g-guess so." I blinked. "He was a good dog. Rosie will miss him. *I* will miss him. He showed me what to do."

"He was a smart dog, all right," Uncle John agreed.

"Can we bury him on the farm?"

"I reckon that'd be fine. I'll tie him fast to the travois and take him down today. Your ma'll gladly care for him. Caleb grew up with Shep. He's like part of the family."

Mention of my missing brother, added to Shep's death, set me off crying.

"Here, now." Uncle John patted my shoulder. "Tears will do no good. You'd best tend to what needs doing. Help me unload the supplies. Remember—Satan finds work for idle hands."

Aunt Margaret had stitched those words onto the

sampler that hung in her front parlor. She was a devout believer in keeping busy every single minute. I supposed she prayed all the while, but how did she keep her mind on Heavenly Father when her hands were so busy doing and making?

After we finished our work, I rested in the shade with a dipperful of cold water. Uncle John fetched something from his saddlebag.

"I near forgot this," he said. "Your ma found it on a straw bale next to the barn. Lucky for you she spotted it before the rain." He handed me the lost charm chain.

I fingered each button. "It must have fallen out when I went up the camp steps."

"Don't know why you want it. No buttons to be found up here. 'Sides, aren't womenfolk supposed to *give* you new charms?" He laughed. "Better follow the rules. You go adding charms yourself, you might end up an old maid!"

Every girl knew the charm chain rules. You could receive or trade a button or charm but never pay money for one. When your chain had one thousand charms, your true love would appear. Molly's mother had a different rule: Stop at nine hundred ninety-nine. Your true love will bring the last button. If you add number one thousand yourself, you'll be a spinster for life.

So far, I only had thirty-nine charms. I'd be a wrinkled old woman before I got to one thousand. A spinster for sure!

Uncle John rummaged in his pockets and pulled out two buttons. "Your aunt cut these off some clothes worn too thin to pass on."

One button sparkled like a diamond. "Is Aunt Margaret sure she wants to part with this?" I held the shining glass circle to the sunlight.

"Came off her favorite dress. It's an early birthday present."

I carefully put the buttons and charm chain in my apron pocket. "Please thank her for me. I'll write a proper note this week."

"That reminds me," he said. "Here's a letter from Molly."

I snatched it from his hand, but then remembered my manners. "Sorry, Uncle. Thank you for bringing it." I slipped the letter in my pocket.

My uncle laughed. "Molly did the same thing when I handed her your letter . . . grabbed it like I'd offered her a bag of peppermints. Go ahead and read it."

> *Dear Hannah,*
>
> *I can't believe you're gone for all summer. How I miss you! Mama and I visited your mother and sisters yesterday. I don't think this summer will ever end. When I finish my chores, I read or draw, but I wish I could race you across the fields or make flower crowns and pretend we're princesses.*

I see our schoolmates at church on Sunday. Matthew comes to visit my brother Aaron near every day. I don't know why Matthew's so friendly all of a sudden. He seems to be learning some manners, but I know it's not from my rascally brother!

A new family is moving to Sego Springs—the Lindstroms. Papa heard they have a daughter named Inga. She'll be in the upper grades with us next year. I can hardly wait to meet her! Her father just came back from a mission in Mexico.

I hope you're not too lonely up there. Always Singing is a pretty name. Can the Blackfeet talk English? Write me back.

Your friend,

PS Mama won't let me come stay with you 'cause it would be dangerous.

❀   ❀   ❀

Her letter was mostly news I didn't care for. Why on earth was Matthew coming to the Tuttles' house every day? Was he sweet on Molly? Inga Lindstrom would surely be Molly's best friend by the time I got back to Sego Springs. Molly's PS was the worst news. I wished *my* mother thought it was too dangerous to send her daughter to the mountains! That was selfish, but it was the way I felt.

Uncle John was straightening the swing ropes when I saw Always Singing and the others coming. I ran to meet them.

"It was a bad storm," Deer Woman said. "Much rain and wind."

"We were happy to get a heavy rain in the valley," Uncle John said. "Good for the crops. The farmers are glad."

"Rain is good," Raven Feather agreed.

"Horsie! Horsie!" Wind pulled on my uncle's jacket.

Uncle John laughed. "Well, now, let's see if I can find that horsie!"

The little ones gathered around, waiting their turn to bounce on Horse Ride's foot.

I pulled Always Singing aside. "Shep is dead." I pointed to his body.

She lifted a corner of the blanket that covered Shep. After a minute she said, "Coyotes. They kill Blackfeet dogs too."

My voice cracked. "Will they come back?"

"They will try," she said. "Our men keep watch." She put the blanket back. "He was a good dog."

"Yes," I whispered. Another blanket corner had come loose. When I bent to tuck it in, the charm chain slipped from my pocket.

Always Singing picked it up. "What is this?"

I told her about the one thousand charms bringing a true love.

"A husband." She smiled.

I felt my face turn red as Mama's strawberry preserves.

"We will find a charm now," Always Singing said.

"Where?"

She gestured toward the ground.

I looked at the spot. No buttons. No charms.

"Look hard," Always Singing said. "Be still."

I stood like a statue and stared at the ground. I saw nothing but rocks.

Always Singing picked up a small, dark orange stone. She held it in her open palm. "See this hole? It will go on your string."

I undid the chain's knot and added the shiny rock to my collection. "It's perfect!" I said. "How did you find it?"

"Look with your heart," she said. "You will see many things."

Look with my heart? This was like the puzzling things Mama sometimes said.

After the Blackfeet had gone, Uncle John and I carefully secured Shep to the travois.

"We'll go slow and careful," Uncle John said. "Shep will rest at home tonight, and we'll bury him in the morning."

Rosie and I watched our old friend leave.

Twelve

Still sad about losing Shep, I tried to follow Aunt Margaret's advice about idle hands keeping busy. I carefully added her buttons to my charm chain. It now held forty-two charms, counting Always Singing's stone. A hodgepodge of colors and shapes stretched across my lap: mother-of-pearl, crimson glass, carved wood, and shiny brass. I tucked the chain under my pillow.

I stepped outside to look with my heart. *What did that mean?* Every few feet, I searched the ground. I saw no pretty stones . . . only mud and rocks. Nothing came close to my favorite—a round enamel button with a hand-painted daisy. I'd traded two of Grandpa's band uniform buttons for that beauty.

My eyes worked just fine, but my heart had no knack for looking.

I settled by the fire pit with Papa's guitar. Plucking the strings took my mind off Shep's passing and the horrible bear attack. The song's hopeful words turned me to good things that had happened here. Blackfeet friends. Mountain sunsets. Time to read and stitch and practice the guitar. The chickadee family. A new language.

I looked at the black-and-white dog sprawled by the fire. "Not everything up here is bad, Rosie. Someday I might even—"

A terrible roar ended my peace. That night it boomed out louder than ever. Without thinking, I looked toward the sound. On the ridge across the canyon, the setting sun silhouetted a bear. Even from a distance, its giant hulk sent chills through me.

I shooed the chickens into their coop, tied up Rosie, and hurried into the camp. Huddled on the bunk, I stroked my charm chain. *Heavenly Father, please protect me from all dangers, seen and unseen.*

Next morning, Rosie's bark got me out of bed. A splash of cold water on my face stirred me to action. I brushed out my tangles, untied Rosie, and let the chickens out. They'd left me two fresh brown eggs. I spotted a cobweb spun between the doorway and a nearby pine. Dewy lace sparkled in the early sun. A fine start to the day!

"We'll have ourselves a tasty breakfast," I told Rosie as we moved the sheep.

I mixed a hard-cooked egg with last night's rice and spooned the mixture into separate pans for the dogs. Rosie looked at the two portions and cocked her head at me. I gulped back a sob. I had forgotten Shep was dead.

I built a pit fire against the chilly morning air and settled on my rock to start a letter.

> *Dear Molly,*
>
> *Thank you for your letter. Every day I feel farther away from you and all the folks I love. I worry that you'll forget me.*
>
> *It sounds like you're seeing Matthew a good deal. You said that he seems more polite, but I can't picture him with manners!*
>
> *Mama found my charm string, and Aunt Margaret sent me two buttons. One of them sparkles like a diamond. Always Singing found a little orange stone with a hole for my chain. She says that if I look with my heart I'll see what my eyes can't find. Isn't that peculiar? I'm not sure what she means, but I plan to try.*

I stopped to whittle my pencil to a sharper point. What should I write next? Something about the new girl in Sego Springs? I worried that she and Molly would become good friends, but it would be selfish to say so.

> *I look forward to meeting Inga when I come home. It will be fun to have another girl in our class next year!*

Mama would approve of what I'd written. I went on.

I guess you've heard that Shep died trying to protect one of the lambs. Rosie and I miss him.

Next time you visit my family, please hug them all for me! I can hardly wait to see you again.

Your friend forever,

Hannah

PS I'm sorry your mother won't let you come for a visit.

Writing the letter reminded me how much I missed life in the valley.

No point in sitting around feeling sorry for myself. I jumped up. "Come on, Rosie! Let's see if we can find some wildflowers for Mama's wool."

Except for moving the sheep, this was the first time I'd ventured from camp. Rosie and I walked by the herd as they quietly chomped their leafy meal. Sweet chickadee songs called from the quakey nest as we passed.

Soon camp was out of sight. Patches of muddy storm water hampered my steps. I rounded a bend and stumbled over a rotten tree lying across the trail. A clump of dark animal hair had caught on the rough bark. I stuck it in my apron pocket to show Always Singing later.

Tangles of chokecherry poked up nearby. The bush's white blossoms reminded me of the lacy edgings Grandma tatted for her linens. By fall, those blossoms would be clumps of dark purple fruit. They'd make a fine dye and be just right for syrup and jam.

I passed a stand of tall, thin plants whose leaves grabbed at my skirts. Some folks used this plant to stuff mattresses. Mama called it bedstraw, but Miss Taylor said its proper name was madder. The roots made a beautiful red dye. I'd send a bagful to Mama in a month or so.

Hot and thirsty, I turned to go back to camp and spotted a flower I'd never seen before. Pale lavender blossoms brightened the brown rocks high above the path. The frilly blooms would add color to my kitchen. I had finished a pint of Mama's pickles the night before, and the empty jar would make a fine vase.

"Maybe I can see with my heart after all," I told Rosie.

I started my climb and stepped from one sure hold to another, creeping across places slick with wet moss. There! The flower was almost in reach. I looked ahead for the next safe foothold but saw only smooth rock. I strained to my tiptoes and reached for the flower.

My fingertips brushed the bottom leaves, and I stretched to yank the plant loose. Suddenly the narrow ledge where I stood crumbled. For a second, I rested on air. Then I fell. My hands scraped down the craggy slope. Tumbling onto my side, I rolled over and over toward the path. Jagged rocks that had helped me climb now reached out to hurt me.

Thud! I crashed against the ground, my face slamming onto a rock. I couldn't find my breath. I rested on my side, eyes closed.

Rosie whimpered and licked my face.

With a grunt, I struggled to sit. I was a mess of dirt and scratches. I spit out a mouthful of grit. Blood and dirt stained my torn dress. My scraped elbows and hands stung with pain. Both stockings were ripped, and blood ran from a gash on my right leg. My right cheek felt as if a door had banged against it.

Now I'd had a *fourth* trouble. What would happen next?

Papa's hat was gone. I crumpled over and sobbed. The brush rustled behind me. A wild animal ready to attack? I held my breath, expecting more pain.

"Woof!" Rosie appeared, pushing that old hat with her nose. She herded it to my side like it was a lost lamb.

"Rosie, you're a fine shepherd! You even guide hats back where they belong!" I hugged the lost hat close and buried my face in Rosie's fur.

After resting for a time, I felt ready to start for camp. I tried to stand, but the pain from my bloodied leg made me cry out. I sank to the ground. Could I walk? If I crawled, my scraped knees would suffer more. I spotted a thick branch lying at the side of the path and used it as a make-shift crutch. I hobbled along the trail.

Finally back at camp, I sank onto the rock and peeled

off my torn stockings. My leg still bled, and I remembered the cobweb I'd seen that morning. Mama used spider webs to stop bleeding. I limped to the camp door and found the web still in place. I gathered it into a sticky bundle and spread it over the cut. The bleeding slowed, but my pain was growing worse.

It was time to move the herd to shade. I sent Rosie ahead and followed on my crutch. "Bring 'em to the quakeys!"

The peppy dog barked her command, and the sheep obeyed.

I hobbled up the camp steps and dropped onto the bunk. Clutching my charm string, I drifted off to sleep, worried how I would feel by nightfall. Papa held that bumps and bruises always felt worse at day's end. If I'd fallen at home, Mama would be there to comfort me. Now I was on my own to take care of the harm I'd caused myself.

❉　❉　❉

"Hannah!" Always Singing's soft voice woke me.

"Oe-keh," I whispered.

I told her about my fall. Deer Woman and Raven Feather came to the doorway. Always Singing spoke to them in Blackfeet.

Raven Feather nodded and left.

"Where is she going?" I asked Always Singing.

"To bring healing."

Deer Woman carried me down the steps and gently laid me on a blanket next to my rock. She rolled another blanket to make a pillow.

She and Always Singing sat with me.

I looked around. "Where are the others?"

"Raven Feather took them back to camp," Deer Woman said.

"I tried to look with my heart." I shook my head. "I found a beautiful flower, and then I fell. I'd best look with my eyes to see where I'm going."

"Your eyes find the path. Your heart finds beauty," Deer Woman said. "Look with your eyes *and* heart."

I started to reply when I saw Raven Feather riding toward us with an older woman. Creamy white braids hung over her beaded dress. Her wrinkled face glowed like polished oak. She sat straight as a schoolyard flagpole. As she came near, I could feel her dark eyes burn into mine.

What would she do to me? More than ever, I longed for my mother.

Thirteen

The woman stopped next to the fire pit. "Oe-keh." She took a buckskin pouch from Raven Feather.

"Oe-keh," I murmured. My insides trembled. What was in that bag? Would her healing be painful?

She stroked my tangled blonde hair. "Nah-toe-seh." The Blackfeet word for *sun*.

"She is White Medicine Wolf. My grandmother," Always Singing whispered. "Strong healer."

White Medicine Wolf spoke to Always Singing and the two women. They nodded and hurried to gather twigs. Without a word, they tossed the sticks into the fire pit. A flame sputtered to life. White Medicine Wolf reached into the leather bag and pulled out something green that was woven into a soft braid.

"Sweetgrass," Always Singing said.

White Medicine Wolf used a forked stick to drag bright embers from the pit and then laid the sweetgrass braid on them. A soothing smell filled the air. Always

Singing's grandmother waved the fragrant smoke toward me and sang in a low, soft voice. I didn't know the meaning of her words, but they comforted me all the same.

"She prays for healing," Always Singing explained.

Heavenly Father, thank you for sending this woman to help me.

White Medicine Wolf sat by my side and moved her hands over every spot of pain. She gently patted my bruises and scrapes with a damp, warm bundle that held the sweet, earthy scent of Mama's sage tea. White Medicine Wolf continued her prayers, and I knew Heavenly Father heard her. My eyes closed as her quiet voice calmed me.

"Iss-oe-tahn." White Medicine Wolf gently rocked me in her arms.

"She calls you granddaughter," Always Singing said.

Resting against my Blackfeet grandmother, I felt her power. I was safe.

White Medicine Wolf spoke to Always Singing.

"Use the sage pack before you sleep," Always Singing told me, "to help pain leave. Be sure it is warm and wet." My friend helped me climb into the camp to rest.

As I lay down, I spied my Bible on the shelf above the bunk. Had it been there all the time? Why hadn't I seen it? Maybe I hadn't looked with my heart.

I turned to Psalm 23. "The Lord is my shepherd. I shall not want." I fell asleep on the verse: ". . . I will fear no evil: for thou art with me; thy rod and thy staff they comfort me."

Rosie's frantic barking woke me. It was time to move the sheep to nighttime grazing. I expected pain to tear me apart, but my aches had eased some. I turned my crutch into a make-do shepherd's staff and followed Rosie.

After supper I settled by the fire pit and picked up Papa's guitar. My fingers set themselves to strum a chord, but pain hit my stiff hands at the first note. No music tonight.

     ✿   ✿   ✿

The next morning I moved stiffly and creakily to look in the tin mirror above the bunk. I gasped at my swollen, purple-red reflection. If he saw me, Matthew Colton would surely guffaw!

When I went to scrub dirt and blood from my clothes, the clump of animal hairs fell from my apron. Later I showed them to Always Singing. "What are they?"

"Sticky Mouth."

"What?" I had walked the same path as a bear! My fingers tingled as I let the bear hairs fall into Always Singing's hand. I vowed never to leave camp again.

"Grandfather says Sticky Mouth is close," Always Singing said. "Watch for signs."

"Signs?"

"Look for scratches on trees. Pressed down grass.

Tracks." She traced a print in the dirt.

The outline showed five claws. Mama's good cake plate would hardly cover the whole paw. I'd have no chance against such a huge animal.

"They move when nah-toe-seh comes up and goes down," my friend said. "Watch and listen. You will know if he comes near."

And then what?

The Blackfeet left soon after my lesson in bear signs. I longed to follow to the safety of their camp.

The next two nights were quiet. Had the bear moved on? I kept my eye out for signs. It seemed every tree carried scratches. I imagined bear prints wherever I looked.

The chickadees had finished their nest. One was always perched there now, a sure sign they were hatching a family.

I woke on the Fourth of July thinking of the celebrations down in Cache Valley. The Sego Springs Brass Band parading from house to house. Folks eating all afternoon. Boys and men playing baseball in the park. Come evening, long speeches and a musical program. The day would end with fireworks.

I would miss it all. Worse than that, my twelfth birthday was little more than a week away, and I'd spend it away from my family.

My spirits were low as Rosie and I gathered the sheep from their overnight spot. "I miss being home," I complained to the animals. As if to say, "We understand," the herd bleated softly, and Rosie nuzzled my leg.

On his last trip, Uncle John had brought homemade sausages, and I fried three for breakfast. "We'll have our own celebration, Rosie." She eagerly gobbled up her share of the spicy meat.

I settled on my rock to practice "Come, Come, Ye Saints." I was so lost in my music that I forgot about dinner. The sheep started up a loud chorus of hungry bleats and noisy bells. They wanted shade and water. Always Singing and the others walked toward me as I came back from settling them.

I slung the guitar strap over my shoulder and ran to meet my friends.

Always Singing studied the guitar as she drew near. Her eyes were wide.

"My father's guitar," I explained. "To make music."

"Show me."

I pretended I was a member of the Sego Springs Band and marched around the fire pit playing the only tune I knew. My audience smiled and nodded.

"Again," Always Singing said. "Please."

I obliged.

Then Always Singing spoke to Deer Woman. As she listened, the woman shook her head. Always Singing seemed determined, and finally Deer Woman nodded. She lifted her baby from the cradleboard. Rocking her son, she sang in soft, low tones.

"Song for babies," Always Singing whispered. "To sleep."

"A lullaby!" I pictured Mama in the parlor, humming one of her made-up melodies to baby Alice. I moved close to Deer Woman. She smiled and handed me her little one. Together we sang our lullabies to the tiny baby sleeping in my arms.

On Saturday Uncle John jumped down from Zeke and stared at my purple-black cheek. "What in thunder happened to you?"

I confessed my flower-picking mistake. "Always Singing's grandmother brought me some cream to ease the pain."

My uncle shook his head. "You've got to stay close to camp, Hannah. Wandering off to pick a pretty flower! You could've run into some wild critters. Supposing you'd hurt yourself bad? Who'd tend the sheep?"

"Sorry, Uncle." Shame and huff settled in me at the same time. I was wrong to leave the camp, but why couldn't my own uncle show concern for *me*? Was he only worried about the sheep?

"Well," he said, "it's good you made it through all right."

I told him about the bear hairs I'd found.

He jumped up. "Glory, Hannah! I'll not tell your mother that you wandered off like that. That bear could have been watching you!"

"Always Singing says the bear is close. She showed me how to look for bear signs."

"You'd best stay right here and not go off looking for tracks and such."

🌸 🌸 🌸

The Blackfeet came after dinner. Always Singing carried a small bundle. "Gopher skin. We'll make a doll tipi."

Another kindness from the Blackfeet.

We drew hopscotch squares in the dirt and played until it was time for my friends to leave.

As he left, Uncle John made a promise. "I'll bring your birthday presents next Saturday. They'll be two days early, seeing as how your birthday won't be 'til Monday, but I guess a body can open her presents early."

His promise cheered me.

🌸 🌸 🌸

The next afternoon, we cut the gopher skin for the tipi. "My uncle will bring birthday gifts next time."

She smiled. "Oh-maht-skah-tah-key to honor you."

"What?"

"A Giveaway." She explained that the Blackfeet held

Giveaways to celebrate special happenings. "Wind healed from snakebite. Our Giveaway honored his healer. We gave food and clothes to those who came."

What an upside-down way to celebrate! To my mind, the presents should have gone to Wind.

"What will your uncle bring?" Always Singing asked.

"I don't know for certain. A surprise is something you don't know before it happens."

She smiled. "Like finding your charm chain."

I agreed. "That was a good surprise."

"Falling was also a surprise," she added.

"But not a good one!"

I'd had enough unpleasant surprises this summer. It was time for a change.

Fourteen

All week I made lists of birthday presents. A copy of *Little Women.* Hair ribbons. Writing paper. A hand mirror. My mind jumped from frills to needs and back to frills again. Waiting was more than a body could stand!

Saturday morning dragged slow as the last bit of honey from a jug. I tidied the camp and fetched fresh water. I even cleaned the chicken cage. By midday, I was near beside myself with nerves.

Dinnertime passed with no sign of Uncle John, but the Blackfeet arrived at their usual hour. Always Singing carried a small leather bag. She and the other children ran to me.

"Oe-keh!" they shouted.

The younger ones looked around. "Horsie!"

"Horse Ride is not here."

Smiles gone, they looked sadly at the "horsie" stump.

Always Singing sat on the ground near my rock and opened the small pouch. "Jackstones." She spilled several small rocks onto the ground. One large stone was bright red. With a smile, she tossed it into the air and scooped one stone from the pile.

I grinned. Jacks was one of my favorite games. I tried the Blackfeet word for being thankful. "Ehn-ee-yeh-tah-keh."

After we had played a round, Deer Woman called us to my rock. "We eat now."

The children crowded around as she offered me a piece of a reddish-brown patty. "Mow-keh-maa-knee."

"Your people call it pemmican," Always Singing said. "It is meat and berries." She explained they pound dried deer meat into powder and then mix that with buffalo berries and suet. "We dry it in the sun."

Deer Woman said, "It gives strength. The men take it when they hunt."

Deer meat and berries? What a peculiar mix! To my surprise, I liked the taste. The berries sweetened the strong meaty flavor.

Deer Woman gave the signal to leave.

Except for the game and treat, this had been like any other day. No visit from my uncle. Rosie and I moved the sheep, and they set to nibbling right away. Like babies, sheep mostly just eat and sleep.

The sunlight faded, and I knew Uncle John would not come. Would he visit on my real birthday?

I climbed into bed with a heavy heart. Faint rumbles

from the mountains added to my gloom. I covered my head and searched for sleep.

On Sunday I tried to pray, but my mind wandered from one feeling to another.

"Why didn't Uncle John come yesterday?" I asked Rosie.

Rosie nuzzled my leg, but she had no answers.

I was vexed. I had no birthday surprises. No fresh supplies. No way to know why my only visitor from home hadn't appeared.

If Mama knew I was worrying, she'd shake her finger. "Either pray or worry, Hannah. No point doing both. Pray and you've no need to worry. Worry just shows you've put no trust in prayer."

I tried to follow her advice, but worry slipped into my prayers.

The Blackfeet brought a bag filled with wild onions and turnips.

"You are sad," Always Singing said. "Horse Ride did not come."

I sighed. "Maybe today."

"Yes," she said. "Maybe today."

We were wrong. My uncle didn't come.

I spent the afternoon darning. When I finished, rough stitches criss-crossed my stockings. Four new patches paraded around my second-best apron.

In bed that night, I remembered last year's birthday. Molly brought a carved wooden button for my string and the drawings I'd hung over my bunk. I had a new lace collar from Aunt Margaret and a wicker sewing basket from Mama. Papa's bookshelf gift came from the wood of an old pine blown over in a storm. We'd enjoyed Mama's molasses fruitcake and the silky vanilla ice cream Caleb churned up. Happy memories.

Hugging Liza Lou, I stroked Molly's wooden button and finally fell asleep.

Rosie's bark woke me in a bad mood. I stumbled from the camp. I wanted Rosie to tend to the herd without me. This was my birthday, and I wanted no part of sheep complaints. I nudged the noisy herd with my make-do staff.

The chickens made me a present of two large brown eggs. For once, I felt almost kindly toward the noisy hens. "I'm obliged, ladies." I let them loose to peck for food while I scrambled the eggs with cheese, potato, and wild onion. The sharp taste cheered me some.

After looking to make sure no bear had scratched nearby trees, I settled on my rock to wait for Uncle John. Surely he'd come for my birthday. To pass the time, I mended my tattered dress.

I was stitching up the hem when I heard the sound of horse hooves on the trail. I jumped up to greet my uncle.

"Howdy!" someone yelled. "Anybody there?"

That wasn't Uncle John's voice.

"Hallo!"

I ran to the camp, where Papa's rifle rested by the door. I snatched it up. Was I to celebrate my twelfth birthday defending myself against an intruder?

I stood at the top of the steps to load my weapon, but the cartridge slipped from my hand. It rolled across the dirt and stopped by the fire pit. I crouched by the door, holding an empty rifle. Would just the sight of a rifle drive the stranger away?

The horse came into sight. When I saw the rider, I gasped.

Fifteen

Matthew Colton. Riding my uncle's horse with two thick packs and a small crate strapped to the saddle. Matthew grinned as he stopped Zeke near the fire pit. "Happy birthday!" he yelled. "Whatcha aiming to do with that rifle? The cartridge ain't gonna do you much good on the ground. 'Sides, you're shaking so hard, you couldn't hit nothing!"

I lowered the useless rifle. My mouth hung open, but no words came. What could I say to this pesky boy? Itchy heat, like a fever, took hold of me. What a terrible birthday surprise—Matthew Colton instead of Uncle John! I braced myself for rudeness. An insult was surely on its way.

Matthew jumped down. "Well? Don't you want to know why I'm here? Where your uncle is? "

"'Course I do!" I snapped. "Is he all right? Is something wrong at home?"

"Word came that Caleb got hurt in a mine accident. Couple of fellows died, but Caleb was lucky."

"No!" I sank to my rock, snuffling back tears.

Matthew sat next to me. "Don't get all glummy. Caleb's gonna be all right. Your uncle went to fetch him. Ma volunteered me to bring your supplies."

I rubbed my eyes. "W-was Caleb hurt bad?"

"Broke a leg. Got banged up some, but he'll soon be fit." He grabbed my arm and pulled me up. "Come on. Help me with these packs."

Matthew unstrapped the saddlebags and carried them to my rock. He looked hard at my face. "Say, what happened to you? How'd your cheek get all yeller and green?"

I told him about my fall, and he turned serious.

"Riding up here alone got me thinking. If Zeke hadn't known the way, I'd a been lost for certain. Takes a lot of gumption to spend the whole summer here by yourself."

Was he poking fun? I waited for him to start in about all the dangers he'd warned me about. Instead of saying something sassy, he handed me a bag. "Food from your ma."

Mama had sent beef jerky and fresh strawberries, along with dried beans and cornmeal. I stored them in the camp. When I stepped outside, Matthew was setting the crate behind the wagon. What was he hiding? He gave me no time to ask.

"A lot of folks sent you birthday presents."

"Glory!" I could hardly believe what Matthew had done. My rock looked like a party table. A circle of packages ringed Mama's bright yellow cake tin. I spied three boxes done up in brown paper, a small cloth bag, a square silver tin, and a large envelope tied with blue ribbon. Oddest of all: a lumpy object wrapped in muslin.

Matthew waved his hat toward the rock. "Well, ain't you gonna open them? I didn't haul 'em all the way up here for you to just *look* at them. I thought girls liked to open presents."

He was right. I longed to open everything, but I wanted Always Singing and the others to be here. "I'll wait for my Blackfeet friends. They'll be coming soon."

"I heard you met up with some Indians. Your uncle said they been real nice to you. Hard to believe."

"You'd best not set your mind about someone 'til you know them," I snapped.

"I reckon so. Ma says I jump to judgment," he admitted.

I remembered my manners. "Would you like some dinner?"

"Yep, sure would." He pulled a dinner pail from behind his back. "Ma packed us a birthday dinner. She's mighty sorry you can't celebrate with your family." His smile showed a space between his front teeth that I'd never noticed before.

Sarah's chicken wasn't fried crispy like Mama's, but her corn bread was moist and sweet.

I struggled to think of what to talk about. "Molly Tuttle says you've been visiting her."

Matthew reddened so that I was sure he was sweet on my friend. "Nope, not Molly. Ma says I need to be around someone like Molly's brother, Aaron." He swallowed a mouthful of chicken. "Says I need to learn some manners. She was right mad the day she caught me teasing you about being a scaredy-cat."

"You *do* seem more polite. It was kind of you to bring my supplies."

He grinned. "Ma didn't give me a choice!"

We laughed together.

Matthew and I ate every last bit and then shared a dipperful of water.

"That was tasty!" I said. I longed to tell Matthew about the crumbs on his chin and the bit of chicken stuck between his teeth. Why did boys make a mess of themselves when they ate? Caleb's place at the table always needed an extra cleaning. I sighed.

Matthew's voice cracked. "Aw, what's wrong now?"

"Thinking about Caleb."

"He's gonna be fine. No reason for you to wor—" Suddenly he jumped up and stared behind me.

My Blackfeet friends walked toward camp but slowed when they saw Matthew.

I waved and smiled. Matthew stepped behind me. *Was he scared?*

Deer Woman held up her hand, and the group stopped. Always Singing motioned me to come near.

When I reached her, she pointed at Matthew. "Your brother?"

"No," I said. "A friend from home." I'd never before called Matthew a friend, but it seemed fitting.

Always Singing spoke to the women. Raven Feather shook her head.

"Where is Horse Ride?" Always Singing asked.

I told her about Caleb's accident. "Uncle John went to bring him home."

Always Singing and the women talked in Blackfeet. Finally, Always Singing turned to me. "Blackfeet do not like their daughters to be with older boys. They worry we will come to harm."

That's why they had stopped! "My mother sent him to bring my supplies. He's a good family friend." I could hardly believe I was talking about the same Matthew Colton who'd been so mean just weeks ago.

Finally, Deer Woman agreed to let everyone come near my rock. Matthew moved away. Was he scared? Nervous?

Wind edged toward him.

Matthew looked at me as if to say, *What should I do?*

Wind tapped Matthew's knee. "Horsie! Horsie!"

Matthew sat on the stump. "I'll be glad to play horsie!"

While he kept the small children happy, Always Singing and the women gathered around my birthday rock display.

"You have many presents," Deer Woman said. She set a hide bag in the gift circle.

First I opened a box. Miss Taylor had sent the book I had hoped for—*Little Women*. Her note read: "For the bravest little woman I know!"

The small bag held a shiny brass thimble from Grandma: "For my dear Hannah. To keep your stitches even and your finger smooth. Blessings on you!"

Deer Woman handed me another box.

I unwrapped it to find a set of Jackstraws from Uncle John and Aunt Margaret. "For you and your friends."

Always Singing picked up the lumpy package. "What is this?'

"Let's find out!" I unwound the cloth and found a dried turkey wing with a note from Sarah: "Feathers to keep your camp clean."

Always Singing giggled when she saw Sarah's gift.

Why was she laughing? "We use wing feathers to dust our home," I explained.

Deer Woman smiled. "Blackfeet use turkey wing too." She reached for the hide bag she'd brought.

I undid the strings and pulled out *another* turkey wing. Beaded leather around the base made a colorful handle.

Deer Woman swept her hand back and forth across her face. "For heat."

A fan! Now *I* laughed, too. "I bet I'm the only girl in

Cache Valley to get two turkey wings for her birthday! Thank you."

The square tin held a batch of molasses taffy.

Matthew spoke up from his stump. "Molly and Inga Lindstrom cooked it up. I helped pull it."

I nearly dropped the tin. Matthew's fingernails were usually caked with dirt.

"Before I buttered my hands, they made sure I scrubbed 'em real good," he said. "You'd a thought I was made of filth the way they acted."

The envelope held Molly's artwork. She had drawn the two of us in a field. We wore flower crowns and skipped in a circle, holding hands. Just last summer we'd pretended to be dancing princesses.

The last box surprised me the most. It was a set of quoits that Matthew had made. "Aaron Tuttle's been teaching me to whittle. He helped me get the rings right, but I did the post on my own."

"Thank you. We'll have a good time with this ring toss."

Mama's cake tin held my favorite sweet—molasses fruitcake. She had made it big enough to share with all my friends. Deer Woman sliced my cake, and I passed around the tin of taffy.

Always Singing bit into her piece of candy. "Oh!" Her eyes grew wide and she licked her lips. The other Blackfeet reacted in the same way. Raven Feather studied her taffy bit as if she was looking for something.

What was wrong? Had Molly's taffy gone bad? I took a bite. It was as delicious as ever.

I soon learned that sugar was a new taste for the Blackfeet. The taffy's sweetness had been a surprise. A pleasant surprise!

While we enjoyed our sweets, Matthew disappeared. What was he up to? He'd been mannerly most all afternoon. Was he about to turn mean?

Before I could follow him, he came back lugging the crate he'd hidden earlier.

"This is from your pa."

Sixteen

"What a horrible thing to say!" I snapped. "How could you be so hurtful?"

Matthew set the crate on my rock. "Hannah, it's true. He started it last winter for your birthday. When he, uh, couldn't finish it, your ma asked Aaron to get it done." His voice cracked again. "Just open it."

It was an oak lap desk. Fancy flower carvings outlined in gold decorated the lid. It opened to make a writing surface covered with green blotter paper. I lifted the ribbon tab. A collection of paper, pens, and pencils rested in separate spaces.

I squeezed my eyes tight, but two tears escaped to form circles on the blotting paper.

Matthew pulled a wrinkled-up red cloth from his back pocket and pushed it at me. "Here, now. Don't cry."

Embarrassed, I snatched the handkerchief.

Mama's gift was last. A shiny wooden brush all my own!

"Your ma said to send back your pa's brush for Caleb," Matthew said.

We ate Mama's cake, chewed taffy, and tried my new games. No one could beat Always Singing at quoits. Every ring landed smack dab onto the post with a solid *thunk*.

Deer Woman and I tried to start a game of Jackstraws, but Rosie stuck her nose in the pile and sent sticks rolling every which way.

Before she left, Raven Feather spoke to Matthew. "You are a good friend for Hannah."

Matthew turned red as his handkerchief. "Thank you, ma'am."

We watched the Blackfeet walk away.

"Never thought Indians could be so nice," Matthew mumbled. "It's lucky you got some friends close by. Must get awful lonely. 'Specially when something bad happens."

"I'm getting used to it, but I miss my family. Mostly at night."

Matthew cleared his throat. "I heard a bear killed a man up here. Didn't that scare you?"

I told him about the hairs I'd found and the nighttime roars. "They're right scary, 'specially when they seem nearby. I don't know what I'd do if I saw a bear up close."

"Hunh?" Matthew snorted. "You got your pa's rifle. If you see a bear, shoot 'im!"

I frowned. "I hope I don't have to."

"Just like a girl! If something happens to you, who's gonna tend the sheep?"

I was plain tired of menfolk reminding me about caring for the sheep! Did they have even one worry about someone caring for *me*?

"Anyways," Matthew said, "you remember the Mortensons that used to live up near Jacob Corner?"

I nodded. Annie Mortenson had been in school with us.

"Well, a bear come up to their house one night when Annie's pa was away. Mrs. Mortenson 'n' all the kids got up on the roof. They hollered and made a racket with pot lids and broom handles and such. Scared that bear away. Never came back."

I'd forgotten that story. Knowing there were ways other than guns to get rid of a bear gave me comfort.

But Matthew snatched it away. " 'Course, the bear you been hearing's pretty mad. Banging a pot likely wouldn't work."

I slumped onto my rock. "I'd rather bang a pot than shoot a gun."

"What's the sense having a rifle if you're not gonna use it? I thought you wouldn't be such a scaredy-cat now you're in charge of a sheep herd."

"Humph!" I said. "I thought you'd changed, but you're as rude as ever. Tell Aaron Tuttle you need more lessons on manners!"

"Just 'cause I say what's true don't make me rude."

Matthew stood and stretched. "Time to head home. Guess you'll be glad to see me go." He threw the saddle over Zeke's back. "You got anything for me to take to your ma?"

"Wait a bit." I rinsed the cake tin and taffy container and wrapped them in muslin along with Papa's brush.

Matthew packed the bundle in a saddlebag. "I reckon your uncle'll come next Saturday."

"I appreciate you bringing my supplies and presents. Please thank everyone for me."

He flicked the reins over Zeke's neck. "So long. Next time I see you will likely be at school."

"Hold up!" I ran inside the camp and grabbed a hunk of cheese and some dried apples. "In case you get hungry on the trail."

"Thank you, Hannah."

Matthew turned the bend, and I glanced at the quoits set he'd made. It had taken a lot of work and patience—two habits I never connected with Matthew Colton.

I hummed as I straightened the camp and put my presents away. I carefully set Papa's lap desk on the table and brushed it with my turkey wing duster.

For supper, I cooked up wild turnips and onions with the salt pork. I was so full of cake and taffy that I didn't have much room for sensible food. Rosie ate her portion and most of mine as well.

The night air brought a chill, so I moved inside. I settled in my rocking chair and began *Little Women*. Of the four March sisters, Amy wouldn't last one hour in a sheep camp. She worried too much about clothes and pretty trinkets.

Rosie's bark woke me as dawn's gray light seeped through the window. I covered my head with Grandma's quilt, my insides quivering with cold. Time to stoke up the cook stove. I dressed under the covers. My icy fingers struggled to work buttons and ties. I stepped onto the freezing camp floor, pulled on my boots and overcoat, and scurried to the doorway.

Oh, no! Not a stick of firewood in sight. I had been too surprised yesterday to notice that Matthew hadn't brought a fresh supply, and I'd used up all the ground kindling. The only wood nearby was my make-do staff, and I'd come to depend on it to move the sheep. No help for it. I'd have to leave camp, but I'd not go the direction of my wildflower hunt. I'd had enough of bear hairs.

When Uncle John and I had come up last month, I'd spotted a giant dead pine fallen across the stream. Its top branches should come loose with little effort. It was farther away than I cared to venture, but chopping a dead tree was the easiest way to get firewood.

I needed enough to last 'til Saturday . . . too much for me to tote in one trip.

"Rosie, I need your help." I hitched her to the Blackfeet

travois and grabbed my ax. I left Papa's rifle in the camp. If I carried it along with the ax, I couldn't bring back an extra armful of wood.

"Come on, Rosie. Let's go!"

Fee-bee-yee! A chickadee said good-bye and flew to the quakey nest.

I hurried down the trail. *Get this trip over with!* My heart pounded. My breath puffed white curls into the chilly air. The ax bumped against my shoulder. Rosie kept ahead, the empty travois poles clanking against the hard ground. We passed a giant cottonwood tree I'd not noticed before.

Finally, the dead tree came in view. The top branches were on my side of the rushing stream. I skidded to a stop. "Rosie, stay!"

I swung the ax high and forced it down. *Whap.* Hacked the dead wood hard as I could. *Oof!* Pain throbbed up my arm. *Whap.* The noise echoed through the woods.

Finally the travois was packed full. A few more chops gave me a load to carry. As we turned to leave, Rosie growled and bared her teeth. Why was she carrying on?

A dark mound moved in the tall grass across the stream. Chills wrapped me tight. Slowly, the mound grew larger and stood.

The bear's eyes fixed on me.

Seventeen

Heavenly Father, protect us!

Had my noisy hacking angered the bear? Fright nailed my feet in place. My arms turned to mush and dropped the wood. I listened for more angry grunts. Waited to feel the earth tremble as the bear charged across the stream.

The bear didn't move. Our eyes locked.

Without my rifle, what should I do? Run? Stand my ground?

Rosie kept barking.

I bent to stroke her back. "Shush!" I hissed.

I looked up.

The bear had disappeared. *Now what?*

Limp as Mama's noodles, I crumpled onto the kindling. Splintery edges ripped a new hole in my stocking and scraped my arms. *Where was the bear?*

Wherever that bear had gone, Rosie and I had to get home. I gathered the wood, pulled my apron corners tight around the load, and picked up the ax.

I looked. Listened. No sound or sight of bear.

"Let's go!"

Rosie strained ahead with the loaded travois. I longed to run, but my burden slowed me. A strong breeze caught us as we neared the cottonwood tree. Fluff drifted onto Rosie's load. *Aa-choo.* Sneezes took hold of me so strong that my eyes filled. The trail ahead blurred.

"Oof!" I stumbled over a tree root. My arms whirligigged. Wood and ax went flying. *Aa-choo.* I landed hard on my backside and rubbed a sleeve across my eyes and runny nose. My throat tightened so much, I couldn't find breath.

Heavenly Father, help me!

Rosie licked my face. I gulped in air and looked around. No bear.

Good!

We were on our way again. My fear imagined bears everywhere. Each tree held deep scratches. Every uneven spot was a paw print. Rustling sounds meant a stalking bear. *How much farther?*

Ahead of me, Rosie barked. Our camp was in view.

Fee-bee-yee! The chickadees welcomed us back.

We were home.

I freed Rosie from the travois, scurried up the camp steps, and bolted the door. A bundle of shivers, I collapsed onto the bunk. *Heavenly Father, thank you for bringing us home safe. I promise to always look before I leap if You'll just keep me from harm. Amen.*

Finally my shaking stopped. I took stock. Torn apron and stockings.

Filthy arms and face. Most important, the bear hadn't harmed me or my dog.

Outside, Rosie barked. Time to move the sheep. I slowly opened the door and searched the campsite. Was it safe? Safe or not, I had to a job to do. I crept down the steps with the rifle and my make-do staff.

As Rosie and I guided the herd, I considered what had happened that morning. I had ventured far from camp. Chopped kindling. Faced a bear.

And thought of my sheep camp as home.

Eighteen

I told Always Singing and the women about the bear. "I just stared. I didn't know what to do."

"Sticky Mouth sleeps in soft grass," Raven Feather said. "You surprised her."

"No," I said. "*She* surprised *me*."

Raven Feather shrugged.

I frowned. "But why did she run away?"

"She follows her spirit."

What did that mean?

Later, as we worked on the doll tipi, I asked Always Singing to explain.

"Sticky Mouth hunts. Eats. Sleeps. Comes close. Goes away."

The next day, Always Singing handed me a small painted pouch. "For you."

I spread the drawstring and looked inside. I shuddered. The bag held the dark bear hairs I'd taken from the log.

"Wear them for power."

Wear them? I threw the pouch to the ground. "I don't want to wear *anything* from a bear!" I snapped.

Always Singing's brown eyes narrowed. She walked away.

My face burned. When would I learn to think before I used hurtful words? I wanted to grab my meanness back, but the harm was done.

Silence. The children stopped playing. The chickadees ended their cheery song. My eyes blurred with shame as I watched the Blackfeet leave.

I fretted the rest of the day. Supper tasted flat. Music held no comfort. The sheep's bleating chatter irked me. A needle prick left a spot of blood on my sampler.

I had acted spoiled and rude—just like Amy March. *Heavenly Father, pardon me. Give the Blackfeet forgiving hearts, especially my friend Always Singing. Thank you. Amen.*

The evening pit fire cast light on the pouch Always Singing had brought. I picked it up. *I'm sorry, Always Singing.* The soft pouch warmed my skin. Was its power working?

I scurried into the camp to huddle with my nightly companions: Liza Lou, my charm string, and the rifle. Were they my only mountain friends now? I prayed again that Always Singing would forgive me.

The bear was quiet that night.

The next morning, a look in the mirror told me it was high time I washed my hair. Grease spatters from the frying pan had trapped dirt in my tangled curls. My itchy scalp stank of dirt and sweat. I filled two buckets from the stream and laid out my new brush on a towel. I looked around. No claw scratches on tree bark. No matted grass nearby. No sign of the bear.

I knelt on the bank and dumped water on my head. Mama's lye soap lathered up fine. *Ouch.* Suds burned into my eyes. I felt along the ground for the towel and snatched it up. *Kerplunk.* Something hit the water. I squinted through the stinging soap and saw my brush hurtle downstream.

I raced along the bank. *No!* My birthday gift was about to disappear in a swirl. I plunged into the freezing water and shot my fingers out until they touched bristles. I grabbed at the brush, but it tumbled away in the stream's rush down to Logan River.

I crawled out of the water. Clothes, hair, every inch of me, dripped onto the bank, turning it to mud. Not thinking had brought me another misery. *Now what?* I rinsed my hair 'til the water ran clear. When I reached up to smooth my headful of kinks, my fingers pulled against the tangles. Snarls caught each other like sheep fleece.

Anger twisted my insides. Why couldn't I have silky hair like Molly? Or smooth, shiny braids like Always Singing?

I stomped up the camp steps to look for a way to settle my hair. *A fork.* Tangles held the tines tight. *Knives.* Could

I carve a wooden comb? My knives cut meat and bread. They shaved off pencil ends. I doubted they'd whittle comb teeth.

One tool would work. Papa's words about my crown of sunshine echoed in my mind. I was about to destroy that crown.

I opened my sewing basket and drew out the scissors. *Snip.* One snarl fell. *Hack.* Another matted curl. Another and another. Yellow hair piled around my feet. One last chop. I looked in the tin mirror and saw a curly-haired boy with sad eyes.

I swept my lost hair out of the camp. Yellow wisps floated through the air. *Fee-bee-yee.* A chickadee swooped to flip around the clothesline. She flew off with a curl.

I peeled off my soaked clothing and toweled myself dry. After I dressed, I set my boots in the sun and hung the soggy clothes on the line. Time to rest. I lay on the bunk fingering my charm string and tried to turn my mind to *Little Women.*

Steps on the camp stairs woke me.

"Hannah!" Always Singing stared at me from the doorway.

I smiled. She was back, in spite of my bad manners.

Instead of smiling, Always Singing rushed to my side. "Who is dead?"

What?

She ran outside. Blackfeet words rushed between her and the women. I stepped to the doorway. Several gasps greeted me.

Deer Woman said, "Someone is dead."

I turned to Always Singing. "I don't understand."

"Your hair is gone."

"Yes. I cut it off."

Raven Feather explained. "Many Blackfeet women cut their hair to show sadness for a death."

Oh! "No one is dead." I told them why my long hair was now on the ground. "My hair has never been cut before."

Raven Feather stroked my short curls. "This is sad for you."

❊   ❊   ❊

Later, Always Singing and I cut sticks for the doll tipi.

"I'm sorry for what I said yesterday," I said. "I didn't understand."

She nodded. "Blackfeet ways are not your's."

I looked at the gopher skin. "How can we decorate it?"

"Paint is there." Always Singing smiled and her hand swept the air, as if she was gathering up the wooded hills and stream.

What did she see in those thickets? Even if I looked with my heart, I would never find paint!

Another puzzle to think over.

Nineteen

Rosie's bark announced a new day, sunny and warm. I had slept through the night without hearing the bear. *Thank you, Heavenly Father, for a quiet night and peaceful morning.*

My peace ended when the herd count showed three ewes missing. Had coyotes left another bloody trail? Was the bear attacking the herd now? I shouldered my rifle and clambered up the hill behind camp, on the lookout for signs of danger. Rosie stayed close by my side.

Faint bleats led us to the wanderers as they munched dewy grass beneath a pine. "You gave us a scare," I scolded.

Rosie used her best stare and barked commands to move them back to the herd.

Chores filled up my morning: tidy the camp with the turkey wing duster . . . rub clothes and sheets against the washboard . . . drape them over the clothesline. Soon sweat rolled down my back, and I was happy to have short hair. My Blackfeet fan nicely cooled the air as I ate beans and rice.

That afternoon, I toted wood to heat the cook stove for baking. My uncle still chided me about the biscuit disaster the day Alice was born. I'd show him I could make a proper batch. I slid the pan into the oven. By then, the camp was hot enough to bake *me*. I went outside to take down the wash.

Fee-bee-yee. A chickadee flew to the nest. *Peep-peep-peep.* The babies had hatched! I dragged the washtub across the rough ground and climbed up to take a look. Not high enough. I added an upturned bucket, wobbled some on the rickety perch and saw five tiny beaks. *Peep-peep. Feed me!*

Rosie set up a high warning bark. My insides flapped around like sheets on the line. Was the bear near camp? As I teetered off the makeshift ladder, my nose wrinkled at an ugly smell. Burnt biscuits!

When I pulled the smoking tin from the oven, black clumps stuck to the charred pan. I longed to throw the whole mess into the stream. Let the gurgling water swallow my biscuits! But Mama expected me to bring home every piece of her kitchen goods. I put the scorched pan to soak.

After supper the sun still hung high over the ridge where I had first seen the bear. Time to fix my blunder. I loaded a bucket with scraping tools and a bag of cleanser sand and carried the burnt tin to my rock.

Rosie stuck her muzzle in the pan and came away with an ashy nose.

"I'll never get this done with you poking about!" I tied her under the camp.

I scraped the hard black crust, scrubbed the pan, and then rinsed it in the rushing stream. The pan looked just the same. I sighed and returned to the rock. Tried again. The second rinse showed no change. I started back to the rock for another try.

Rosie barked.

Goose flesh tingled up my arms. Was the bear near?

Growl!

Clutching the pan, I turned toward the noise. The bear stood at the edge of the stream. *My* side of the stream. No farther away than the distance from our privy to the back door at home. *Too close.*

She reached one massive paw toward me.

I froze.

Rosie near went crazy barking.

The powerful giant stopped. Her dark eyes burned into mine. Long snout sniffed the air. Triangles of pale fur marked her forehead. An enormous hump swelled between her shoulders.

Think.

The bear plodded one step nearer.

Shivers ran through me. What should I do? The rifle rested against a camp wheel. Out of reach.

The bear lumbered so close I could hear her breathing.

Do something!

The huge animal reared up on her hind legs. Larger than any nightmare monster I'd ever dreamed, her size filled me with terror. Grunts wheezed out in loud huffs. She watched me. Waited.

What should I do? Jumbled words crowded my mind: *Aim straight . . . look before you leap . . . Sticky Mouth follows her spirit . . . Heavenly Father always with you . . . ain't you scared? . . . look with your heart . . . the Mortensons got on the roof.*

That was it!

Watch the bear. Don't look away. I shuffled backward. Those dark eyes followed every move.

I carefully sidled onto the upturned washtub.

Slow, slow. Climb up. Make a racket.

I banged the biscuit pan with my ash scoop. Stomped my boots on the metal tub. Always Singing's bear pouch bumped against my chest.

Bang. Thunk. Stomp.

The bear stared. Menacing claws dug the air. Sunlight spread her shadow until it near reached the tub.

I shrunk into myself. What other noise could I make? *A made-up song.*

Powerful One, listen to me.
Whack.
Strong One, hear my song.
Boom.

Go home, Mighty Spirit! Go home!
Whomp.

I kept on and on.
Sing. Stomp. Bang.

The bear dropped to all fours. Sniffed. Stretched a paw so close that I could count all five claws.

"No!" I sang so loud that my chest hurt. "Go home, Mighty Spirit!" I whacked the biscuit pan against the oak tree. "Go home."

The bear turned. With a soft grunt, she disappeared into the pines.

I kept up my rumpus like a wind-up toy. Over and over. Where had the bear gone? Was she waiting out of sight?

Don't stop. Bang. Stomp.

My feet burned. Hollering seared my throat. Smacking the pan numbed my hands. Worn out, I stopped to listen. No grunt. No roar. Rosie was quiet. The bear had gone.

Go!

I jumped off the tub and scrambled into the camp. Bolted the door and crawled under the covers . . . boots, clothes, and all. I piled on more blankets to quiet my shivers and burrowed into the farthest corner of the bunk. *Thank you, Heavenly Father.* When my trembles slowed, I dragged my charm string from under the pillow and fingered the black button from Grandma's coat. My bear's eye button. Liza Lou huddled with me as I stroked the smooth circle.

I spent the night awake, thinking about the danger I'd faced. I had sent the bear away without hurting her.

Without hurting me.

Twenty

D*ear Molly,*
Last night a giant grizzly came close enough to touch.

I stopped. Thinking about last night made my writing tremble across the page. I took a deep breath and went on.

> *I've never been so scared! When that bear reared up and came at me, I set up a terrible loud ruckus. I couldn't think what else to do. The bear turned and ran. It's true! I know that Heavenly Father helped, but I stood up to that grizzly myself. I felt like I grew five years in five minutes last night. I was in such a state that I left my rifle outside and went to bed with all my clothes on—even my boots.*
>
> *I didn't want to go outside this morning, but Rosie's bark reminded me I had work. I sure took a good look around for bear signs before we moved the sheep. When*

I saw the paw prints where the bear stood last night, I shivered all over again. I'll never . . .

I jerked my pencil off the paper. Much as I longed to tell Molly that I'd faced that bear and made it leave, I'd best keep the whole thing to myself. If I told Molly, she'd tell her mother, who would tell Mama. It wouldn't do for my mother to know how close I'd come to a grizzly. She'd only add that danger to her cares. I crumpled the letter and threw it into the cook stove fire.

> *Dear Molly,*
>   *Thank you for the pretty picture. I hung it above my bunk. The taffy was delicious. I shared it with my Blackfeet friends, and it disappeared quick as a wink! I was a mite worried when Matthew said he'd helped make it. I'm sure glad you made him scrub good.*

There. That was better. I owed my friend a thank-you letter. I'd keep my bear story until I could tell it in person.

> *You were right about Matthew acting more polite. Your brother's a good teacher. Please thank him for finishing my lap desk. It's beautiful.*
>   *I'm glad you're having a good summer. I miss you every day.*
>   *Love,*
>   *Hannah*

I sealed the letter in an envelope and drew a heart on the flap.

Outside, I searched in all directions for signs of the bear. My noisemaking tools were scattered where I'd dropped them. The beat-up pan would never be fit for baking again, but I rinsed it in the stream just the same. The cold water would feel mighty good on my sore feet. Keeping the rifle close, I peeled off my stockings and boots to soak my blistered soles. Rosie sat nearby as the icy stream carried my pain away.

Fee-bee-yee. The chickadees flew back and forth, caring for their babies.

When the Blackfeet came, I told them about my night-time visitor. "I made such a noise!" I repeated the words of the song I had made up.

Raven Feather smiled. "You honored Sticky Mouth with music. That was brave."

Honored the bear?

"You listened to your heart," Always Singing said. "She knew."

"Yes," Deer Woman said, "she felt your courage."

"I couldn't think what else to do."

"It is a reason to be happy." Deer Woman smiled.

She was right. I thought of how her family had shown their happiness when Wind recovered from snakebite. "I'll have a Giveaway!"

"A good idea," Always Singing said. "When?"

When? I needed time to make gifts. "Soon."

Later I thought about my invitation. How could I give something to each person? Rosie and I hardly had enough for ourselves. Sewing notions, baking supplies, writing paper, pen, and pencils. Not much for a Giveaway.

After puzzling a bit, I made a list: vinegar candy, molasses fruitcake, and homemade toys. Miss Taylor often showed us how to make toys when bad weather kept us inside for recess. Whirls, paper hats, thaumatropes. That last one was my favorite. It twirled until the drawings on both sides blended into one picture.

The bear was quiet that night. Had she gone away for good? Every snap or thump clenched my heart.

Uncle John arrived the next morning while I was searching for tiny stones to weight the whirls. He yanked Zeke's reins up short when he saw me. "Where in thunder did your hair go?"

He *tsk*-ed and shook his head when I explained.

"I'm purely sad about losing that brush," I said, "but my hair will grow back."

I told him about my Giveaway plan.

Uncle John smiled. "That's right nice of you, Hannah. What are you celebrating?"

I described my meeting with the bear.

"Glory!" He whacked his hat against the water barrel. "What were you thinking, Hannah? Making music to scare a bear! That's what you got a rifle for."

"I couldn't reach it."

His groan shook the air. "Have you seen the bear since?"

"No, sir. No sign at all." I made sure of that every time I ventured out.

"It's a good thing Caleb's back."

What did that mean?

He hugged me close. "We'll credit Heavenly Father tomorrow in church."

"No!" I pulled away. "Please don't tell Mama. She has enough care with Caleb and the little ones."

Finally, he agreed. "I'll leave you to tell her."

Without talking more, we unloaded the usual supplies from Flint's travois, plus something new. Heavy string held a bundle of *Sego Springs Gazettes*, our little town's weekly newspaper.

"Your aunt sent these. Thought you'd like to catch up on Cache Valley news."

"I would, indeed." And then I'd turn those newspapers into paper hats.

We finished unpacking and sat in the shade of the oak tree to eat dinner.

"Tell me about Caleb," I said. "Will he be all right?'

"Caleb's fine. He had it hard, waiting for help in that mine shaft, but he's put that mostly behind him. Just a bad memory." He handed me an envelope. "He sent this."

Dear Hannah,

Sorry you had to take summer grazing. Seems you've had a bad time of it, putting up with Indians and all. I'm real regretful about losing Shep. Watch out for yourself. Be careful of the Blackfeet. I've heard tales to make your hair stand on end.

I stared at Caleb's words. Why on earth did he think I was *putting up* with Indians? Why think so poorly of folks he hadn't even met?

Ma says none of my letters got home and she feared I was dead. Pa's passing near broke my heart. My leg's mending fast—good enough to hobble around with Rosie. I'll take over for you next week so you can be safe at home for the rest of the summer.

Your loving brother,

Caleb

Uncle John hugged my shoulder. "I know his offer makes you happy. We asked too much of you to take the sheep all alone."

I jerked away. "That's not what you said when you sent me here! I've done everything you asked. I kept the sheep safe and only lost one lamb to a coyote. I've taken care of myself, cooked, and washed, and chopped wood. . . even stood up to a grizzly. 'Cept for the Blackfeet, no one helped me. I've made friends here. Why should I go home?"

"Because—"

"I *won't* go home!"

"Watch how you talk to your elders, missy!"

"I'm sorry, Uncle, but I want to finish my job."

Uncle John's face was set as stern as that night in June when he told me I had no choice about how I'd spend my summer. "Lookit here, Hannah. You're just a little girl."

I straightened up. "I was big enough when you needed me for the sheep. I'm plenty big enough now."

He patted my back. "'Course you are." His voice softened. "But your ma misses you something terrible, Hannah. You owe it to her to come home."

I shook my head. "I miss Mama too, but Caleb's been gone almost a year. He'll be company and comfort for her 'til I bring the sheep down. 'Sides, he can help you with the crops." Surely my uncle could see the reason of this.

He shook his head. "Your mother worries about you."

"Why can't you tell her that I'm doing the job I was sent to do?" I asked.

Instead of answering, he turned away and saddled Zeke. After some short words of good-bye, he left.

As I watched him go, I prayed that he and Mama would let me finish my summer in the mountains.

Twenty-one

I was still stewing over Caleb's letter when the Black-feet came. I took Always Singing aside. "My brother's coming to take over the sheep and send me home," I sputtered. "I don't want to leave!"

She nodded. "You want to finish your work."

"Yes!" It was some comfort to know she understood.

"Soon Grandfather will give the sign to move." Always Singing linked her arm in mine. "It is hard to say good-bye."

We stood together under the oak tree, watching chickadee babies peek over the nest edge. Even the little birds would have to leave soon.

"Knee-poh-mah-key," Always Singing said. "I am one."

"You're a chickadee?" Something else to puzzle over.

"Our Chickadee Society is for the children. We learn Blackfeet ways."

I smiled at the thought of my sweet friend being a chickadee.

Always Singing handed me a bunch of paintbrush flowers. "Tipi paint." We folded the flowers inside the gopher skin and weighted it down with heavy rocks. I could hardly wait to see the design the bright red blossoms would leave.

I decided to hold my Giveaway on Friday. If Uncle John took me home the next day, I'd have no other chance to honor the Blackfeet.

"The Giveaway is in six days," I announced.

Always Singing smiled. "Good! We will bring a surprise."

"What is it?'

She laughed. "You said that a surprise is something you don't know until it happens."

"You're right. I'll have to wait."

After the Blackfeet left, I fingered the orange stone on my charm chain. It would always remind me of Always Singing's words: "Look with your heart."

Rumbling baas and Rosie's bark startled me awake Friday morning. A quartet of ewes ignored the command to move, but Rosie stared them down. They complained loudly as I nudged them along with my make-do staff. They quieted when they reached fresh grazing.

I mixed the last of my dried apples and raisins into the fruitcake batter. This time I watched over my baking instead of reading or wandering off to look at chickadee nests. The cake came out fine. Rosie and I moved the sheep to shade, and I set out my Giveaway presents.

Next step: vinegar candy. I boiled sugar, vinegar, and water. Then I added butter and baking soda and spread the mixture to cool on a buttered pan. It would be ready to pull when the Blackfeet came. Next to eating, pulling candy was the best part of sweet-making.

Just in time! My friends moved across the rocky ground toward camp. *Fee-bee-yee!* The chickadee parents perched on the clothesline to sing a cheery welcome.

I tried not to think about how much I would miss my friends as I greeted them: "Welcome. I hold this Giveaway to thank the Great Spirit of Heavenly Father, to honor the Blackfeet, and to celebrate my meeting with the bear." I pointed to the paper hats and whirls that I'd arranged on my rock.

I showed the little ones how to make their whirls spring up and down in the breeze. Then I passed out the hats. The children giggled as my newspaper gifts slipped over eyes and ears or teetered to the ground.

While they played, I turned to Always Singing. "I need your help." I brought out the pan of taffy and a dish of butter. We washed our hands in the stream, then coated them in butter. I carefully peeled the vinegar candy from the pan. "Take one end," I said, "and pull."

The little ones made a circle around us as we worked.

Always Singing and I stretched out the candy and

folded it back in. Pulled out, folded in. Moved back, stepped forward, away, then together, over and over 'til our hands grew tired. Finally, the candy hardened enough to cut.

We took it in the camp and cut bite-size pieces with my sewing scissors. I stacked the sweets on a plate and started for the door.

"Wait!" Always Singing held my arm. "We should taste one to be sure it is good." Her dark eyes sparkled.

We chewed away, and soon drops of sugary juice dribbled down our chins.

"Sticky mouths!" I declared.

Always Singing giggled agreement.

I brought the candy, and she carried the cake outside. Everyone gathered around the rock, and we ate our fill. We took turns on the ridy-bob and swing and tossed Matthew's rings. Then everyone ran to the stream. We cupped our hands and drank the clear, cold water.

Arm in arm, Always Singing and I walked back to my rock.

Deer Woman motioned everyone to stand. "The Blackfeet want to honor your courage, Hannah."

A flutter of excitement ran through me.

Always Singing touched my arm. "We told Grandfather of your bravery."

Her mother nodded. "You honored Sticky Mouth by showing her no fear. Now my father honors you with the name Makes Strong Music."

"Make music!" the little ones shouted.

"Yes," Deer Woman said. "Let us hear your music."

I felt foolish making such a racket when there was no bear to scare away, but I wanted to show my friends how pleased I was with my new name. I fetched the beat-up pan and a wooden spoon from the wagon and climbed up on the stump. Banging away, I danced and sang:

> *Powerful One, listen to me.*
> *Stomp.*
> *Strong One, hear my song.*
> *Boom.*
> *Go home, Mighty Spirit! Go home!*
> *Whomp.*

I beat out a rhythm and hopped from one foot to the other. Soon everyone was clapping the same beat and dancing around the stump. I finished with one loud *thump* and jumped down.

"Your music has power." Deer Woman stepped forward and pulled something from her leather bag. "For you." A leather strip held a small bear claw. She slipped it over my head.

"Thank you! I am honored." Hot tears welled at the thought of leaving. I squeezed my eyes to hide them. Tomorrow I'd be sent down the mountain and never see my friends again.

"We will come tomorrow," Raven Feather said.

"It will be the last time I'll see you," I told her. "My uncle will take me away." Sobs burst out of me.

Deer Woman touched my shoulder. "A change may come. Wait to cry when it is time."

Trying to save my tears for later, I watched them leave. Their kindness had warmed me from my first day in the mountains. I was sure I'd never see them again after tomorrow. I attacked the battered pan with my wooden spoon, pounding it as hard as I could. Too much had been snatched away from me: Caleb and Papa, my summer in the valley with Mama and my sisters, Shep, and now the Blackfeet. Just when I'd got the hang of my summer job with the sheep, I was losing it too.

I clutched my charm string and felt for the peach-stone button that Caleb had carved. I loved my brother, and I was glad he was home safe, but I didn't want him to take my job.

❈   ❈   ❈

On Saturday morning, I heard a horse clopping up the path. Just one horse! I jumped up to thank Uncle John for letting me stay.

Caleb sat on Zeke. He was alone. Did that mean he would stay and I was to ride Zeke home? A mix of anger and sadness gripped me.

Twenty-two

"Howdy, little sister!" Caleb shouted. "You're a sight with that short hair. Folks'll take you for a boy—a mighty pretty one."

Rosie went crazy, barking and jumping up on Zeke. I rushed to my brother's side. Caleb might've come to send me home, but I was powerful glad to see him.

"Help me down. My leg's stiff as a plank."

I led Zeke to the stump. Caleb swung his good leg over the saddle and slid down. For a minute he tottered back and forth, and I braced to help him catch his balance.

He hugged me tight. "Whew! Still haven't got the hang of getting off a horse with this bum leg."

"Does it pain you much?" I clung to my brother. He'd grown considerable since I'd last seen him.

"Naw, just locks up if I hold it the same way too long." He looked toward the sound of baas. "Herd sure sounds content. Never thought a girl could do this job, but Uncle John says you're handling it fine."

Did that mean I could stay?

I helped him settle on my rock and fetched a dipper of water. "What was it like in the mines? Being so far away and all."

Caleb shrugged. "Pretty country. Mountains—like here. Hard work, for sure. In the bunkhouse, I heard every language you could imagine . . . French, Swedish, German, Polish, and like that. Drinking water was bad and I got sick more 'n' once. There was a breakout of diphtheria. I worked with fellas that took sick one day and were dead a few days later. I was lucky. Never came down with it." He took a long drink. "Then an accident near killed me." He fell quiet and stared across the stream.

I waited, not knowing what to say.

"Me and two other fellas were working in a side tunnel when the roof caved in. I was close to the entryway and fell out into the main tunnel. A timber pinned my leg so's I couldn't move. I heard the other two moaning, but I couldn't get to them. Then their moaning stopped." He sighed. "They didn't make it."

I chilled at the awful things my brother had been through. "I'm glad Heavenly Father brought you home, Caleb."

He shook his head. "I did a fool thing, going off like that to make money. Money don't mean nothing if you're crippled—or worse, dead." He patted my knee. "It's good to be back in the valley, Hannah." He stared off again.

Was he going to tell me now? To hold back hearing the bad news, I chattered away about losing Shep and meeting up with the bear and cutting my hair and making new friends. I talked so fast the words bumped against each other. ". . . and the sunsets are a sight up here, and I've never seen so many kinds of flowers, and there's a nest of chicka—"

"Hold up!" Caleb raised his hands. "You're going to talk yourself clean out of breath!"

I took in a gulp of air. Waited to be told I was going home.

"I come to tell you something."

My fists clenched, along with my innards.

"Uncle John said your mind's set to finish summer grazing. Ma put up a fuss at first 'cause she worries you're not safe. She worr—"

I jumped up. "But I *am* safe. I scared off a big grizzly—by myself."

"Thunderation, Hannah! Let me finish."

I slumped against the oak tree.

"Uncle John stood up for you. He sat Ma down in the parlor and told her about the bear and how plucky you are. Said you've done a fine job taking care of things. Held that you oughta stay here, and I oughta stay on the farm to help him."

I tried to picture the scene in our parlor. Ma in the rocker, her mouth in a thin line. Uncle John on the settee, leaning forward as he talked.

"It took a while, but Ma finally saw the reason for it. To tell the truth, I'm right glad to stay home for a while. Summer'll be over in a few weeks, anyways."

I stared at Caleb. Had I heard right?

"What's wrong?" he asked. "Thought that's what you wanted."

I hugged him tight. "Oh, it is!"

"Well, then, let's unpack your supplies. I got to get back."

"Can't you stay to meet the Blackfeet?"

"Nope. Ma's countin' on me to drive the wagon to Logan this afternoon to pick up a load of barbwire and lumber. Now that I'm back, there's plenty for me to do."

I pulled on his sleeve. "I wanted you to meet Always Singing and her family."

"Sorry," he said. "Not this time. I hear they've been real nice to you, and I'm glad for that. I guess there's good folks everywhere."

"If you come next week, you can see for yourself."

"You've my word that I'll stay for a time," he said. "It's good to be home, little sister, and it's a blessing to see you doing so well."

"It's more a blessing to see you," I said. "I feared I'd never lay eyes on you again."

"Well, here I am." He laughed. "And you'll be seein' me regular from now on."

He hobbled over to Zeke. "Reckon I'd better get going."

"Take care, Caleb. Give Mama and the little girls my love." I helped him climb into the saddle.

He looked down at me. "Remember how Pa was always telling you to look before you leap?"

I swallowed hard. "I remember."

He smiled. "I reckon you've learned to do that this summer."

"I reckon so, Caleb."

I watched my brother out of sight and then turned to look at my summer home. Rosie dozed under the camp. Chickadee babies teetered on their nest. The stream rushed by, gurgling over its rocky bed. Soon the Blackfeet would make their daily visit. The sheep bleated their complaints about the midday heat. Time to move them to shade.

I picked up my make-do staff.

"Come on, Rosie, let's get to work."

Twenty-three

After Rosie and I tended to our herding chores, I set out a chunk of salt pork to reward her hard work. "You've truly been a good friend, girl."

Busy with her treat, she paid my compliment no mind.

"Hannah!"

I turned to see Always Singing running ahead of her mother and aunt. "We heard a man's voice. I worried that your uncle had taken you away." She looked around the campsite. "Where is Horse Ride?"

"My brother Caleb brought my supplies, but then—"

"Where is he?"

"He went back to our farm. Mama needs his help."

I wished Molly could be here to draw every look that raced across Always Singing's face. *Worry. Puzzlement.*

"I'm to stay with the sheep 'til summer's end," I told her.

Relief. Happiness.

"You will not leave?"

"No!" I squealed.

We joined hands and spun around and around in a wild, hopping dance. Always Singing's braids flew in the summer air, but my short curls stayed put. The little Blackfeet joined us, and soon our circle ringed the fire pit.

When we dropped to the ground, dizzy and out of breath, Raven Feather and Deer Woman sat with us. Always Singing told them my happy news.

I smiled at Deer Woman. "You were right to tell me to save my tears. I had no need to cry about leaving too soon."

"I am glad that your family honors your strong spirit. It will be good to finish your work."

"We thought today we would say good-bye. No ridy bob. No swing," Always Singing said. "No races or games."

How different the day had turned out! Instead of leaving, I had a good visit with my brother; I learned that I could stay and finish my job; and I enjoyed time with my Blackfeet friends.

After they left, Rosie and I moved the sheep. Then I ate cheese and bread while Rosie chewed on a meaty beef joint that Caleb had brought. I cooped the chickens and settled by the fire to read from my Aesop book.

I drifted off to sleep that night, thanking Heavenly Father that I had three more weeks in the mountains.

The next few days followed my usual pattern. Rosie and I woke to the chickadee's song and did our work. The chickens pecked away all day and rewarded me with fresh eggs. We moved the sheep to fresh, grassy spots and then to shade. Always Singing and her family visited in the afternoon. I spent evenings reading and working on my sampler. I had finally decided on a Bible verse:

All things have their season.
Ecclesiastes 3:1

How true. Last year, my everyday chores had been simple. Minding my sisters. Gathering eggs. Sweeping the parlor rug. Work I could manage easily. This summer was my season to take over grown-up work managing our herd.

Thursday night I put in the last stitches and pressed the sampler cloth between two books to keep it smooth.

Caleb came up early on Saturday with fresh supplies and a letter from Molly. He laughed when I put it in my pocket. "Go ahead, little sister. Read your friend's letter. I know you're itchin' to get at her news."

No sense arguing. Caleb knew me too well. I ripped open the envelope.

Dear Hannah,
I'm glad you liked my birthday present. I told Inga Lindstrom all about you and about your taking the

*sheep up for the summer. She thinks you're very brave
and bold. I told her you were just plain old Hannah
as far as I was concerned and that soon she'd find out
what a good friend you are.*

*Now here's the BIG news from Sego Springs. Miss
Taylor won't be teaching us next year. She's getting
married and moving to Montana!*

*The rumor is that we'll have a man teacher, but no
one knows who.*

Things keep changing so fast it makes me dizzy!

*I can hardly wait to see you. Hurry on down to
Cache Valley!*

Your loving friend,

Molly

Molly's letter eased some of my worries about losing
her friendship to the new girl Inga. I hoped I'd be able to
see Miss Taylor before she left. I had so many questions
for Molly. Who was Miss Taylor marrying? Would her
wedding be in our little church in Sego Springs? Would
her students and their families be invited? Too bad that
the temple in Salt Lake City wasn't yet finished. That
would be a grand place to be married.

"Who're you thinking about, Hannah?" Caleb whispered in my ear. "Reckon it's that Matthew Colton. Uncle
John said Matthew was real eager to come up here in his
place. He's sure Matthew's sweet on you."

My face burned. "I'm certainly *not* thinking about Matthew Colton! Molly's letter is just chock full of news, that's all." I cleared my throat. "Our teacher is getting married, for one thing."

Caleb picked up a stick and threw it for Rosie to fetch. "You have enough firewood?"

"I think so, but I can gather more if I need to." I showed him Rosie's little travois.

"That looks right handy. Let me try it out." He hitched up Rosie and they went down the path while I read Molly's letter again.

I heard someone coming and looked up. Always Singing raced toward the camp. Alone. Early.

Something was wrong.

Just inches from me she bent over to catch her breath and pant out three troubling words: "We . . . are . . . leaving." She waved toward the ridge where I had first seen the Blackfeet men. "Grandfather says it is time. My mother and aunt are taking down our tipi. They send good wishes to you." She touched my arm. "Now I must go help them."

"Wait!" My mind raced. I couldn't believe that in a minute, my friend would be gone. Maybe forever. "Don't leave right away."

Always Singing shook her head. "No time. Tonight's camp is far away."

"Please, wait just a minute!" I ran to the camp and pulled my sampler from between the books. One corner was turned back. No time to smooth it. No time to wrap my gift.

My voice choked as I read the words to Always Singing. "This summer was the season for our friendship."

"We are friends always," she said. "Grandfather says we will come here next year. It is a good place for summer camp." She folded the sampler carefully, put it in her pouch, and held out her arms.

We hugged hard and long.

"Let me go a ways with you." A few more minutes with my friend.

We linked our arms and walked as far as the path's turning. Then Always Singing called a soft good-bye and raced away.

Tears blurred my last sight of her as she disappeared into a stand of fir trees. Then I stumbled back to camp.

I told Caleb the reason for my tears. "I'm real sorry, Hannah." He put his arm around my shoulders, and we sat together on my rock. Rosie came to nuzzle against my leg as if she knew my sadness. As I cried myself out, I remembered all the times I had spent there with Always Singing.

Caleb turned to look at me. "I been thinking, Hannah. Things have changed now that your friends have left. Maybe you'd best go home and save yourself from being up here all alone."

I jerked up straight. The thought of being home with Mama and my sisters tugged at me. Caleb was right.

Things *had* changed, but *I* had changed as well. I was bound to finish what I was sent to do. "No!" I stood up. "I'm staying."

He looked hard at me. "You're a whole different Hannah than the little girl I left last fall. I can tell there's no use arguing with you."

As we unloaded the rest of my supplies, Caleb cheered me some with his stories of our little sisters' wandering ways. "Mama spends most of her day trying to keep track of them. Sometimes she throws a rope over the clothesline and ties 'em to the ends. They can move back and forth while she hoes the garden. Elsewise, those little girls travel right along behind her, pulling up a carrot here or picking a bean there."

"Sounds like they take after you," I teased my brother.

"Yep. I never was one to sit still."

We shared the fried chicken and corn bread that Mama had sent for our lunch. Soon Caleb stretched his legs. " 'Bout time for me to leave."

I hugged him hard and waved until he was out of sight.

Twenty-four

Three weeks later Rosie and I got up extra early to move the sheep in the gray light before dawn. Then we ate the last of the biscuits and cheese for our breakfast.

"Good-bye, sweet chickadees." I tried to copy their song as I packed flour and salt into the storage boxes. The night before, I'd folded up the extra blankets and put away my skillet and kettles. Caleb would come soon, and I wanted things to be ready for our trip home. Now that the going-down time was near, I was excited to see my family and friends in Cache Valley.

As the sun grew brighter, I took the lantern down from the oak tree and fastened it to its hanger on the camp's side.

"This time tomorrow, Rosie, we'll be home."

Rosie growled. Her back fur stood in a ridge.

"What's wrong, girl?"

She pulled her mouth back in a snarl and stared across the stream.

I followed her gaze, fearing the worst.

The bear had returned.

The stream was between us, but she could cross it easily and quickly. I looked around in a panic. I'd stored my noise-makers out of reach. The tree stump where I had performed my bear dance was far behind me. Shakily, I edged backward.

The bear watched. In a croaky voice, I called to her. "Mighty Spirit, why have you come?" I tried to remember the Blackfeet words after I'd faced the bear:

"You honored Sticky Mouth with music. That was brave."

"Yes, she felt your courage."

"You listened to your heart."

Had I really learned to be brave? To have courage? To listen to my heart? I watched the bear, my heart racing.

She moved to the stream's edge. Stood on her hind legs. Roared. Then dropped to all fours and lumbered away.

I slumped onto my rock, shaking with relief.

"What's goin' on up here?" Caleb rode into camp on Zeke. Lucky followed, along with Flint. "Rosie's barking her fool head off, and you look like you've seen a ghost."

I told him about the bear's visit.

Caleb shook his head. "Let's get you packed and take Rosie and the sheep down where it's peaceful and quiet. No bears in sight. Least not lately."

An hour or so later, we headed down the mountain trail. Soon I could see our farm in the distance. Once we were on level land, I wanted the horses to gallop.

"Can't they hurry more?" I asked Caleb.

"Sure they can. And they'll turn us over when we hit a bump or a bad hole. Don't you want to get home in one piece?"

As we neared the Tuttle place, I saw Molly in the garden.

"Halloo! Molly!"

She dropped her hoe. "Hannah! I can't believe you're finally home. I've missed you so much."

"Whoa!" Caleb pulled the horses over.

I climbed down to give my friend a hug. "Can you ride the rest of the way with us? We can have a catching-up talk. I've so much to tell you."

"I'd best not." Molly frowned. "Matthew came over with his new piebald pony, Dan, and I got way behind on my Saturday chores."

For some reason my stomach churned.

"Mama'd sure be mad if I left now," Molly said. "I'll see you in church tomorrow. I want to hear *everything* about your summer."

We were about to hug when Matthew walked from the barn with Aaron. They were leading a brown-and-white spotted horse.

"Hannah!" Matthew waved. "Wait up."

"I'm in a rush to get home," I called.

"Aw, you can give me a minute or two. Your ma and sisters aren't going anywheres."

Caleb chuckled. "I reckon we can spare you a little time, Matthew."

I didn't care for the know-it-all grin on my brother's face.

"Well, here I am," I huffed. "What do you want?"

"Just wanted to say I'm glad you're home. I missed teasing you."

"I'm not so easy to poke fun at as I was last spring," I pointed out.

"True," he said. "Reckon I'll settle on being your good friend then. I'll come over after church tomorrow and let you ride Dan."

Now Molly was grinning too.

I climbed back on Lucky, and we were on our way again.

Finally our farmhouse was in sight.

"I can't wait!" I jumped down and raced toward home. My heart pounded. I had so much to tell Mama. I could hardly wait to see my little sisters.

The front door flew open. Mama swooped up Alice and rushed down the porch steps. Catherine toddled after her.

"Child, I'm so happy to have you back! Heavenly Father watched over you." Mama's hug smelled of sugar and peaches, and I knew she'd made her special cobbler for my homecoming.

I was sad to see Alice stare at me like I was a stranger 'til I remembered she'd been just a baby when I left.

"Hannah home!" Catherine pulled my skirt, and I lifted her high.

We were chattering away when Caleb joined us. "'S there room in that hug for another Turner?"

We sat on the porch to enjoy a pitcher of Mama's lemonade. Then Uncle John and Aunt Margaret came for supper. We talked and laughed all the way from my aunt's fried chicken to Mama's cobbler.

I was enjoying a second helping when Uncle John cleared his throat. "Hannah, your ma and I have come to an important decision. You proved yourself this summer— more than once. From now on, it will be your job to take the sheep for their mountain grazing."

I was so surprised, I forgot to finish my cobbler. I rushed to Mama's chair and gave her a long hug. I turned to my uncle. "Thank you! I promise to do my best."

He smiled. "We know you will."

Before the little ones went off to bed, I joined my family in evening prayers. "Thank you, Heavenly Father, for bringing me safe home. Please help me follow Your path. And watch over my Blackfeet friends until we meet again."

It was twilight when I climbed to our family's hillside burying-place. I sat under the oak tree and told Papa all about my summer in the mountains.

Author's Note

W *asatch Summer* began with a true story I heard several years ago. The girl in the original story was only eight when she took her family's sheep to the mountains in 1889. Her story captivated me, and I knew that some day I would write a book about her. When I started researching the late 1800's history of Cache Valley, I learned that Hannah was not unique. Every Pioneer Museum I visited held similar stories of courageous children who took up heavy responsibilities to help their families survive. I owe a tremendous debt to those young people from the past and to those who shepherd their stories and artifacts in the museums scattered throughout Utah and Idaho.

The American Indians in *Wasatch Summer* are Blackfeet, as were the friends in the original story. Although it is true that Shoshone lived in Cache Valley during this time period and that some had become Latter-day Saints, the Blackfeet often camped in the mountains above the valley. They were known to have made salt treks to the

Great Salt Lake to gather that essential mineral.

Sego Springs is a fictitious place I created for Hannah's Cache Valley home. I attempted to make it typical of the small towns of that period. The church and school served town residents and farm families from the surrounding area. Each community had its own marching band, and Hannah imagines the Sego Springs Marching Band performing on July 4th.

The story of the Mortensons fending off a bear by clapping and hollering comes from a true incident included in the Christenson-Jorgenson family story.

I've spent time with the Latter-day Saints in Utah and Idaho and the Blackfeet in Montana and found both to be hospitable and generously willing to share their stories and cultures.

Discussion Questions

1. Hannah lived over one hundred years ago, when life was very different. Compare Hannah's chores with those expected of children today. (The "real" Hannah was only eight when she undertook the summer grazing.) Do most children today have this kind of responsibility? Why or why not?

2. Before Hannah leaves for her summer duty, Matthew Colton reminds her that she's a "scaredy-cat." What events in *Wasatch Summer* show that Hannah is learning to face and overcome her fears?

3. Who is your favorite character? Why?

4. Hannah worries about being alone in the mountains, away from family and friends for the summer. How does she cope with this problem? If you were Hannah, what would you do to keep from being lonely?

5. Family is important to Hannah. Choose a member of the Turner family. How did Hannah show her love for that person?

6. Hannah is constantly being told to look before she leaps. What actions show Hannah leaping without looking? How do you see her change? Do you think she's completely over this tendency to act first and think later?

7. Music has always been an important part of Latter-day Saint life. What role does music play in Hannah's story?

8. Relationships form a strong thread in *Wasatch Summer*. Compare Hannah's friendship with Molly to her friendship with Always Singing. How does each friendship change as the story progresses? How does her relationship to Matthew change? How does Hannah feel about the new girl in Sego Springs? About Matthew spending time at Molly's home?

9. In what ways are Hannah and Always Singing alike? Different? Both Latter-day Saints and Blackfeet have strong religious and spiritual beliefs. Hannah realizes some ways in which those beliefs are similar. What are they?

10. When Caleb returns, Uncle John tells Hannah that her brother will take over the summer grazing. How does she react? How is her response different than her reaction at the beginning of the summer?

11. At the book's close, Hannah is twelve. What do you think her teen years will be like? What do you think she'll be like as a grown woman?

About the Author

As a third grader, Anola Pickett discovered how much fun writing stories could be. She kept writing in high school. In college, she majored in English and creative writing and continued to turn out stories and poetry. It was always a thrill when her work appeared in print. After teaching and then working as a school librarian, she now writes full time and is pleased that Hannah's story has come to life for young readers. Anola lives in Kansas City, Missouri, with her husband Peter Doyle. As often as possible, they try to visit their journalist son and daughter-in-law in whatever faraway place they're currently living. Every trip brings another story idea! Visit the author at www.anolapickett.com.

Kedamono Damono Volume 1
Created by Haruka Fukushima

Translation - Michelle Kobayashi
English Adaptation - Jamie S. Rich
Retouch and Lettering - Star Print Brokers
Graphic Designer - John Lo

Editor - Carol Fox
Digital Imaging Manager - Chris Buford
Pre-Production Supervisor - Erika Terriquez
Art Director - Anne Marie Horne
Production Manager - Elisabeth Brizzi
Managing Editor - Vy Nguyen
VP of Production - Ron Klamert
Editor-in-Chief - Rob Tokar
Publisher - Mike Kiley
President and C.O.O. - John Parker
C.E.O. and Chief Creative Officer - Stuart Levy

A  Manga

TOKYOPOP and 🌑 are trademarks or registered trademarks of TOKYOPOP Inc.

TOKYOPOP Inc.
5900 Wilshire Blvd. Suite 2000
Los Angeles, CA 90036

E-mail: info@TOKYOPOP.com
Come visit us online at www.TOKYOPOP.com

ISBN: 978-1-59816-823-5

First TOKYOPOP printing: March 2007
10 9 8 7 6 5 4 3 2 1
Printed in the USA

KEDAMONO damono ™

Volume 1
by Haruka Fukushima

HAMBURG // LONDON // LOS ANGELES // TOKYO

HELLO!!!

I'M A DOG.

Vroom

I want a big bike license.

I'M FUKUSHIMA.

Vroom

NICE TO MEET YOU! AND LONG TIME NO SEE! THANK YOU FOR BUYING *KEDAMONO DAMONO!* ♥SMOOCH♥♥♥ LOVE YOU!!!

><)/

THIS IS ALREADY MY EIGHTH COMIC.

YAAAY! CLAP CLAP CLAP AND STUFF.

...working hard.

I'll keep on...

LAST YEAR, WHEN THE OPPORTUNITY TO DO MORE COMICS AROSE, I SAID, "I THINK I'LL WRITE A STORY THAT'S A LITTLE MORE MATURE." THIS IS WHAT I CAME UP WITH.

How is this "a little"?

KEDA-MONO.

OOMPH!

IT'S A TAD MORE EXTREME THAN USUAL, BUT PLEASE DON'T GET A NOSEBLEED...

Ugh. Buy your own.

KEDA-MONO.

GO

OKAY! LET'S GET STARTED!

HARUKA ☆ FUKUSHIM

HARUKI (♀)

MY NAME IS KONATSU NARUMIYA (16 ♀). I'M THE MANAGER OF THE BOYS' BASKETBALL TEAM.

AND THIS SUMMER...

I AM GOING TO BECOME A WOMAN!

KEDAMON damon

LET ME GO, KONATSU!

YOU'RE THE MEANEST MANAGER EVER!

ザザーーン

ずる

ずるっ

THERE'S NO WAY I'M GOIN'.

NOT TO SOME STUPID OVERNIGHT CAMP!

YAMAGUCHI-SENPAI SAID EVERYONE HAS TO BE THERE, AND THAT INCLUDES YOU!

HARUKI! WHY ARE YOU BEING SUCH A FREAK ABOUT THIS?

THE BASKETBALL TEAM STARTS TRAINING TODAY.

KONATSU!

YAMAGUCHI-
SENPAI!

HMPH.

NO PROBLEM! I'VE APPREHENDED THE FUGITIVE!

HA!

THANKS!

HUH?

HEY, HAVE YOU SEEN HARUKI?

...AND I WAS GOING TO ASK HIM TO BRING ME AN EXTRA T-SHIRT.

DID HE ESCAPE AGAIN?

NO, WE'RE SHARING A ROOM...

AH!

DON'T WORRY. I'LL TAKE CARE OF IT!

WHOOOA!

THIS IS SENPAI'S ROOM!

Yeek!

WELL, SINCE NO ONE'S HERE...

I SMELL SENPAI! HEH HEH HEH. THIS T-SHIRT MUST BE HIS.

WOW! I'M ON SENPAI'S BED!

SHOVE

AAAUGH!

AAAUGH!!!

AAUGH!!

AAAUGH!

14

WHO WAS THAT?

huff huff

hrn
hrn
hrn
hrn

WH— WHAT'S THE BIG IDEA?

And what is she doing in my room?!

Ack!

WHERE'D YOU COME FROM?

I'M HARUKI SUGIMOTO.

WHO? ME?

HUH?

...I TURN INTO A GIRL.

BUT...

HARUKI'S A BOY.

I-IS THIS SOME SORT OF A JOKE?

...WHEN THE SUN GOES DOWN...

...AND THE MOON COMES UP...

SURE, DURING THE DAY.

16

...HAVE JUST BEEN KISSED!

YAMAGUCHI-SENPAI...。

...OR HARUKI?

WHICH ONE DO I REALLY LIKE?

HUH?!

WHAT SHOUL I DO?

WILL WE REALLY BE...

sigh

...ALL ALONE?

UMM, LISTEN.

SENPAI JUST...

KONATSU...

HARUKI!

...INVITED ME TO WATCH THE FIREWORKS TONIGHT.

AND BESIDES...

...WHY SHOULD I CARE WHAT HARUKI THINKS?

MIND IF I JOIN YA? ♡

G-GO RIGHT AHEAD! ♡

TRICKED YA.

NO WAY!

WHO IN THE HELL ARE YOU?

GRRR...

...I'D WANT TO HOOK UP WITH A SKANK LIKE YOU?!

AND WHAT MAKES YOU THINK...

HMPH!

WHO YOU CALLIN' A SKANK?

chirp
chirp
chirp...

KEDAMONO damono™

MY NAME IS HARUKI SUGIMOTO (16 ♀). I'M A MEMBER OF THE BOYS' BASKETBALL TEAM.

AND THIS WINTER...

...I AM GOING TO BECOME A MAN!

KEDAMONO damono™

I, UH...

SAY WHAT?

...I'LL MAKE YOU COFFEE.

IS...

IS SHE SERIOUS?!

THEN... WE'RE ALONE?

NOW'S MY CHANCE!!!

OH!

SORRY TO IMPOSE--

Huh?

NO ONE'S HERE. YOU DON'T HAVE TO BE SO FORMAL.

HMMM...

1-B

PART-TIME JOBS
A How-To Guide
Special collection of short-term winter jobs!

kabuki

POKE

I'LL NEED A JOB...

...TO PAY FOR IT.

FROM 7:00 P.M. DEC. 31st UNTIL 7:00 A.M. JANUARY 1st!

HEY, LOOK AT THIS!

25,000 YEN!

Wow!

Gettin' a job?

What's up, Hanabi?!

WHAA--?

A GIRL?!

A GIRL?! I KNOW A GIRL! A GIRL NAMED HARUKO!

WE'RE LOOKING FOR A GIRL MIKO*, NOT A BOY.

YES. I'M VERY SORRY.

I KNOW SHE'LL WANT TO DO IT!

Yeah!

Yeah!

Yeah!

Dad!

WHAT?

*An attendant at a shrine.

THANK YOU VERY MUCH!

THEN ASK HARUKO-SAN TO COME ON DOWN.

I WON'T LET YOU GO UNTIL YOU TELL ME!

HEY!

WHO'S HARUKO-CHAN?

IS SHE YOUR GIRLFRIEND?

NOPE. I CAN'T DATE MYSELF!

68

72

I'LL GIVE YOU A RIDE

REALLY?

THAT'S RIGHT.

THANK YOU!

FROM NOW ON...

...DON'T SPACE OUT IN CLASS.

I HOPE I CAN GO...

SWEET!

YOU'RE SO LUCKY YOU'RE ALLOWED TO WORK.

THERE'S A SPECIAL SESSION ON NEW YEAR'S EVE, RIGHT?

...WITH HARUKI THIS YEAR.

IN THAT CASE...

AFTER CLASS IS DONE, I'M GOING TO THE SHRINE.

...MAYBE I CAN TAG ALONG?

I-I'M SORRY!

SORRY!

bow
bow

IT WAS JUST A JOKE.

Heh...

HUH?

THAT WAS SO MEAN!

HA HA HA HA!

BUT...

A-AKANO?

REALLY?!

BATHUMP

URK!

...I'LL SEE YOU ON NEW YEAR'S EVE.

URRGH!

SHE CAN'T KNOW THE TRUTH!

NEW YEAR'S EVE? SHE'LL CATCH ME AT MY JOB!

IT'LL TIP HER OFF ABOUT THE RING!

UM... THAT'S NOT A GOOD DAY FOR ME.

TH- THEN...

KONATSU!

NEVER MIND.

I HAVE CRAM SCHOOL ANYWAY.

OH... I SEE.

I HAVE RELATIVES VISITING.

HOW ABOUT THE DAY AFTER NEW YEAR'S?

CRAP...

SHE'S MAD AT ME AGAIN.

WHY CAN'T I DO ANYTHING RIGHT?

KONATSU HAD TO ASK MY MALE SIDE OUT!

I'M SO MUCH BETTER AT THIS WHEN I'M A GIRL.

HARUKI! LET'S GO TO THE ARCADE!

A LIMITED EDITION RING!

WHOA!

"HARUKO" CAN ALWAYS EXPLAIN THINGS BETTER THAN HARUKI. *

*Haruko=female version of Haruki.

THAT WOULD LOOK FABULOUS ON KONATSU.

I'm so happy!

Thank you, Haruki!

THAT'S THE ONE!

HARUKI AND MIYA WERE CLINGING ALL OVER EACH OTHER!

COULD IT BE....?

SHUFF

WHAT WAS THAT?

SHUFF

SHUFF

I'M SO PISSED!

AND THEN...

HARUKI, YOU IDIOT!

SOB...

SOB... SOB...!

ARE YOU OKAY?

SOB...

HUH?

SLAP
シ₁ッ

UM...

...AKANO?

NARUMIYA-SAN...

87

92

I... I WAS EMBARRAS- SED.

WHEN I'M WITH THE GIRL VERSION OF YOU...

...I DON'T KNOW WHAT HAPPENS TO ME.

I'M SORRY...

KONATSU...

MY IMPULSES...

...CAN'T BE CONTAINED.

...FOR FIGHTING WITH YOU.

ESPE- CIALLY ON CHRISTMAS EVE.

AND MY URGES ALSO GET THE BETTER OF ME.

IT WOULDN'T BE SO BAD TO BE A GIRL ALL THE TIME.

HEY, HARUKI...
WHAT KIND OF RELATIONSHIP DO WE HAVE?
Coming to My House?!
KEDAMONO damono

Coming to My House?!

KEDAMONO damono

HELLO!

MY NAME IS KONATSU NARUMIYA (16 ♀).

I'M A JUNIOR IN HIGH SCHOOL!

How do you do?

This is me, Konatsu!

I'm in class 2-D!

AND THIS IS HARUKI SUGIMOTO (16 ♂). HE'S ON THE BOYS' BASKETBALL TEAM.

BY DAY, HE'S JUST A REGULAR HIGH SCHOOL BOY.

Good morning!

Daytime

Boy Haruki

Eating an early lunch!

He's in 2-C.

I DISCOVERED HIS SECRET ...

...LAST SUMMER AT BASKETBALL CAMP.

OH! NO!

Me, naked for some reason.

Boy Haruki, wearing my bra.

...HE TURNS INTO A SUPER-RAUNCHY GIRL!

← Night

Girl Haruki

Big breasts! (It pisses me off)

Long flowing hair

BUT AT NIGHT..

Note: Haruki stays the same inside!

Really good at basketball

HE INTRODUCED ME AS...

...HIS GIRLFRIEND.

IT'S NO BIG DEAL. HIS FAMILY WAS THERE.

2 - D

ISN'T THAT THE STRANGEST THING YOU'VE EVER HEARD?!

YOU WENT TO SHINAGAWA-KUN'S HOUSE?!

WHAT FOR?

WEREN'T YOU NERVOUS?

...YOU'RE GOING OUT WITH SHINAGAWA-KUN?

DOES THAT MEAN...

DID HIS FOLKS APPROVE OF YOU?

WHOA!

YEAH... I GUESS I AM!

MUST... BE... NICE...

W-WAIT A MINUTE!

I SAID NO!

MY HOUSE IS A MESS, AND MY FAMILY'S STRANGE.

SO?

GRAB

SHOCK

WHAT?!

I'VE DECIDED ON OKONOMIYAKI!*

See ya!

*A sort of cross between a pancake and an omelet, typically made with flour, eggs, vegetables and any of several optional ingredients.

I JUST THINK...

...THAT YOU AND I...

LOOK, I DON'T WANT YOU COMING OVER!

wheeze wheeze

Lemme go!

What happened? Tell me!

NO WAY...

HARUKI CAUGHT A COLD?

HUH?

MIYA-CHAN...

GAH!

NOW I CAN MAKE UP...

...FOR MISSING MY CHANCE BEFORE!

YUP.

HARUKI LEFT EARLY?

I'LL GO TO HIS PLACE RIGHT NOW!

DID YOU SAY HARUKI?

HE COLLAPSED BEFORE LUNCH.

121

YOU'VE CHECKED. NOW LEAVE!

KONATSU! I TOLD YOU NOT TO COME TO MY HOUSE!

UH-OH.

B-BUT..

YOU CAUGHT A COLD BECAUSE OF ME...

...SO I CAME TO CHECK UP ON YOU!

ちゃぷ — — ●……ん…

KERSPLSSSH

SIIIGH…♡

YES! HARUKI…

…REALLY LIKES YOU, KONATSU-SAN!

DOESN'T IT, KONATSU-SAN?

WOW, THIS FEELS GREAT!

:
:

OH! YEAH.

HEY, LISTEN!

HE DID?

"KONATSU… KONATSU…"

…HARUKI KEPT MUTTERING IN HIS SLEEP.

BEFORE YOU CAME OVER…

S-SPONGE BATH?

HUH?!

...UM. UH...

OH, AND WHILE YOU'RE AT IT...

...CHANGE HER UNDERWEAR TOO, M'KAY?

WELL, HARUKI'S A GIRL NOW, SO... NO HARM, NO FOUL, RIGHT?

ARE...

I THINK YOU SHOULD SPONGE HIM OFF.

YUP.

HARUKI'S ALL SWEATY.

I'M GOING OUT SHOPPING.

WILL YOU TWO BE OKAY?

WHAT?!

I'M GOING TO BED!

chirp
chirp

HARUKI!

DID I REALLY SLEEP HERE ALL NIGHT?

Ughhh...

LOOKS LIKE HE'S BETTER. ♡

GOING
HOME?

UH-HUH.

HUH?

AAUGH! I'M SORRY! I'M SORRY!

ck!

Ack!

TEE HEE. ♡

I THOUGHT YOU WERE RYO-SAN!

Ack!

Ack!

Aaugh...

LET'S TAKE ANOTHER BATH TOGETHER!

WAIT... YOU'RE NOT MEG-CHAN!

M-MEG-CHAN!

KONATSU-SAN! ARE YOU GOING HOME?

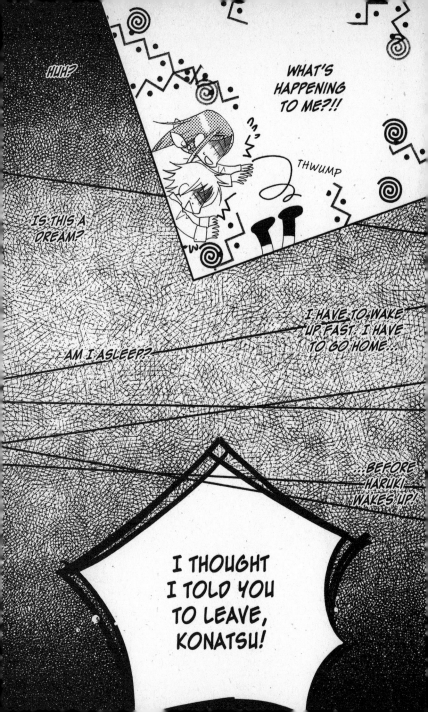

HIS KISS...

...IS SO GENTLE.

ARE YOU MAD AT ME?

I DON'T REMEMBER A THING, SO I HOPE--

KONATSU!

ARE YOU WONDERING IF YOU...

...TURNED INTO A GIRL AND MOLESTED ME?!

HMM.

OF COURSE N-NOT!

WHY WOULD I DO THAT?

MY BEAST.

WELL, RIGHT NOW, THIS...

...IS THE ONLY WAY I CAN DESCRIBE IT.

Continued in Vol. 2!

Like a bolt from the blue, it's KEDAMONO CHAT!

Fukushima

Dog

yahooooo!

Wherein I discuss my memories of writing Chapter 3 of Kedamono Damono.

KEDAMONO DAMONO - SUMMER, 2003 Summer

☑ IT ALL STARTED IN A CONVERSATION WITH THE EDITOR, WHO WE WILL CALL "KIPPY."

Whaaat?

Sounds interesting!

WHAT ABOUT A BOY WHO TURNS INTO A GIRL AT NIGHT? WOULDN'T THAT MAKE A GREAT STORY?

?

Seriously?

Hee hee

Zusshi, another editor

Fuku-→ shima

← Kippy the Editor

Well, she really liked senpai.

I love stories that involve gender swapping, so I immediately wrote up a plot with Haruki as the main character.

BUT... When it got down to it, the story wasn't coming out very well. So at the last minute, I changed the main character to Konatsu...I was so relieved that it worked!

£3

"First Sunrise of the New Year!" Kedamono Damono, Winter 2004.

☑ People who read this title are like, "What the heck?!" But I'm fine with it. (laughs) People always ask me about it. Is that strange? Eh heh heh...

Zusshi's best work!

Heh heh!

Winter

☑ I guess you could say that I wrote the New Year's chapter entirely because I wanted to draw Haruki in his female form dressed up as a miko!

BUT...

☑ I don't exercise enough, so when I went to the local shrine to do a little research, just climbing the stairs was enough to make my legs feel like rubber. They were even shaking a little...

Why do shrine stairs have to be so high?!

wobble

I won...the 100 meter... dash...

wheeze wheeze

And I used to be on the track team!

With a teacher like this, I wouldn't mind going to cram school!

★ KEDAMONO CHAT CONTINUES ON PAGE 169!

MY QUEST FOR HAPPINESS

COME AT ME WITH WHATEVER YOU'VE GOT!

I'VE BEEN GETTING MY FORTUNE TOLD REGULARLY!

HA HA HA! HARUKA FUKUSHIMA HERE! MY SIGN IS ARIES, AND MY BLOOD TYPE IS A!

BY THESE GUYS!

CHIZURU HAYASHI-SAN, FENG SHUI FORTUNETELLER

HIDEKI YASHIRO, CRYSTAL FORTUNE-TELLER

Gaiennishi Street

Nisseki Medical Center

Tokyo Women's School

Hiroo Garden Hills

West Azabu Intersection

House of Fortunes Shaman Minami Aoyama

Roppongi Street

SEE? THE SHOP IS RIGHT HERE!

TO BE HONEST, I DON'T REALLY CARE ABOUT ALL THIS HOCUS POCUS.

BUT I'M DEFINITELY GOING TO HAVE MY FORTUNE TOLD!

You seem kinda down. Why don't you have your fortune read, too?

No thanks!

TAROT, CRYSTALS... OH! FORTUNE TELLING THROUGH DANCE? WHICH SHOULD I DO?

Z-san

S-san

Editors

Fortunes

166

PART 1: LUCK IN LOVE

I CAN SEE IT, I CAN SEE IT! I CAN SEE YOU IN A WEDDING CEREMONY, SURROUNDED BY MANY PEOPLE...OOH! IN THREE YEARS!

HA HA HA!

HAAAAAA!!!

Whooooo!

ばっ ばっ ばっ ば!

REBOOT POWER!

PUT ALL YOUR POWER INTO THE CRYSTAL.

YASHIRO-SAN IS REALLY GETTING INTO IT.

I WONDER WHAT IN THE WORLD HE SEES IN THAT JEWEL...AN IMAGE? WORDS? DOES HE HEAR SOMEONE'S VOICE?

staaaare

Please be more cooperative.

I WAS SO ENTHRALLED BY THE CRYSTAL THAT I DIDN'T ASK HIM ANYTHING.

...AND AROUND 2003, YOU'LL BECOME POPULAR!

ESCAPE FROM POVERTY!!! ← RICH! ← INCREASED POPULARITY

PART 2: LUCK IN WORK

Oh... uh... yeah.

I SEE YOU'RE BUSY AT WORK RIGHT NOW.

Am I the one bossing her around?

Oh!

YOU'RE BEING BOSSED AROUND AND JUST DOING WHAT EVERYONE TELLS YOU, BUT...

...STARTING IN THE FALL, YOU'LL GET NEW WORK...

That one's right on the mark!

Wow!

OH HO HO HO HO!

YAHOOO!

Really?

Oww...

BUT RIGHT NOW, YOU'RE POOR.

...you'll at least be able to open a savings account.

If you work hard all through next year...

I'LL JUST BELIEVE IN THE GOOD PARTS!

Wa ha ha!

Wa ha ha!

SO THAT'S ONE WAY PEOPLE GET HOOKED ON FORTUNETELLING.

You'll meet someone, but don't make your move this year.

Umm...am I going to get married?

AND THIS IS ANOTHER.

Because you spend it too fast.

NO MATTER WHERE YOU WORK, YOU WILL NOT HAVE ENOUGH MONEY...

Gyaah!

SHE'S RIGHT!

★★End★★

168

Kedamono Chat!

"Coming to My House?!" Kedamono Damono, Spring 2004.

I think I can write a lot more stories with these two characters.

My ear hurts. Let's call it quits for today.

Same here...

← Zusshi

Idiot.

Yeah, yeah.

☑ If Haruki transforms, it only makes sense that his family does, too. I worked really hard on Ryo's (♂) bean-sprout-like hair, and the scene where Haruki (♂) is naked, and the kiss scene.

☑ 60 pages...It was long. I always talk with the editor Zusshi over the phone, and no matter what I do to cut the calls short, they always go for at least three hours. When I'm on the phone, my ear starts hurting, and I have to take a break sometimes. I'm sorry...Please move closer to me...

This was the hardest part...

OKAY...

GO

For pages 164 and 168, I did a Fortunetelling manga. I researched for these strips...twice! Do you like fortunetelling? As for me...well...

MY QUEST FOR HAPPINESS

part 2

NO WAY! WE GOTTA GET OUR ROMANCE FORTUNES! ♡

LET'S HAVE HER LOOK AT THE FUTURE OF OUR CAREERS!

Sudacchi, a.k.a. the guy who edits the fortune-telling corner.

THESE WERE OUR GOALS FOR THIS SESSION.

---

college de

Welcome!

purchase on the NOVE

MBER

CATHERINE-SAN! (WESTERN ASTROLOGY)

THIS PERSON HERE IS OUR FORTUNE-TELLER!

An American born in San Francisco who is fluent in Japanese.

long ago output

THIS IS THE PLACE!

TARIM

IN A POPULAR SPOT CLOSE TO HARAJUKU STATION!

YUP... A PC...

IT'S A PC...

Doesn't like stability. Likes to explore new places

OH MY! IN YOUR PREVIOUS LIFE, YOU WERE A EUROPEAN IMMIGRANT!

Whoa...   Amazing...

Uses a PC to search data

YOU HAVE TO MEET SOMEONE FIRST, DON'T YOU?

I WONDER WHEN I'M GOING TO GET MARRIED...

heh heh

NEW GUINEA!

Where in the world is that?

SO YOU SHOULD GO ON A TRIP ALONE FOR THREE WEEKS!

This is sudden.

HUH? WHERE?

THEY WERE ALL IMPOSSIBLE FOR ME!

Ha ha ha ha

OKAY, MAYBE THAT'S TOO FAR OUT OF THE WAY. HOW ABOUT MEXICO OR THAILAND? EVEN HAWAII WOULD WORK.

UMM...

WHEN? WHERE? WHO IS IT?

OH! YOU'RE GOING TO MEET SOMEONE GREAT THIS YEAR!

UM... WHAT ABOUT LOVE? WILL I GET LUCKY?

THANK YOU FOR READING THIS FAR!

AND SO...

Sakura mochi...
Kusa mochi...
Kinako mochi...

End of volume hur-ri-cane!

KONATSU (?)

☑ How was it?
I tried some new things with *Kedamono Damono.*

I'm really interested in hearing the opinions of the readers!

Don't make too much of it.

bleh

write write

My stomach!

☑ I'd never drawn many kissing scenes, so the ones in this manga are so pathetic that even when the work is finished and the book (lovely) goes on sale, I can't bear to look at them!

Moron.

Lovely

TH-THEY'RE KISSING!

Of course, kissing scenes in other people's manga don't bother me at all.

☑ It goes without saying that the story progresses quickly from Chapter 1 to Chapter 2, from Chapter 2 to Chapter 3, and so on.

Eh heh...

☑ Drawing kissing scenes is hard, so I have to work on them carefully. But the hardest part is...

HER! ➡

☑ Haruki's (♀) flowing hair! Siiiigh... I don't really understand hair. I so admire artists who can effortlessly draw their characters with flowing locks. Someone, please teach me the trick!

He's transforming again... Sigh...

More and more panels ➡ with female Haruki...

By the way, I like Konatsu's hair. (Though it's a pain to draw when I'm in a hurry.)

☑ Because Kedamono Damono was a short story, I figured I'd just collect it all into this one volume. Urk! If I get the chance, I hope to complete the whole series one day!

HARUEI (8)

I am terribly ashamed of myself for delaying my responses to your letters. However, if you have any comments, please send them to the following address:

Kedamano Damono Fanmail
c/o TOKYOPOP
5900 Wilshire Blvd,.
Suite #2000
Los Angles, CA 90036
USA

Letter
Love!

Until next time!

Bye-bye!

Special Thanks!

- ☐ T · Katada
- ☐ S · Hironaka
- ☑ K · Asakura
- ☐ M · Etō
- ☑ K · Ueyasu
- ☐ M · Yasumura
- ☑ M · Fukushima

- ☑ My family
- ☑ My friends

2004. 6. 13.

In the next

KEDAMONO
damono

Haruka Fukushima

②

More trials await this star-crossed,
cross-gendered couple! For starters,
Haruki forgets an already frustrated
Konatsu's birthday...but another,
more handsome guy doesn't! Then
when Konatsu and Haruki win a trip
to the hot springs, girl-Haruki can't
wait to pack her bags, but boy-Haruki
wants no part of the excursion!

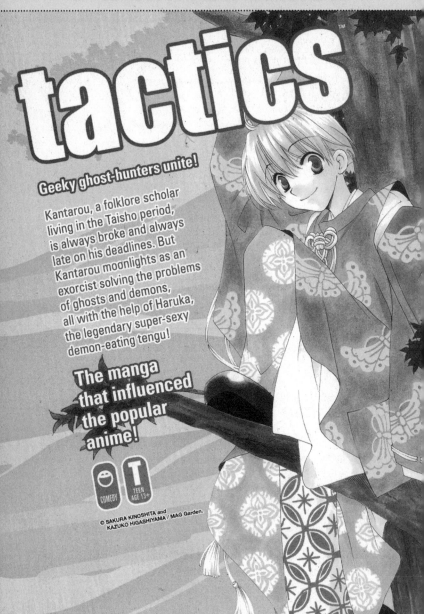

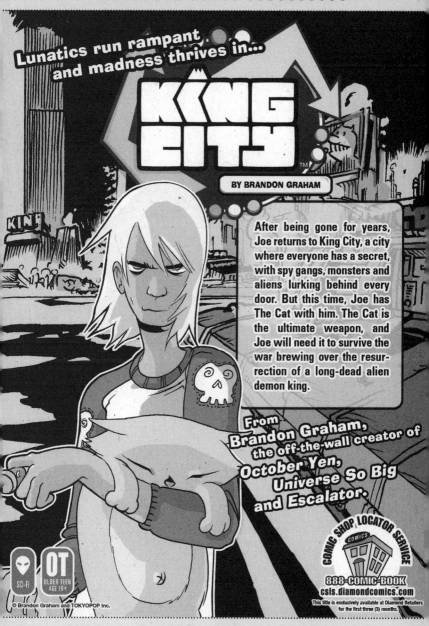

STOP!

This is the back of the book.
You wouldn't want to spoil a great ending!

This book is printed "manga-style," in the authentic Japanese right-to-left format. Since none of the artwork has been flipped or altered, readers get to experience the story just as the creator intended. You've been asking for it, so TOKYOPOP® delivered: authentic, hot-off-the-press, and far more fun!

DIRECTIONS

If this is your first time reading manga-style, here's a quick guide to help you understand how it works.

It's easy... just start in the top right panel and follow the numbers. Have fun, and look for more 100% authentic manga from TOKYOPOP®!

THE MAKING

BIBLE GUIDES
The twenty-two volumes

1	THE MAKING OF THE BIBLE	*William Barclay*
2	IN THE BEGINNING	*Bernhard W. Anderson*
3	THE LAW GIVERS	*R. A. Barclay*
4	NATION MAKING	*Lawrence E. Toombs*
5	HISTORIANS OF ISRAEL (1)	*Gordon Robinson*
6	HISTORIANS OF ISRAEL (2)	*Hugh Anderson*
7	PROPHETS OF ISRAEL (1)	*George Knight*
8	PROPHETS OF ISRAEL (2)	*William Neil*
9	PROPHETS OF ISRAEL (3)	*John Mauchline*
10	SINGERS OF ISRAEL	*G. S. Gunn*
11	THE WISDOM OF ISRAEL	*John Paterson*
12	TRACTS FOR THE TIMES	*William McKane*
13	THE GOOD NEWS	*C. L. Mitton*
14	WORLD OF ST. JOHN	*E. Earle Ellis*
15	THE YOUNG CHURCH	*G. E. Ladd*
16	FREEDOM OF THE CHRISTIAN	*B. S. Mackay*
17	PAUL AND HIS CONVERTS	*F. F. Bruce*
18	LETTERS TO THE CHURCHES	*Morton S. Enslin*
19	EPISTLES FROM PRISON	*Donald Guthrie*
20	EPISTLE TO THE HEBREWS	*William Barclay*
21	GENERAL EPISTLES	*G. R. Beasley-Murray*
22	DREAMS OF THE FUTURE	*T. S. Kepler*

BIBLE GUIDES

General Editors: William Barclay and F. F. Bruce

No. 1

THE MAKING
OF THE BIBLE

by

WILLIAM BARCLAY

Professor of New Testament in the
University of Glasgow

Published jointly by

LUTTERWORTH PRESS
LONDON

ABINGDON PRESS
NEW YORK AND NASHVILLE

First published 1961
Second impression 1962
Third impression 1963
Fourth impression 1965

Printed in Great Britain by
Cox & Wyman Ltd., London, Fakenham and Reading

ABBREVIATIONS

R.S.V. (Revised Standard Version of the Bible). Most of the Biblical quotations in this book are from the R.S.V.

A.V. (Authorized Version, or King James Version of the Bible).

GENERAL INTRODUCTION

THE AIM of Bible Guides is to present in 22 volumes a total view of the Bible, and to present the purpose, plan and power of the Scriptures.

Bible Guides are free from the technicalities of Biblical scholarship but are soundly based on all the generally accepted conclusions of modern Bible research.

They are written in clear, simple, straightforward English. Each author has worked to a comprehensive editorial pattern so that the 22 volumes form a concise conspectus of the Bible.

THE AIM

The aim of Bible Guides is to offer a "guide" to the main themes of each book (or group of books) rather than a commentary on the text of the book. Through Bible Guides the Bible itself will speak its message, reveal its power and declare its purpose.

Bible Guides is essentially an undertaking for non-theologically equipped readers who want to know what the Bible is about, how its various parts came to be written and what their meaning is to-day. But the preacher, teacher, educator and expositor of all ranges of the Christian Church will find Bible Guides a series of books to buy and study. They combine the modern knowledge of the Bible together with all the evangelical zeal of sound Biblical expression—and all done in a handy readable compass.

EDITORIAL PLAN

In our suggestions to the writers of the various books we were careful to make the distinction between a "commentary" and a "guide". Our experience is that an adequate commentary on a book of the Bible requires adequate space and on the part of the student some equipment in the scholarly lore and technicalities of Biblical research. A "guide", however, can be both selective and compressed and do what it sets out to do—guide the reader in an understanding of the book. That has been, and is, our aim.

As general editors we have had a good deal of experience among the various schools of Biblical interpretation. We are constantly surprised at the amount of common Biblical understanding which is acceptable to all types of Christian tradition and churchmanship. We hope that our Bible Guides reflect this and that they will be widely used, and welcomed as a contribution to Biblical knowledge and interpretation in the twentieth century.

THE WRITERS

The writers of Bible Guides represent a widely selected area of Biblical scholars, and all of them have co-operated enthusiastically in the editorial plan. They conceive their work to be that of examination, explanation and exposition of the book(s) of the Bible each is writing about. While they have worked loyally to the pattern we suggested they have been completely free in their presentation. Above all, they have remembered the present power and appeal of the Bible, and have tried to present its message and its authority for life to-day. In this sense Bible Guides is, we think, a fresh venture in the popular understanding of the Scriptures, combined as it is with the scholarly skill of our company of writers. We owe our thanks also to our publishers and their editors, Dr. Emory Stevens Bucke of the Abingdon Press of New York and Nashville, and Dr. Cecil Northcott of the Lutterworth Press of London. Their careful management and attention to publishing detail have given these Bible Guides a world wide constituency.

WILLIAM BARCLAY

F. F. BRUCE

CONTENTS

INTRODUCTION TO BIBLE GUIDES—THE EDITORS

AUTHOR'S FOREWORD

1. THE MAKING OF THE OLD TESTAMENT   *Page 11*

The Three Sections—The Grandeur of the Law—The Start-ing-point of Scripture—Some Discrepancies—The Holiness Code—Other Additions—The Prophets—The Prophets Es-tablished—The Writings—Attributed Authorship—Establish-ing The Writings—The People of the Book—The Emergence of Sacred Scripture.

2. THE MAKING OF THE NEW TESTAMENT   *Page 43*

The Old Testament, a Christian Book—Apostles, the Living Books—End of the Oral Tradition—The Need of a Written Literature—The Words of Jesus—The "Forms" of the Gospel—How the New Testament Emerged—The Apostolic Authority—The First Christian Books—Collecting Paul's Letters—Making the Collection—The Gospels Win their Place—A Written Gospel—Authoritative and Sacred—Dis-carding the Old Testament?—The Church's Decision—Closing of the Books—The Final Completion.

3. THE FINAL TEST   *Page 89*

Authority of the Books—Does the Book speak of Christ? Faith in a Living Saviour.

BIBLIOGRAPHY   *Page 95*

AUTHOR'S FOREWORD

IN ANY undertaking of study the first essential is to define the area of the study. This is precisely what we seek to do in this book. The area of study in this whole series of books is the Bible, and in this initial volume we seek to define the Bible, and to see how it came to be in the form in which it exists to-day.

To give it its technical name, this book seeks to deal with the Canon of Holy Scripture, and to tell the story of the Formation of the Canon. For some reason or other the study of the Canon of Holy Scripture has come to be looked upon as one of the dry and less interesting fields of Biblical study. That is a great pity, for it is by the study of the formation of the Canon that we come to see the essential greatness of Scripture.

As we study the history of the Bible, and as we come to see how it came to be what it is to-day, we see God speaking to men in every age and generation through men whom His Spirit inspired, and through events through which He was making His will known to men. We see that word of God establishing itself in the hearts and in the minds of men. We see the necessities of the human situation driving men to seek and to study and to cling to the word of God. We see the events of history and the needs of the human heart sending men for strength and for guidance, for help and for comfort to the word of God.

Above all we come to see how the Bible came to be the Bible, how these books came to be regarded as Holy Scripture, how they came to be regarded, not simply as great books, but as holy books, how they came to be regarded, not simply as the products of the mind and pen of great men, but as products of the divine inspiration of the Spirit of God. We come to see quite clearly, when we study the formation of the Canon of Scripture, that the Bible and the books of the Bible came to be regarded as the inspired word of God, not because of any decision of any Synod or Council or Committee or Church, but because in them men found God. The supremely important thing is not what men did to these books, but what these books did to men. These books, as the story plainly shows, became Scripture, because nothing could stop them doing so. Their unique inspiration was self-evidencing through their ability to meet the needs of the human heart, especially in times when life was an agonizing thing.

To study the Canon of Scripture is not to come away with a lesser view of Scripture, but with a far greater view, for it is to see the unanswerable power of the word of God in action in the minds and hearts of men.

It is my hope and prayer that, as people read this book, they will come more and more to realize the self-evidencing power of the word of God. All through my own life my experience has been that, the more I knew about the Bible, the greater the Bible became, and it is my prayer that the reading of the story of how the Bible came to be what it is to-day may convince those who read it even more that the Bible is the word of God to men.

WILLIAM BARCLAY

THE MAKING OF THE OLD TESTAMENT

To THE JEWS the Scriptures were indeed the Holy Scriptures. They expressed this special holiness in a very curious way. "All the Holy Scriptures," says the *Mishnah*, "render the hands unclean" (*Yadaim* 3:5). When a man had touched an unclean thing he had to go through a process of the most meticulous cleansing and washing of his hands to remove all possible defilement. The law was that he must do exactly the same after he had touched any of the rolls which contained the books of Scripture. The intention of that strange regulation was to make it very difficult to handle the rolls of Scripture at all; they were so holy that they must be fenced about with rules and regulations which made it difficult even to take them within the hands.

The process by which the Old Testament came to contain the books which it does to-day contain is a long story. It began with the emergence of the Book of Deuteronomy in 621 B.C. and finished with the decisions of the Council of Jamnia in A.D. 90 or thereby. It took seven hundred years and more to build up the divine library of the Old Testament; and it is the story of that long process which we are to study.

The Three Sections

As the Jews regarded it, the Old Testament fell into three sections—the Law, the Prophets and the Writings, the *Torah*, the *Nebiim*, and the *Kethubim*. That division goes at least as far back as about 180 B.C., when the Greek translation of *Ecclesiasticus* was made. The original author of the Hebrew version of that book was Jesus ben Sirach, and the Greek version was made by his grandson. In the Prologue to the Greek translation the grandson speaks of the many good things which were given to Israel for wisdom and instruction by the Law, the Prophets, and by the others who followed in their steps; and he tells how his grandfather gave himself much to the reading of the law and the prophets and the other books of our fathers.

These are the earliest references to the threefold division of Scripture which became so familiar to the Jews.

The Law consisted of the first five books of the Old Testament—Genesis, Exodus, Leviticus, Numbers, Deuteronomy. *The Prophets* fell into two sections. First, there were *the Former Prophets*, which we reckon rather as historical books—Joshua, Judges, Samuel, and Kings. The last two books were generally, but not always, reckoned as two books and not four, as in our reckoning. Second, there were *the Latter Prophets*—Isaiah, Jeremiah, Ezekiel, and The Twelve. The Twelve, which we sometimes call the Minor Prophets, were reckoned as one book. It ought always to be remembered that when we speak of the *Minor* Prophets, the word does not imply any kind of inferiority in wisdom or quality or authority, but simply means that the books of these twelve prophets were *shorter* than the books of the great prophets. *The Writings* were a much more miscellaneous and loosely connected group, and were composed of Psalms, Proverbs, Job, Ecclesiastes, the Song of Solomon, Ruth, Lamentations, Esther, Ezra-Nehemiah, Chronicles, Daniel. Of these eleven books, five were known particularly as the *Five Rolls* because they were specially connected with certain great Jewish festivals at which they were always read. The Song of Solomon was read at the Passover, and allegorically interpreted to tell of the exodus from Egypt. Ruth, the harvest idyll, was read at the Feast of Weeks, which was a harvest-thanksgiving festival. Lamentations was read on the ninth day of the month Ab, which was the day of fasting in memory of the destruction of the Temple. Ecclesiastes was read at the Feast of Tabernacles, because, as Cornill puts it, "it preaches a thankful enjoyment of life, united with God and consecrated by the fear of God, as the ultimate aim of wisdom." Esther was read at the Festival of Purim, for the existence of which it was the warrant and authority.

Jewish practice did not enumerate the books as we do, nor did it always enumerate them in the same way. The commonest method of enumeration, which is usual in the *Talmud*, is to number the books as twenty-four. In the *Talmud* the Old Testament is frequently called *the twenty-four holy Scriptures,* or the *twenty-four books.* In 4 Ezra (2 Esdras), an apocryphal book written towards the end of the first century A.D., there is an imaginary story of how Ezra the scribe restored from memory the books of Scripture, when they had been lost, and how he received other books from God along with them; and the story finishes with God's command: "The twenty-four books that thou hast written publish, that the worthy and unworthy may read therein; but the seventy last thou shalt keep, to deliver them to the wise among the people" (4 Ezra 14: 45, 46). The twenty-four books were made up exactly according to the list that we have already given—five books of the Law, four books of the Former Prophets and four books of the Latter Prophets, and eleven books of the Writings. This may be said to be what we might call the official enumeration.

I. THE GRANDEUR OF THE LAW

Although the Jews regarded all these books as sacred and holy, they did not give to all of them quite the same place. It was in the Law that the greatness of Scripture reached its full height and grandeur. It was the Law which was Scripture *par excellence*. Using the layout of the Temple as a parallel, they said that the Writings were like the Outer Court; the Prophets were like the Holy Place; but the Law was the Holy of Holies. The Law, they said, was created one thousand generations before

Moses, and nine hundred and seventy-four generations before the creation of the world, and was, therefore, older than the world itself. When the Messiah came, they said, the Prophets and the Writings would be abrogated, but the Law should endure for ever and ever. The Law, they said, was delivered to Moses by God complete and entire, and he who said that Moses himself wrote even one letter of it was guilty of sin; it was literally and completely the word of God. Jewish boys were taught the Law from their first consciousness, and had these laws, as it were, "engraven on their souls" (Josephus, *Against Apion* 2: 18). They learn them from their earliest youth, so that "they bear the image of the laws in their souls" (Philo, *Embassy to Caius* 31). From their swaddling-clothes they were instructed in these sacred laws (Philo, *Embassy to Caius* 31). The Jew might in his national misfortunes lose everything, but he could not lose the Law; and, however far from his native land he was, and however hostile a ruler might be, he feared the Law more than any man (Josephus, *Against Apion* 2: 38). History was full of examples of Jews who had chosen to die rather than to be disloyal to, or to abandon, or to disobey the Law (Josephus, *Against Apion* 1: 8). In the Law there was concentrated the very being and essence of Scripture. Great as the Prophets and the Writings might be, they were only *quabbalah*, tradition, explanation, or interpretation of the Law. It is, therefore, with the story of the canonization of the Law that we must begin.

When we make a careful study of the Law, the first five books of the Old Testament, the Pentateuch—the word means the five rolls—as it is called, we come to see that it is a composite document, and that it must have been the product of a long growth and development. Jewish tradition ascribed every word of it to Moses, but there are clear signs that others besides Moses must have had a hand in its writing. Deuteronomy 34 tells of the death of Moses—the story of which Moses himself could hardly have written. Genesis 36 gives a list of the kings of Edom, and then says that all these reigned before Israel had a king, which takes us down to the days of Saul at least (Genesis 36: 31).

14

Genesis 14: 14 tells us that Abram pursued those who had taken Lot captive as far as Dan, but from Judges 18: 29 we find that Dan did not receive its name until long after Moses was dead. We find in the Pentateuch repeated references to the Philistines (Genesis 21: 34; 26: 14-18; Exodus 13: 17), and the Philistines did not come into Palestine until about 1200 B.C., long after the time of Moses. There are quite certainly sections of the Pentateuch which come from a time long after Moses. Further, we find that the Pentateuch contains differing accounts of the same incident. There are, for instance, two stories of how Beersheba got its name, one tracing it back to a covenant between Abraham and Abimelech, the other to an incident in the relationships between Isaac and Abimelech (Genesis 21: 31; 26:31). There are two stories of how Bethel got its name, the one tracing it back to the vision of Jacob on the way to Padanaram, the other to an incident years later when Jacob was returning from Padanaram (Genesis 28: 19; 35: 15).

These are small points, but often the difference is more important. There are two distinct accounts of the banishment of Hagar. In the one she is banished before her child Ishmael is born, and in the other she is banished when Ishmael has grown into a lad (Genesis 16: 6 ff.; 21: 9 ff.). Still more important, there are two quite distinct accounts of the creation story. In Genesis 1 man and woman are created at the end of creation after all the animals and the rest of the world have been formed. In Genesis 2 man is created first, then the animals and finally woman. There are two quite distinct accounts of the Flood story. In the one Noah is commanded to take into the ark two of every beast (Genesis 6: 19), in the other seven of each clean animal and two of each unclean (7: 2), a difference which is underlined when the narrative goes on to say that all the animals went into the ark in pairs (7: 8, 9). It is clear that in these stories the men who put the Pentateuch into its final form found two accounts of these incidents and events, and with complete honesty and fidelity to their sources they included both.

Perhaps most surprising of all is the difference in the use of the

15

name of God. To see this clearly we must note that when the Authorized Version uses the word L~~ORD~~ in capital letters, it is translating ~~Jehovah~~ in the original Hebrew. In Exodus 6: 2 we see God encouraging Moses for his contest with Pharaoh. "God spake unto Moses and said unto him: I am the LORD; and I appeared unto Abraham, unto Isaac, and unto Jacob, by the name of God Almighty, *but by my name Jehovah was I not known to them.*" And yet in Genesis 15: 2, 8 we find Abraham calling God by the name Jehovah. We find both Sarah and Laban using that name (Genesis 16: 2; 24: 31). We find the name used in the days of Seth (Genesis 4: 26); and we even find Eve using the name Jehovah when she had borne a child (Genesis 4: 1). There is quite clearly more than one source here, and to note these discrepancies is not in the least to belittle or criticize the compilers of the Pentateuch; it is rather to underline the meticulous honesty with which they dealt with the sources and documents with which they worked.

We must now go on to see the process by which the Law grew up, and by which it came to be accepted by the Jews as the very word of God.

To the Jews God was characteristically a self-revealing God. As G. F. Moore puts it, the outstanding characteristic of Judaism is that it conceived of itself as a *revealed religion.* God, as the Jews thought of Him, is a God who desires to make Himself and His will known to men, and who continually takes steps to bring that knowledge to men. The natural result of this point of view is that in Judaism the supreme figure is the *prophet*, for the prophet is the messenger of God to men, and it is through the prophet that the revelation of God to men is commonly made. The promise made through Moses is that God will always give to the nation a prophet (Deuteronomy 18: 15). The claim of Amos is that God does nothing without revealing His secret to His servants the prophets (Amos 3: 7). God by His Spirit sent His word to men in the prophets, and it was the sin of the nation that men refused to hear (Zechariah 7: 12). That is why Judaism ranked all the great national figures as prophets. Abraham, Isaac, Jacob,

David, Job, Ezra, Mordecai were all prophets; the Jewish scholars enumerated forty-eight prophets and seven prophetesses in their national history. This means that the revelation of God was conceived of as essentially a *spoken* revelation. God spoke to the prophets, and then the prophets spoke to men. The question then is, in a world of religious thought in which the supreme figures were inspired *men* how did the idea of an inspired *book* emerge? "How," as Pfeiffer asks, "did the Israelites come to believe that God not only spoke but also dictated a book?"

The Starting-Point of Scripture

It is just here that we are fortunate enough to have a fixed date which is a starting-point for the whole idea of canonization and of sacred Scripture. It is to be understood that what follows is a reconstruction of events, as we think that they happened, and, although in our narrative we state the events as facts, we are none the less well aware that it is reconstruction and not indubitable history which we are presenting. In the year 621 B.C. a book which can only have been the Book of Deuteronomy was discovered in the Temple (2 Kings 22: 8–20). At the time the young Josiah was king, and he was a good king, and a true seeker after God. This book which had been discovered was accepted as the word of God, and was deliberately taken as nothing less than the law of the nation (2 Kings 23: 3). Here is the beginning of the whole process. A book has been accepted as the revealed word of God, and it has been openly and deliberately and publicly taken as the law of the nation and of the individual. "For the first time in the history of mankind," says Pfeiffer, "a book was canonized as sacred scripture."

But we must follow the process further. The publication of Deuteronomy very naturally stimulated the interest in written books, and there was another great book lying ready to hand.

This was a great epic story which told of the history of Israel down to the death of David, and which was itself a compilation, which had been made somewhere about 650 B.C. To this document has been given the name of JE, because it is formed by the coming together of two documents called respectively J and E. These documents have been given these identifying initials because one of them calls God by the name *Jehovah* right from the beginning, while the other calls God by the name *Elohim*, which is the general Hebrew word for God, down until the revelation of the name of Jehovah to Moses in Exodus 3: 11–18. It is precisely because these two documents have been put together that there were the discrepancies which exist in certain sections of the Pentateuch.

Some Discrepancies

As a brief illustration of this let us look at the discrepancies which we noted in the Flood story. In Genesis 6: 19 Noah is bidden to take two animals of every kind, and we note that this instruction occurs in a passage in which the speaker is God, that is, *Elohim* (Genesis 6: 13). In Genesis 7: 2 there is the instruction to take sevens of the clean beasts and twos of the unclean beasts and we note that this instruction occurs in a passage in which the speaker is the LORD, that is, Jehovah (Genesis 7: 1). Further we note that the passage which says that the beasts went into the ark two by two is a passage in which the divine name is God, that is, *Elohim* (Genesis 7: 9). This is an illustration of how the two documents were put together, and how in their earlier sections they can be distinguished by the name of God which each of them uses.

J, the document which calls God Jehovah from the very beginning, is one of the supreme religious documents of the world's literature. H. H. Rowley says of it: "The literary genius of its author will make it live, if only as literature, so long as men read literature." It thinks and speaks of God with a lovely childlike simplicity. Jehovah makes man from the dust of the earth and breathes life into his nostrils (2: 7). He makes woman, man's partner, from a rib taken from man (2: 22). Jehovah plants a garden and walks in it in the cool of the day (3: 8). When Noah has embarked his cargo and himself safely into the Ark, Jehovah shuts the door after him (7: 16). There never has been any book which has spoken with such a lovely, childlike simplicity about God. When we further study this document called J, we find that it is specially interested in Judah and in the Southern Kingdom of Israel. It is in Hebron that Abraham dwells, and it is to Hebron that the spies go when they enter the land, and in the story of Joseph it is Judah who is the leading figure. We, therefore, may say that this document is the document which was produced in the land of Judah and in the Southern Kingdom to tell of the early history of Israel.

The document which is called E, as we have seen, does not call God Jehovah until after the revelation of that name to Moses. That is why in the Pentateuch we find one line of thought which says that, although Abraham and the patriarchs knew God, they did not know Him by His name Jehovah, and another line of thought in which the name Jehovah is used from the days of Eve. E does not begin with creation; it begins with Abraham. It is not so simple and childlike as J is; it is specially interested in dreams and angels and in blessings and farewells. When we study it, we find that it is specially interested in Northern Israel. In its version of the Joseph story it is Reuben who plays the leading part. In the time of the Exodus it gives special prominence to Joshua who was from Ephraim; and in the Jacob story the centres are Bethel and Shechem. We, therefore, may say that this document is the document which was produced in the Northern Kingdom to tell of the early history of Israel. It is convenient for memory to make the letters J and E stand not only for Jehovah and Elohim, but also for Judah and Ephraim, so that they may also remind us of the parts of Israel from which these two documents came.

So, then, when Deuteronomy emerged, the Israelites already

possessed the incomparable epic history contained in JE; and, since Deuteronomy was taken to be the work of Moses, it was amalgamated with JE, and inserted in the narrative, before the death of Moses. Thus slowly the Pentateuch was being built up, and the divine library was taking its first steps to growth.

The Holiness Code

Now there follows still another addition. The great basic sentence which in itself contains the very essence of the religion of Israel is: "Ye shall be holy, for I Jehovah your God am holy" (Leviticus 19: 2). Bit by bit there had grown up rules and regulations and principles governing this holiness, and laying down in what this holiness consists. These holiness laws are embodied in a document which is known as the *Holiness Code,* which is contained in Leviticus 17–26, and which is usually denoted by the letter H. This was compiled and published somewhere about 550 B.C., and it was natural that it, too, should be added to the growing sacred literature of Israel. So, then, the Holiness Code was, as it were, the next volume to be added to the divine library of the Old Testament.

There remains one great volume to be added, and then the Pentateuch is complete. This last section of the Pentateuch is called P, because it contains all the great ritual and sacrificial practice in the second Temple, and it is essentially a priestly document. It is composed of the remaining part of Leviticus, in which the sacrificial laws are set out. It also contains the rest of the history of the Pentateuch, and it is characterized by certain features. It can be noble and austere, as it is in Genesis 1, when it tells its story of creation. It often tells stories to explain how the great religious practices and festivals of Israel came into being. For instance, its creation story explains the supreme importance of the Sabbath day. It is very fond of genealogies, for to a priest purity of lineage was essential, and it is to it that the long genealogies of the Pentateuch belong, and it became the great framework into which all the other parts of the Pentateuch were fitted. It was completed somewhere about 500 B.C.

So, at last, after more than a century under the guidance of the Spirit of God, the great divine library of the Pentateuch stood complete. It had begun with Deuteronomy; it had embraced the precious history of J and E; it had taken in the great Holiness Code; and finally it had found its unity in the setting of the laws and the history of the great priestly document called P. To put it in very brief form, we might say that the Law, the Pentateuch, equals D + JE + H + P.

But we have now to ask, when did this great document become sacred Scripture? When did it cease to be simply a great and precious book, and when did it come to be regarded and accepted as in a special and unique sense nothing less than, and nothing other than, the word of God? A first step was that the part of it which told specially of the great laws of Israel became separated from the rest. That is to say, the Law proper, the first five books of the Bible, became separated from Joshua, Judges, Samuel and Kings. It was the Law of God which was of supreme importance. Three things help us to fix a time when the Law became Scripture in the full sense of the term.

i. One of the great events in religious history was when the Old Testament was translated into Greek, and when the Greek Old Testament, which is known as the Septuagint, and which is denoted by the letters LXX, first emerged. The importance of it was that the Old Testament was no longer hidden away in the Hebrew language, but became available to almost the whole world, for at that time almost all men spoke Greek as well as their own tongue. That translation was made under the auspices of Ptolemy the Second Philadelphus, who was king of Egypt from 285–246 B.C. It was originally only the Law which was translated, and we know that by that time the Law was *par excellence* the sacred book of the Jews. It was for them *Scripture* in the full sense of the term. We can then say with certainty that by

21

250 B.C. the Law was Scripture. But can we trace the story further back?

ii. To this day the Samaritans accept only the Pentateuch as Scripture, and do not accept the other books of the Old Testament. That can only mean that when the Samaritans split from the Jews, and when the great national schism took place, the Scriptures consisted only of the Law, for it was only the Law that the Samaritans took with them. When that great and lasting schism took place is not accurately certain, but there is good evidence that it at least began to threaten in the days of Nehemiah, that is, at some time not very long before 400 B.C.

iii. Finally, in Nehemiah 8–10 we have the story of Ezra, the scribe, reading the sacred book of the Law to the assembled people. We need not take that story absolutely literally; but what we can say is this. When the people returned from exile under Ezra and Nehemiah, it must have become clear to them that political greatness was not for them. They, therefore, chose to find their greatness in religion and in spiritual things, and it was then that Israel became in a unique and special sense The People of the Book.

Everything points to the probability that the Law acquired the status of fully sacred Scripture, that it became in a special sense the binding word of God for Israel, in the time of Ezra and Nehemiah, that is, about 400 B.C.

So, then, by 400 B.C. the first stone in the edifice of Scripture is well and truly laid; the first great volume is deposited in the divine library; the canon of the Old Testament has begun. By that time the Law (*Torah*) has become Scripture, never to lose its place, to gain throughout the years an ever higher and higher place, a place for ever kept before the eyes of the people because the Law became the book whose reading was the centre of every Synagogue service.

Other Additions

As the years went on other books were to be added to the divine library, but no book was ever to be on a level with the Law; the Law was to stand in Judaism for ever without an equal or even a rival.

Whatever else was to be added to the Jewish Scriptures in the days to come the Law stood alone in all the splendour of the fulness of its revelation.

II. THE PROPHETS

But something was added to the divine library of Scripture. The Old Testament has a second part, and that part is the Prophets. We must now go on to see how that part of it became canonical. There is a sense in which the Law could not stand alone. If it sought to, it lacked that very thing which gave it birth—prophecy. It was the prophets who had been God's messengers to men, and who had been the guides and the directors of the nation, who had moved the people to walk in the ways of God and had warned and restrained them when they went astray. As Dillmann puts it, without prophecy "the Law was a body without a soul". As we shall see, it was the conviction of the Jews that with Malachi, midway through the fifth century B.C., the voice of prophecy had fallen for ever silent, for, as Ryle puts it, "it needed more than the Law to fill the gap."

We must first remind ourselves of what the Prophets are composed. They were composed of the *Former Prophets*, which are the books of Joshua, Judges, Samuel, and Kings, and of the *Latter Prophets*, which are composed of Isaiah, Jeremiah, Ezekiel, and the Twelve.

To us it seems strange to find Joshua, Judges, Samuel, and Kings classed as prophetic books. There is more than one explanation of their inclusion. It is suggested that they are reckoned prophetic because they tell of the works and words of the older prophets, of men like Samuel, Nathan, Ahijah, and above all, Elijah and Elisha. According to Jewish tradition these books were written by prophets. Joshua himself is said to have written the book which bears his name. Samuel is said to have written Judges and Samuel. Jeremiah is said to have been the author of Kings. But the truth is that, although these books are apparently history books, their real aim and function is to set out the principles of the prophets in action. As H. H. Rowley reminds us, to the Hebrew the will of God always became known through concrete experience. These books proclaim the prophetic principles as clearly as the prophets did, for their one aim is to show in every incident which they relate that the way of wisdom and of happiness and of prosperity lies in obedience to God, and disobedience to God is the inevitable way to disaster. These books are not history books; they are demonstrations of prophetic truth in action. The writers were not annalists interested in events as such; they were interested in events only as the working out and the demonstration of the will of God. They are concerned to depict history as the action of God, and to show that the words of the prophets, warnings and promises alike, are true.

There were many reasons why the canonization of these books was natural and inevitable.

They had already existed for many generations, for many of the prophets had committed their words to writing. "Bind up the testimony, seal the law among my disciples," said Isaiah (Isaiah 8: 16), and Ezekiel knew and quoted the words which God had spoken by His former prophets (Ezekiel 38: 17). Throughout the years these prophetic books had been the devotional literature of the devout in Israel. These were not books which had their place to make; their place was made; and they were already enthroned within the hearts of men.

It was during the dark days of the exile in distant Babylon

that the prophets became indispensable to the heart of a devout Jew. These were days of national disaster. What more natural than that a Jew should turn to the prophets? As Wildeboer puts it: "The deportation (to Babylon) itself would necessarily present itself to the people in the light of a fulfilment of the prophetic warnings. Now they searched the same oracles, which their fathers had spurned, for light in the darkness. If these had proved themselves truthful in their presages of punishment, they would also in Yahwe's time prove themselves faithful in their predictions of a blessed future." As Robertson Smith has it: "In the time of the Exile, when the national existence with which the ancient religion of Israel was so closely intertwined was hopelessly shattered, when the voice of the prophets was stilled, and the public services of the sanctuary no longer called the devout together, the whole continuance of the spiritual faith rested upon the remembrance that the prophets of the Lord had foreseen the catastrophe, and had shown how to reconcile it with undiminished trust in Jehovah, the God of Israel." They became "the main support of the faithful, who felt, as they have never felt before, that the words of Jehovah were pure words, silver sevenfold tried, a sure treasure in every time of need". Even when they returned from exile these older books were a necessary stay and support, for even then their condition was wretched in the extreme. So they read eagerly the story of the ancient and the glorious days. They knew that their sufferings had been caused by their sin, and in the history of the Former Prophets and the promises of the Latter Prophets they gained the certainty that, if they walked in the ways of God, the great days would come again. In the days of the Exile and the return the Prophets had been the food on which men fed their fainting souls. So in the circumstances of the Exile and the troubled days of the return the Prophets became to men the very word of God.

There was another factor in the situation which was significant and influential. It was a fixed Jewish belief that with Malachi, midway through the fifth century B.C., the voice of prophecy was silenced and never spoke again.

There are signs of this belief even within the Old Testament itself. In Deuteronomy the hope and the belief is that God will always raise up a prophet for His people (Deuteronomy 18:15), but in Malachi all that can be expected is not the emergence of any new prophet, but the return of Elijah (Malachi 4:5). Zechariah envisages a time when anyone who claims to be a prophet must be necessarily an impostor. "If anyone again appears as a prophet, his father and mother who bore him will say to him, You shall not live, for you speak lies in the name of the Lord; and his father and mother who bore him shall pierce him through when he prophesies" (Zechariah 13:3). In Psalm 74 there is a verse which is probably not a part of the original psalm but rather a comment of some editor, and it is a verse of this latter-day despair: "There is no longer any prophet, and there is none among us who knows how long" (Psalm 74:9).

In 1 Maccabees we repeatedly come on this belief. That book speaks of a sorrow in Israel "such as there has not been since the days that the prophets ceased to appear among them" (1 Maccabees 9:27). It describes how the people put aside the stones of the polluted altar, not knowing what to do with them, and waiting until a prophet should arise in Israel to tell them (1 Maccabees 4:46). It tells that they agreed to make Simon high priest until such time as a prophet should appear (1 Maccabees 14:41).

It is the same in the writings of the Rabbis. One passage says that up until Alexander the Great—Ezra was not very long before Alexander—the prophets prophesied through the Holy Spirit, but from that time onward all that a man could do was to listen to the wise, that is, to the scribes. Rabbi Akiba, writing in the Christian era, declared that any Jew who read in the Christian books had no share in the life to come. He went on to say that books, like that of Ben Sirach and others such, which had been composed after the age of the prophets had closed, might be read, but only as a man reads a letter.

Just because the days of the prophets were held to have ended with Haggai and Zechariah and Malachi, the works of the great prophets were of extreme preciousness. They belonged to an age of inspiration which no longer existed. The "Thus saith the Lord" of the prophets was something that a man could never hope to hear again. In view of that fact it was only natural that the works of the great prophets should be lovingly collected, and carefully preserved, and diligently studied. The very fact that men were conscious of living in an age of lesser inspiration gave to the great prophets a new place in life and thought. We must now go on to ask when the works of the prophets were collected and edited and issued.

Here we are in the realm of tradition and legend, but even in the case of legend and tradition it may be possible to penetrate to the truth which lies behind them. There are three main lines of such legends which we must take into account.

i. 2 Maccabees begins with a letter which is certainly a work of fiction. In that letter there is a statement about Nehemiah. It says of him that he founded a library, "and gathered together the acts of the kings, and the prophets, and of David, and the epistles of the kings concerning the holy gifts and sacrifices" (2 Maccabees 2 : 13). It is hard to say what, if any, truth lies behind this; but in this statement Nehemiah is credited with collecting the prophetic writings.

ii. Jewish belief always gave Ezra an all-important place in the formation of the Old Testament. The *Talmud* says of him that he would have been worthy that the Torah should have been given to Israel through his hand, if Moses had not preceded him. The legend comes to its peak in the apocryphal book known as 2 Esdras, which belongs to the latter part of the first century A.D. According to that book the Law was lost and burned in the national disasters. Ezra prayed to God that he might be enabled to write down all that God had done in history, and all that God was still to do, as it had been written in the Law. He was told to withdraw from men for forty days, taking five skilful penmen with him. He was given a cup to drink, and he spoke continuously for forty days and nights. In that time ninety-four books

27

were produced, seventy of which were to be handed over to the wise, and twenty-four of which were to be published for all to read, and these twenty-four were the canonical books of the Old Testament (4 Ezra 14: 19–48). Once again this is pure legend, but it ascribes to Ezra the preservation and the promulgation of the whole Old Testament.

iii. In Jewish tradition we meet with a body called The Great Synagogue. In the *Sayings of the Fathers* we read that, "Moses received the *Torah* from Sinai and delivered it to Joshua, and Joshua to the elders, and the elders to the prophets, and the prophets to the men of the Great Synagogue." This Great Synagogue was said to have been a body of men convened by Ezra and numbering one hundred and twenty, and including amongst others Haggai, Zechariah, Malachi, Nehemiah, Daniel, and Mordecai. The Great Synagogue was the spiritual ruler of Israel. It is said that the men of the Great Synagogue wrote Ezekiel, the Book of the Twelve Prophets, Daniel, and Esther, and that at the same time Ezra wrote the book which bears his name, and the genealogies in Chronicles up to his own time. If we say that the Great Synagogue *edited* and *published* these books rather than *wrote* them we will come near to the meaning of this tradition. Once again we are in the realm of legend, and it is very doubtful if the Great Synagogue ever existed at all.

The Prophets Established

Jewish traditional and legendary accounts lay it down very definitely that the books of Scripture were assembled and collected and even canonized in the days of Ezra and Nehemiah. It may well be that none of these legends and traditions is anything like accurate history, but it seems to us certain that they do preserve the memory of the fact that it was in the days of Ezra and Nehemiah that the Law became canonical and that the Prophets were assembled and collected. Throughout the exile men had fed their souls on the Prophets. In the deep disappointments and the heart-breaking problems of the return they had found their help and their support in the prophetic writings; and it was then that the prophetic writings were deliberately collected and preserved. It is to be noted that at this stage it is not a matter of declaring the prophets sacred Scripture, and not a matter of placing them in the canon beside the Law; it is still a matter of collecting well-loved books, and ensuring that they will never go lost. Canonization was still to come. Have we any indication as to when it did come?

We may begin our investigation with one pointer which provides us with a date at which the Prophets were almost certainly regarded as canonical and as Holy Scripture. The Book of Daniel appeared about 165 B.C. Now Daniel is quite clearly a prophetic book and yet never at any time did it appear amongst the prophets, and always it was included among the Writings. That can only mean that by the time Daniel appeared the number of the prophets was closed; the prophetic literature was a fixed and settled body into which no other book, however well qualified, could find an entry. It is safe to say that that means that the Prophets were regarded as Holy Scripture at least by the time of Daniel in 165 B.C.

So, then, by the beginning of the second century B.C. a further stone has been added to the edifice of Scripture; a further section has been added to the divine library of the Old Testament, and now beside the Law there stand the Prophets.

And now there arises a rather significant fact. At no time did there ever arise among the Jews any question or any dispute in regard to any part of the Law. It was unquestionably and un-arguably divine from beginning to end. But among the prophets two books came under discussion. The first was Jonah, which was described as "a book by itself", and which was questioned because it has to do exclusively with the heathen and does not mention Israel at all. To some of the Jewish scholars it seemed strange that a book which, as they saw it, had nothing to do with Israel had a place within the canon of Israel. They failed that in many ways Jonah is the greatest book in the Old Testament, because it lays down the missionary task of Israel as no other book does. The other book which was questioned was the book of Ezekiel. It was never suggested that Ezekiel should be ejected from the canon, but it was argued sometimes that Ezekiel should be "put away", that is, that it should be withdrawn from general circulation, and that it should not be read in the Synagogue. That was due to two things. It was due to the difficulty of the beginning and the end, especially the passage about the chariot of God.

It was not that anyone wished to eliminate either Jonah or Ezekiel from the canon of Scripture. It was simply felt that they raised difficulties and the difficulties were openly discussed; and it must be noted that, although that could happen with the Prophets, it could never happen with the Law, which was so divine that it was beyond question and beyond discussion.

III. THE WRITINGS

We have now arrived at the third part of the Old Testament, the part which was known as the *Writings* or the *Hagiographa*. In the case of the Writings the story is much less simple and much less straightforward. The Writings do not form a homogeneous whole like the Law or the Prophets. They are rather what has been called "a miscellany of independent books". They did not enter the canon of Scripture as a whole as the Law and the Prophets did, but one by one they came to be regarded as sacred Scripture, rather by popular acceptance than by official decision. For long they were not so much Scripture as "religious literature". They were not intended to be used, and they were not as a whole used, for public liturgical reading at the worship and service of the Synagogue; they were rather meant for homiletic exposition. They formed what Ryle calls "an informal appendix to the Law and the Prophets".

Their secondary quality can be seen in that to the end of the day the Old Testament was commonly referred to as The Law and the Prophets. In the preface to Daniel Jerome writes: "All Sacred Scripture is divided by them (that is, the Jews) into three parts, into the Law, the Prophets and the Hagiographa." That is true, but it none the less remains true that Scripture was commonly called the Law and the Prophets. We need go no further than the New Testament for abundant evidence of this. "Think not," said Jesus, "that I am come to destroy the Law or the Prophets" (Matthew 5: 17). The Golden Rule that we should do to others as we would have them do to us is the essence and summation of the Law and the Prophets (Matthew 7: 12). The Law and the Prophets existed until John; thereafter it is the time of the Kingdom (Luke 16: 16). It was from Moses and all the Prophets that Jesus expounded the Scriptures (Luke 24: 27). In the Synagogue in Antioch in Pisidia it is the Law and the Prophets which are read (Acts 13: 15). In every Synagogue on every Sabbath day Moses is read (Acts 15: 21). It was from the Prophet Isaiah that Jesus read in the Synagogue at Nazareth (Luke 4: 17). It was the Law and the Prophets which were read at the public worship of the Synagogue, and it is as the Law and the Prophets that the Old Testament is commonly described. Obviously the Writings, the Hagiographa, do not stand on this same level.

In the same passage as we have already quoted, Jerome goes on to say that there are five books of the Law, eight of the Prophets, and eleven of the Writings. The eleven books of the Writings do not fall into any natural and inevitable sections, and they were divided in different ways. They were divided into three books of *poetry*—Psalms, Proverbs, and Job; five rolls, the *Megilloth*, which were, as we shall see, specially connected with five great national occasions—The Song of Solomon, Ruth, Lamentations, Ecclesiastes, and Esther; one book of prophecy—Daniel; two books of history—Ezra-Nehemiah and Chronicles. Sometimes, as the prophets were, they were divided into the *Former Writings,* the *Rishonim*—Ruth, Psalms, Job, and Proverbs; *the Latter*

31

Writings, the *Acharonim*—Daniel, Ezra-Nehemiah and Chronicles; and the five *Megilloth*. Sometimes they were divided into *The Major Writings*—Psalms, Job, and Proverbs; *the Minor Writings*—The Song of Solomon, Ecclesiastes, and Lamentations; *the Latter Writings*—Esther, Daniel, Ezra-Nehemiah, Chronicles. They are a highly varied miscellany falling into highly varied sections. Our task is to trace how these eleven books became part of the sacred literature of Israel, and part of the Old Testament. We may begin with certain general facts.

In the ancient world a book had to be popular and had to be read before it could even survive. We are thinking of an age when books were not printed, but when each copy had to be made by hand; and, if a book was not popular enough to be read, it simply ceased to be copied, and vanished out of existence. These Writings must, therefore, in the first place have been popular works, known and read widely by the ordinary people.

Second, it became a first principle of the Jewish view of sacred books that a book to be Scripture had to be written in Hebrew, or at least in Aramaic, and, if it dealt with history, the history must be the history of the great classical period of the Hebrew story.

Attributed Authorship

Third, we will remember that it was the Jewish conviction that all true prophetic inspiration had ceased with Malachi, and that since about 450 B.C. the divine voice was silent. At first sight it would, therefore, appear that any book must be written prior to Ezra to have even a chance of entering into the canon. But there is one extremely interesting exception to that. If a book was anonymous, if no one knew who had written it, and, if it had become a book dear to the hearts and minds of people, it was possible that it could be attributed to one of the great figures of the past, and, therefore, could become canonical. That is to say,

32

if a book's author was known to be after Ezra, it had no hope of becoming canonical. That is what turned the scale against Ecclesiasticus (in the Apocrypha). There are few who would care to deny that Ecclesiasticus is a very great book, and that it is greater in moral and spiritual power than certain books which gained an entry into the canon, but it had never any hope of entry, because its author was known to be a man called Jesus ben Sirach who had lived not long after 200 B.C. Many of the Writings were written in the fourth and the third centuries B.C., and at least one—Daniel—in the second century B.C., but their authors were unknown, they were anonymous, and, therefore, it was possible to attribute them to the great figures of the past, and so to make it possible for them to enter the canon. So Ruth was ascribed to Samuel, who was traditionally the author of Judges and the books which bear his name. All the Psalms were ascribed to David. Jeremiah was said to have written both Kings and Lamentations. Proverbs and Ecclesiastes were said to be the work of Solomon. Job was assigned to Moses. Ezra and Nehemiah were the work of Ezra, who was so respected that it was said: "The *Torah* was forgotten by Israel until Ezra went up from Babylon and re-established it." And Ezra had at least a share in the writing of Chronicles. The Song of Solomon might actually be Solomon's, or at least it was held to belong to the time of Hezekiah. Esther was the work, or at least the editing, of the men of the Great Synagogue. The Writings could only become canonical, because, when their supreme value was realized, they were seen to be anonymous, and could, therefore, be held to be the work of men within the period to which inspiration was said to be confined. This is true even in the case of Daniel. It was well known that Daniel had actually emerged about 165 B.C., but it was held to be the actual work of Daniel, the great figure of the exile. It was thus that it was possible for these books to become canonical at all.

When did they come to be regarded as Holy Scripture?

The process was a long one. We must begin by returning to the enigmatic statement about Nehemiah in the admittedly spurious letter at the beginning of 2 Maccabees. There it is said that Nehemiah collected into a library the books about the kings and the prophets, and *ta tou Dauid*, which literally means "the things of David", and which in the context can most naturally mean the books, or the writings, of David (2 Maccabees 2: 13). It may be impossible to place very much stress or reliance on that statement, but it may mean that Nehemiah began the whole process by the collection of the Psalms—by no means the whole book as we possess it—which go under the name of David.

It is when we come to Ecclesiasticus (now in the Apocrypha) that the existence of this third division of Scripture becomes quite clear and certain. Writing in or about 132 B.C. the grandson of the original writer of Ecclesiasticus, Jesus ben Sirach, wrote a prologue to his Greek translation of his grandfather's book. There he speaks of the great things handed down to us by the Law and the Prophets and *the others who have followed in their steps*. He tells how his grandfather gave himself to the study of the Law and of the Prophets and of *the other books of our fathers*. And he speaks about the Law, the Prophecies, and *the rest of the books*. He does not use the term Writings; he does not define what these other books are. It is clear that they are not nearly so well defined a body of literature as the Law and the Prophets are; but it is also clear that by the second century B.C. there stands beside the Law and the Prophets a body of literature less well defined than they are, but none the less an essential part of the sacred literature of the Jews.

Our next witness comes from the New Testament itself. In Luke's Gospel we read that the risen Christ told the disciples about the things which must be fulfilled in Him, which were written in the Law of Moses and in the Prophets and in the Psalms (Luke 24: 44). Here we see that the Psalms are included in, or perhaps are taken as typical and representative of, a body of sacred literature other than the Law and the Prophets. Once again the existence of the Writings is assured, although their constituent parts are still undefined.

When we come to the end of the first Christian century we can call two much more definite witnesses. We have already seen the tradition that Ezra rewrote the whole of the sacred literature; and in that tradition we read that the books which were to be open to all men numbered twenty-four, which by Jewish reckoning is exactly the same number of books as are in the Old Testament (4 Ezra 14: 44–46). 4 Ezra (Apocrypha) was written under Domitian about A.D. 90, and here we have proof that by that time the list of the books was settled, and, therefore, the number of the Writings must have been as firmly fixed as the number of books in the Law and in the Prophets.

The second witness is Josephus who wrote about A.D. 100. He says that, unlike the Greeks who have vast numbers of conflicting and mutually contradictory books, the Jews have only twenty-two. He arrives at this number by reckoning Ruth and Judges as one book, and Jeremiah and Lamentations as one book. He goes on to say that there are the five books of Moses, the thirteen books of the Prophets, and four books with hymns or precepts for practical help for life. He arrives at this classification by including Daniel, Job, Chronicles, Ezra-Nehemiah, and Esther with the prophetic books. He then goes on to say: "There is practical proof of the spirit in which we treat our Scriptures. For although so great an interval of time (since they were written) has now passed, not a soul has ventured either to add, or to remove, or to alter a syllable; and it is the instinct of every Jew, from the day of his birth, to consider these books as the teaching of God, to abide by them, and, if need be, cheerfully to lay down his life for them" (Josephus, *Against Apion* 1: 8). Here is the proof that by the time of Josephus the number of books in the Writings was regarded as fixed and unalterable, because the number of books in Scripture was so regarded.

It remains to see the final step in the actual time process of the making of the Old Testament.

Somewhere about A.D. 90 at Jamnia, which was also called Jabne, and which was near Jaffa and not far from the sea, an authoritative council of the Jewish Rabbis and scholars met, and at that council the books of the Old Testament were at last finally settled, and the number was laid down as we have it to-day. From that time forward, although a scholar here or there might express doubts about this or that book amongst the Writings, there was never any real question or argument about the contents of the sacred Scriptures of the Old Testament. The process which had begun with the emergence of Deuteronomy in 621 B.C. had ended with the Council of Jamnia in A.D. 90. The divine library of the Old Testament had taken more than seven hundred years to assemble.

The People of the Book

History has a strange way of repeating itself. It was at Jamnia in A.D. 90 that the Old Testament canon was finally fixed. And Jamnia came only twenty years after the supreme disaster of Jewish history, the disaster from which the nation never recovered, the destruction of the Temple and the near-obliteration of Jerusalem in A.D. 70. Once again in the time of disaster it was to the word of God that the nation was driven. With every worldly hope shattered, faced with a future in which humanly speaking they had nothing to hope for, the Jews had to become *the people of the book,* and for that very reason it was then that the book had to be definitely and finally defined. With nothing else left to live for the Jews began to live for the study of God's word. The Jews clung to the sacred Scriptures not because of any theological theory of inspiration, but because they found in them the comfort of God in their sorrow, the hope of God in their despair, the light of God in their darkness, and the strength of God in a world where for them the foundations were shaken.

It remains briefly to look at the individual books within the Writings and to see how they fared, and in particular to note which of them had questionings and opposition to face.

To the Book of Psalms there was never any opposition, and doubtless it was the first of all the Writings to fix itself on the hearts of men. It was the hymn-book of the Temple, and the prayer-book of the community, as Cornill described it. The order of the Psalms in the daily worship of the Temple was as follows. On the first day of the week Psalm 24 was sung—"The earth is the Lord's and the fulness thereof"—in commemoration of the first day of creation, when "God possessed the world and ruled in it". On the second day of the week Psalm 48 was sung—"Great is the Lord and greatly to be praised"—because on the second day of creation "God divided His works and reigned over them". On the third day of the week Psalm 82 was sung—"God standeth in the creation of the mighty"—"because on that day the earth appeared, on which are the Judge and the judged". On the fourth day of the week Psalm 94 was sung—"O Lord God to whom vengeance belongeth"—"because on the fourth day God made the sun, moon, and stars, and will be avenged on those that worship them". On the fifth day of the week Psalm 81 was sung—"Sing aloud unto God our strength" —"because of the variety of creatures created that day to praise His name". On the sixth day Psalm 93 was sung—"The Lord reigneth"—"because on that day God finished His works and made man, and the Lord ruled over all His works". Lastly, on the seventh day, the Sabbath day, Psalm 92 was sung—"It is a good thing to give thanks unto the Lord"—"because the Sabbath is symbolic of the millenial kingdom at the end of the six thousand years dispensation, when the Lord will reign over all, and His glory and service will fill the earth with thanksgiving".

From the beginning the place of the Psalms was never questioned, for they had a unique place in the public services of the Temple and in the private devotions of the hearts of men.

Certain others of the Writings had their place in public services. The High Priest read in public from Chronicles, Job, Ezra-Nehemiah, and Daniel on the evening before the Day of Atonement. The five *Megilloth*—the word *megilloth* means *rolls*— were read at the great Jewish festivals. The Song, which was allegorized to symbolize the deliverance from Egypt, was read on the eighth day of the Passover. Ruth, the harvest story, was read on the second day of Pentecost. Lamentations was read on 9th Ab, which was the anniversary of the destruction of Solomon's Temple. Ecclesiastes was read on the third day of the Feast of Tabernacles, to remind men to remember God in the midst of the enjoyment of material blessings. Esther was read at the Feast of Purim, for which it is the warrant. The five *Megilloth* were the only books of the Writings to be read in the Synagogue, and they were read only on their special occasions; and, as we shall see, certain of them were very far from being undisputed.

As we have seen, the place of Psalms was never in doubt. Job, too, was never questioned. Job was attributed to Moses, in accordance with the belief that every prophet described his own period, for Job was taken to belong to the patriarchal age. Ruth and Lamentations were never questioned, because Ruth went with Judges and Lamentations with Jeremiah. Daniel was never questioned, because in spite of its late emergence its authorship was ascribed to the great Daniel of the exilic period.

On some very few occasions Proverbs was questioned. It was questioned on two grounds. First, it was argued that Proverbs contains apparent contradictions. Proverbs 26: 4, 5 reads: "*Answer not a fool according to his folly,* lest thou also be like unto him. *Answer a fool according to his folly,* lest he be wise in his own conceit.*" Second, it was argued that a passage such as Proverbs 7: 7—20 presented ethical problems which were difficult of solution. The argument about Proverbs was never at any time very serious, and it must be remembered that it was never suggested that Proverbs should be discarded, but only that it should be withheld from ordinary people who might be puzzled and even misled by the apparent difficulties and contradictions.

It was with difficulty that Esther gained a final place in the canon, and, even after it had gained its place, as late as the third century there were those who were not happy about it. The straits in which the supporters of Esther found themselves are illustrated by a Rabbinic tradition about the book. It was said that Rabbi Samuel had said that Esther did not defile the hands, that is, that it was not a sacred book. Rabbi Judah in speaking of this tradition said: "Did Samuel mean that Esther was not spoken by the Holy Spirit? Samuel undoubtedly taught that Esther was spoken by the Holy Spirit, but it was spoken to be recited and not to be written." Such a statement shows the difficulties which Esther encountered. The problem in regard to Esther was twofold. First, from beginning to end it never mentions the name of God, a truly extraordinary fact in a sacred book. Second, there was in some ways an even more difficult problem. Esther tells of the foundation of the Feast of Purim, and it was at the Feast of Purim that Esther was read in the Synagogue. Now the trouble was that the Feast of Purim is a Feast which finds no warrant and no justification in the Mosaic Law, and the Mosaic Law was taken as a first principle to be absolutely complete (Leviticus 27: 34). Here, indeed, was a difficulty. It was circumvented by the tradition that, although the instructions for the Feast of Purim are not written down in the Law, they were nevertheless given to Moses by God *verbally* during the forty days and forty nights on the mountain, but were not written down until the days of Mordecai. But the fact remained that for long Esther was in dispute, and there have always been those who doubted its right to a place in the canon of Holy Scripture.

Serious controversy in regard to the Writings also centred round two books—Ecclesiastes and the Song. Not unnaturally the weary pessimism of Ecclesiastes and the fact that the Song is one of the world's great love poems, which has to be allegorized to become a religious book at all, presented problems.

It may be said that Esther, Ecclesiastes and the Song were the books about which controversy was most real, for even after the Council of Jamnia there were those who were unwilling to accept them; and it is not without significance that these are three of the very few Old Testament books which are never quoted or referred to in the New Testament.

The Emergence of Sacred Scripture

This then is the story of the building up over seven hundred years of the divine library of the Old Testament.

From this story one thing stands out with unmistakable clarity. It was in the dark days of the Exile that men discovered the Prophets as the word of God. It was in the agony of the time of Antiochus Epiphanes that the Writings began to emerge as sacred Scripture. It was when life had taken everything else away that the Jewish scholars at the Council of Jamnia defined the content of Scripture, accepted the fact that Israel was the People of the Book, and dedicated their lives to the study of the word of God. Here is no human work. The books of the Old Testament took their place as sacred Scripture, not because of the *fiat* or decision of any council or committee of the Church, but because history and experience had manifestly and effectively demonstrated them to be the word of God. These were the books in which men had met God in the times which tried men's souls, and in which they had discovered the strength and the comfort of the Almighty. When any council gave any decision in regard to any book or books of the Old Testament, it was simply repeating and affirming that which experience had already proved. Such councils did not make these books into sacred Scripture and into the word of God; they simply recorded the fact that men had already mightily found them so.

And in these books men continued to find God. There have always been times from Marcion onwards when men wished to lay aside the Old Testament as outdated and outworn. One of the extraordinary features of the early Church is the number of men who were converted by reading the Old Testament. Tatian tells us how he was initiated into the Mysteries and how he had tried all that heathen religion and philosophy had to offer, and had come away empty. Then he goes on to say: "I happened to meet with certain barbaric writings, too old to be compared with the opinions of the Greeks, and too divine to be compared with their errors; and I was led to put faith in these by the unpretending cast of the language, the inartificial character of the writers, the foreknowledge displayed of future events, the excellent quality of the precepts, and the declaration of the government of the universe as being centred in one Being" (Tatian, *Address to the Greeks* 29). These writings were the writings of the prophets and in them Tatian found the voice of God. Theophilus of Antioch tells us of his vain search for God. "At the same time," he says, "I met with the sacred Scriptures of the holy prophets," and it was through them that he was led to God (Theophilus, *To Autolycus* 1 : 14). Justin Martyr writes: "There existed long before this time certain men more ancient than all those who are esteemed philosophers, both righteous and beloved by God, who spoke by the divine Spirit, and foretold events which would take place, and which are now taking place. They are called prophets. These alone both saw and announced the truth to men, neither reverencing nor fearing any man, not influenced by a desire for glory, but speaking those things alone which they saw and heard, being filled with the Holy Spirit" (Justin Martyr, *Dialogue with Trypho* 7). Athenagoras, presenting his plea for the Christians to the Emperor Marcus Aurelius and his colleague Lucius Aurelius Commodus, actually says to these Emperors: "I expect that you who are so learned and so eager for the truth are not without some introduction to Moses, Isaiah and Jeremiah, and the rest of the prophets" (Athenagoras, *Embassy for the Christians* 9). So well were the prophets known that Athenagoras does not think it ridiculous to assume that even the Roman Emperors were acquainted with them. And of this same Athenagoras Philip of Sidē tells us that he planned to write an attack on the Christians. In order to do so he read the Holy Scriptures, and at the end of the reading the would-be attacker had become the defender of the faith.

The books of the Old Testament were accepted as Holy Scripture because in them men found God and God found men. Through all the centuries that continued to happen, and it can still happen to-day. Men can never afford to discard the books in which God speaks.

FOR FURTHER GUIDANCE

F. Buhl: *The Canon and Text of the Old Testament*, 1892.

J. A. Bewer: *The Literature of the Old Testament*, 1947.

F. V. Filson: *Which Books Belong in the Bible? A Study of the Canon*, 1957.

R. H. Pfeiffer: *Introduction to the Old Testament*, 1941.

H. Rowley: *The Growth of the Old Testament*, 1949.

H. E. Ryle: *The Canon of the Old Testament*, 1892.

G. Wildeboer: *The Origin of the Canon of the Old Testament*, 1895.

THE MAKING OF THE NEW TESTAMENT

THE MOST surprising thing about the making of the New Testament is the length of time which it required. The first time that we meet a list of New Testament books exactly the same as our list to-day is in the Thirty-ninth Easter Letter of Athanasius which was written in A.D. 367. That is to say, it took more than three hundred years for the New Testament to reach its final form.

From the very beginning it could be said that Christianity was the religion of a book. It was in Judaism that Christianity was cradled; all the first Christians were Jews; and it was, therefore, natural and inevitable that the Christian service should follow the pattern of the service in the Jewish Synagogue. The Synagogue service fell into three sections. The first section was a service of prayer and worship; the second section was the reading of Scripture; the third section consisted of teaching and explanation of the Law. It was for the second section that the whole service existed; it was in the reading of the Law that the whole service reached its centre and its peak. It was that service which the Christian Church took over. Even in the New Testament itself there are signs that the reading of Scripture was very much in the forefront. In the Pastoral Epistles the message is sent to the Church: "Till I come, give attention to *reading*, to exhortation, to teaching" (1 Timothy 4: 13). In the Revelation the promise is: "Blessed is he who reads, and they who hear the words of this prophecy" (Revelation 1: 3), and the reference is not to private but to public reading. There are plain indications that, at least within the congregations to which they were addressed, the letters of Paul were to be read in public. "I charge you," he writes to the Thessalonians, "that this letter be read to all the holy brethren" (1 Thessalonians 5: 27). He writes to the Colossians: "When this letter is read among you, cause that it be read also in the Church of the Laodiceans; and that you likewise read the letter from Laodicea" (Colossians 4: 16).

In the First Apology of Justin Martyr there is the first description of a Christian service: "On the day called the Day of the Sun all who live in cities or in the country gather together to one place, and the memoirs of the apostles or the writings of the prophets are read, as long as time permits; then, when the reader has ceased, the president verbally instructs, and exhorts to the imitation of these good things. Then we all rise together and pray" (Justin Martyr, *First Apology* 67). Right in the centre of the service is the reading of the word.

But for long the Christian Church had no literature of its own, and the book which was read was the Old Testament, for, when the Church began, there was no such thing as a book called the New Testament or any part of it, for the books of the New Testament had still to be written. And here we come upon another surprise. Clearly the centre of the Christian message is the life and death of Jesus, and the extraodinary thing is the long delay before the Gospels were written. Mark is the earliest of the Gospels, and Mark cannot be dated before A.D. 60; Matthew and Luke were written between A.D. 80 and 90; and John dates to about A.D. 100. That is to say, the first Gospel which we possess was not written until about thirty years after the death of Jesus. Here, then, is the first problem which we must solve. Why was there this long delay in the production of a specifically Christian literature? Many reasons combined to bring about that delay.

The Old Testament—A Christian Book

i. For long the Church was content with the Old Testament; the Old Testament had become a Christian book. Had not everything that the Old Testament hoped for and foretold come true in Jesus? Had not the great promised Messianic age dawned in him? This was made all the easier because the first Christians were Jews and were, therefore, trained in the technique of the interpretation of Scripture for special purposes. It was a Jewish belief that all Scripture had four meanings—*Peshat*, which was the simple meaning which could be seen at the first reading; *Remaz*, which was the suggested meaning and the truth which the passage suggested to the seeking mind; *Derush*, which was the meaning when all the resources of investigation, linguistic, historical, literary, archaeological, had been brought to bear upon the passage; *Sod*, which was the inner and allegorical meaning. The initial letters of these words, P R D S, are the consonants of the word PaRaDiSe, and to enter into these three meanings was as if to enter into the bliss of Paradise. Now of all the meanings *Sod,* the inner, mystical meaning was the most important. The Jews were, therefore, skilled in finding inner meanings in Scripture. It was thus not difficult for them to develop a technique of Old Testament interpretation which discovered Jesus Christ all over the Old Testament.

We take an instance from the *Letter of Barnabas* (9: 7, 8). It is there argued that when Abraham circumcised his household (Genesis 17: 23, 27), he did so looking forward in the Spirit to Jesus Christ. The number circumcised was 318. In Greek there are no signs for the numerals, and the letters of the alphabet are used as numerals as well as letters. So a = 1 and b = 2, and so on. Let us then take this number. 318 is denoted by the two letters *iota* and *eta*, which are the first two letters of the name *Jesus*, and, therefore, the number 18 stands for Jesus; 300 is denoted by the letter *tau,* which is the shape of the Cross, and therefore the number 300 stands for the Cross. Thus in the number 318 is discovered a message of Jesus and His Cross. When the Old Testament was consistently treated like this, it was not difficult to use it as a Christian book which everywhere spoke of and foretold Jesus Christ. It is not to be wondered at that for some considerable time the early Church found the Old Testament enough.

45

ii. In Palestine the early Church came into a non-literary situation, and there were at least three reasons why the Church was unlikely to produce books.

(a) It was long before the days when printing had been invented and book production was slow and laborious and book distribution was very limited. Even when books were produced and copied by hand it was an expensive process. A book consisted of papyrus sheets joined horizontally to form a roll. Papyrus cost from over a shilling to about fourpence for a sheet ten inches by eight. That is why poorer people often used *ostraca*, broken pieces of pottery, and the back of papyrus sheets which had already been used, for their writing.

Copying was by no means a cheap process. For the purposes of copying a manuscript was divided into *stichoi*. The Greek word *stichos* means *a line*. In poetry the line is an obvious unit of measurement, but in prose an artificial unit had to be adopted. So the *stichos* for the purpose of copying was reckoned at the average length of an Homeric hexameter line, which is fifteen or sixteen syllables. In manuscripts the number of *stichoi* is often given at the end. In one manuscript Matthew has 2,480 *stichoi*; Mark 1,543; Luke 2,714; John 1,950; Acts 2,610; 3 John 31: Revelation 1,292. The Edict of Diocletian issued in the middle of the third century fixed the prices of most things, and it fixed the price of copying at 20–25 *denarii* per 100 *stichoi*. A *denarius* was worth about ninepence, so that it cost not far short of a pound to copy 100 *stichoi*. On this basis a professional copyist would charge about £50 or $150 to copy Luke–Acts alone. It is quite clear that for ordinary people books at that price were out of the question.

(b) Especially in Palestine the normal way of transmitting knowledge was by oral transmission. The Rabbis had in fact a dislike of writing. "Commit nothing to writing," they said. For centuries they passed down the Oral Law by word of mouth, and a good student had to have a good memory so that he would be like "a well plastered cistern" which never loses a drop. It was not until sometime in the third century that the Oral Law was written down. It was called the *Mishnah* and in English translation it makes a book of about 800 pages, and all of it had for centuries been orally transmitted. Papias, who was a great collector of information in the early Church, says that he questioned everyone he could find who had come into contact with Jesus and with the apostles and their companions, "for," he says,"I did not think that what was to be gotten from books would profit me as much as what came from the living and abiding voice" (Eusebius, *The Ecclesiastical History* 3. 39. 4). The Church grew up in a situation in which it was more natural to transmit knowledge orally than to commit it to writing.

(c) The great majority of the early Christians did not, in fact, come from educated circles. Not many wise men after the flesh, not many mighty, not many noble were called (1 Corinthians 1 : 26). When Celsus attacked Christianity in the early part of the third century he said that the attitude of the Christians was : "Let no cultured person draw near, none wise, none sensible, for all that kind of thing we count evil; but, if any man is ignorant, if any man is wanting in sense and culture, if any man is a fool, let him boldly come." As Celsus saw the Church it was "the simpletons, the ignoble, the senseless, slaves, womenfolk and children" whom the Christians wished to persuade (Origen, *Against Celsus* 3. 44). Celsus, of course, was attacking Christianity as a hostile critic, but it was true that the Christian community was the last kind of community to be likely to produce literary works.

The situation of the early Church was a non-literary situation in which books in any case would not be readily or easily produced.

Apostles—the Living Books

iii. So long as the original apostles survived there was no need for written records of the life and words of Jesus. The apostles were the eye-witnesses who knew. They were at once the repositories and the guarantors of Christian truth. They were the living books on which Jesus had written His message. Further, as Floyd V. Filson points out, the recitation of the facts of Jesus' life, and the words of Jesus' teaching, was not enough; the events of Jesus' life and the substance of His teaching needed more than transmission; they needed also *interpretation*, and it was that authoritative interpretation that the apostles alone could supply.

There is another side to this. The first age of the Church was far more an age of the Spirit than an age of books. As Filson puts it: "God was writing the gospel on the hearts of the converts to the faith." The message was being demonstrated and passed on far more by persons than by pages in a book.

iv. One of the things which was most influential in delaying the production of a Christian literature was the Christian belief in the imminence of the Second Coming. The Christians expected the return of Jesus at any moment. In 1 Corinthians Paul recommends against marriage, because the Christians, as he at that time thought, were living in a situation in which it was unwise to enter into any ties or obligations. "The time is short . . . The fashion of the world is passing away" (1 Corinthians 7: 29, 31). The whole belief in these early days was that men were living in a quite impermanent situation, which might last only a few days or even a few hours, and in a situation like that books were an irrelevancy. There was no point in recording things for a posterity who would never be there to read the records. The belief in the immediacy of the Second Coming produced a situation in which books could not be regarded as anything else but unnecessary.

Such were the main circumstances in the situation which prevented and delayed the production of a Christian literature, but as time went on the production of that literature became a necessity.

i. The time of oral tradition was bound to end with the death of the apostles, and with the exception of John all the apostles were dead by A.D. 70. Something had to be found to take the place of "the living and abiding voice", and that something could not be anything other than a written record. There are many descriptions and accounts of the writing of the Gospels in the works of the fathers, and again and again the implication is that the written Gospel was a substitute for the living apostle. Eusebius in his account of the writing of the Gospels (*The Ecclesiastical History* 3. 24. 5) tells us that Matthew preached to the Hebrews, and when he was about to leave them and to go to preach to others, he committed his Gospel to writing, and thus "compensated by his writing for the loss of his presence". It is the consistent tradition of the early Church that Mark was "the interpreter" of Peter and that his Gospel is nothing other than the preaching material which Peter used, and that Luke's Gospel is really the gospel which Paul preached. Irenaeus (*Against Heresies* 3. 1. 1, 2) speaks about the preaching of Peter and Paul and of their foundation of the Roman Church. He then goes on to say: "After their death, Mark, the disciple and interpreter of Peter, handed down to us in writing the things preached by Peter. Luke also, the follower of Paul, put down in a book the gospel preached by that one." The clear implication is that the written Gospel was an attempt to compensate for the death of the great preachers. The Monarchian Prologue to the Fourth Gospel says that John wrote "when he realized that the day of his departure had come," and Jerome says that he finished his Gospel "with fortunate haste" before death overtook him (Jerome, *The Prologues to the Four Gospels*).

The written Gospels were meant to compensate for the loss of the living voice of the apostles.

ii. When Christianity left the narrower bounds of Palestine and went into the Greek-Roman world, it entered a world where books were familiar things and where publishing and book-selling were part of big business. Atticus, Cicero's friend and publisher, was the first man to reproduce books in a big way. The bookshops of Rome were covered with advertisements for new books, and became the literary *salons* of their day. Books were multiplied by being dictated to fifty or even a hundred slave scribes at the one time; and this made for speed in copying, even if it did produce books in which mistakes were all too frequent. In this way a book like Martial's epigrams could be copied in about seventeen hours, and an edition of a thousand copies could easily be produced in a month. Book selling and book-distribution were also highly organized and books penetrated everywhere. Varro wrote a series of seven hundred short biographies, and Pliny said that he had succeeded in conferring omnipresence on the people of whom he wrote. *The Life of Martin of Tours* by Sulpicius Severus was a best-seller. A friend of the author found people reading it in Carthage; he went on to Alexandria and found people reading it there; everywhere he went in Egypt he found the book; and even came upon an old man reading it in the midst of the desert. Further, books so copied and so distributed were naturally not nearly so expensive. The first book of Martial has 119 epigrams comprising some 700 lines, and it could be produced and sold for five *denarii*, which is about four shillings.

When Christianity went out to a literary world like this, it, too, began to see the immense value of the written word; and it is not without significance that Mark the first Gospel was almost certainly written and issued in Rome.

iii. The written word was of immense value for the missionary work of the Church. In the very earliest days the class of Church officials called the *teachers* (1 Corinthians 12 : 8) must have been of primary importance. They must have been the people trained and instructed in the facts of the gospel story and in the basic doctrines of the faith, and it is to them that new converts must have been handed over for instruction in the faith. But when Christianity was sweeping across Asia Minor and Europe, it is clear that the travelling missionaries and evangelists could not spend any very long time in one place, and it must have been of immense value to them to have a written account of the life and teaching of Jesus, which they could leave with their converts when they were compelled to move on. To this day it is one of the first tasks of the missionary to learn the language of the people amongst whom he works, and then to translate the gospel story into that language, even if it means, as it often does, that an alphabet has to be invented and a grammar and syntax created. It is easy to see that in its missionary work the Church has no greater instrument and weapon than a written account of the gospel which it seeks to sow among men.

iv. As the years went on, men began to see that the Second Coming was not going to be so immediate as once they had expected it to be. That is to say, they began to see that they were living in a more or less permanent situation. This would completely change their attitude to the written word. Books, which had once seemed to be irrelevant, became of the greatest importance for the teaching of the facts of the gospel story and the setting out and the explanation of Christian belief and the Christian ethic. As the hope of the Second Coming receded more and more into the distant future, the written book became more and more important in the life and work of the Church.

v. As time went on, the Church began to need a prophylactic against heresy. A vital Church will always be a Church liable to produce heresies and deviations. There will never be any heresy when men do not think for themselves, and when they do think for themselves there will always be the danger that they will adventure down the wrong pathways. So in the early Church there were those who misunderstood, and those who twisted and distorted the gospel. Many of them claimed that they had their own private revelations and their own private Gospels. Jerome, thinking of the preface to Luke's Gospel, says that Luke wrote "to correct those who had written with too much haste". He speaks of those who had "attempted without the Spirit and grace of God to draw up a story rather than to defend the truth of history". He compares them to the false prophets who followed their own spirits rather than the Spirit of God. Clearly the Church needed a touchstone of orthodoxy against which false Gospels, distorted theologies, and unethical ethics could be judged; and for that purpose nothing could be so efficacious as an official written Gospel. The rise of heresies made an orthodox account of the facts and the faith of Christianity nothing short of an essential.

The Need of a Written Literature

vi. The Church needed a written literature for apologetic purposes.

(a) It needed a written literature for apologetic purposes in regard to the Jews. We have only to read Acts to see that the Church is founded on the Resurrection. The Church was the Resurrection community; the Resurrection was "the star in the firmament of Christianity". An account of the Resurrection would, therefore, be needed. But the Resurrection was preceded by the Cross, and the story of the Cross would need to be told. Here is the fact which explains the "shape" of the Gospels. Any careful reader must be struck by the apparently disproportionate place the last days of Jesus' life occupy in the Gospels. It is only in the last week that we can anything like follow Jesus day to day. Eight out of Matthew twenty-eight chapters, six out of Mark's sixteen, eight out of Luke's twenty-four, are taken up with the story of the last days; and in John Jesus arrives in Jerusalem in chapter 10 and never seems to leave it again. The explanation of this is that the Gospels, as it were, were written and built up backwards. It was from the Resurrection and the Cross that the story began, and the rest was introduction to that. The supreme events were set down first and set down at most length.

Now here in regard to the Jews there was an acute problem. For the Jews a crucified Messiah was a complete impossibility, for cursed was every man who hung upon a tree (Deuteronomy 21 : 23; Galatians 3 : 13). There was only one argument which could convince the Jews, and that was to take the life and the death of Jesus and to show that every part and action of it was in fact a fulfilment of prophecy, and that all this had long since been foretold. To do this there was needed an account of the outstanding events in Jesus' life, and a record of the prophecies of which they were claimed to be the fulfilments. It may well be that before there ever was a consecutive Gospel there was a book of *Testimonies* which did exactly that. And this is the explanation of the ever-recurring phrase in Matthew that this and that event happened that the saying of the prophet might be fulfilled.

To convince the Jews that Jesus was the Messiah, although He had been crucified, it was necessary to have an account of His life in which it was shown that from beginning to end it was the fulfilment of prophecy; hence a written Gospel became imperative for apologetic to the Jews.

(*b*) When persecution arose, as Jesus said that it would arise, a written account of the life of Jesus was necessary for two reasons. First, it was necessary to have an account of the life and teaching of Jesus to show to the Roman government in order to convince the Romans that Jesus was a good man, and that Christianity was a sound and useful influence, and to convince them that Jesus was not a criminal and that the Christians were not revolutionaries. The written Gospel became a necessity that it might be used as a brief in the defence of the Christian faith, when it was attacked by the state. Second, such an account was necessary for the sake of those who were persecuted. If they could be helped to see that what had come upon them was something of which Jesus had given warning and which He had foretold, and if they could be enabled to see that in their agony Jesus was with them, and that He never called on any man to suffer that which He Himself had not suffered, then the Christians had a

53

great help and support when life became an agonizing thing. The written Gospel was a precious help in time of trouble in the days when the Church was under fire.

(c) When the Christian preachers went out to the world, it would be of the greatest help to them to have an account of Christianity which they could put into the hands of intelligent, thinking people who were interested in this new faith. This is, for instance, what the Prologue to the Fourth Gospel seeks to do. It seeks to express Christianity in language and in categories of thought which the educated Greek could grasp and understand, and with which he was familiar. The Gospel became an apologetic weapon with which to appeal to the thinkers among the Romans and the Greeks. It made the Christian faith something which was not altogether dependent on the voice of a preacher, but which they could ponder and study in their own homes, and in their own groups, and at their leisure.

vii. A written Gospel was of the greatest use for ecclesiastical purposes. The Church was bound to have its problems; the leaders of the Church were bound to have to come to their decisions; the local Churches would inevitably arrive in situations which were puzzling and difficult. On such occasions it was of incalculable help to have a book in which some relevant word or command of Jesus could readily be found. The written Gospels provided the Church with a law by which all problems could be illuminated and by which all actions and all situations could be judged.

It is true that the circumstances of the early Church for long delayed the production of a written Christian literature, but it is also true that the day came when the circumstances of the Church rendered the production of such a literature nothing less than completely essential.

The Words of Jesus

There are still two more particular reasons why a written Christian literature was bound to emerge.

First, there was the supreme reverence for the words of Jesus. The Church emerged from a Jewish society which was accustomed to handing down the most precious teaching by word of mouth; but once the Church had gone out into the larger world the time was bound to come when the words of Jesus would be written down, lest anything of these words of life should be lost. To commit a thing to writing is the most certain way to its fixed preservation, and, for that, if for no other, reason the words of Jesus were bound to be written down.

Second, there was the basic idea of a covenant. A covenant is a relationship between God and man, entered into on the sole initiative of the grace and love of God. But that covenant has its conditions; obedience to the law of God is essential, if it is to be maintained. The covenant, therefore, needs its book of the law (Exodus 24 : 7). The older covenant, the covenant between God and the people of Israel, had its book. But Christ was the end of the law (Romans 10 : 4). The law came by Moses, but grace and truth came by Jesus Christ (John 1 : 17). As Harnack puts it, if the handwriting that was against us was blotted out (Colossians 2 : 14), the handwriting that is for us had to be written down. Hence the new covenant needed its book, just as the old covenant had its book. The idea of a covenant brings along with it the necessity of a book of the covenant, and the New Testament is that book.

At this stage a necessary, and extremely important, question arises. There was this lengthy delay in the production of a written Christian literature. Mark, the earliest Gospel, dates to not earlier than A.D. 60. What was happening to the story in the between time? Was it being in any way falsified, elaborated, distorted? In view of the thirty-year delay can we trust the story in the Gospels? Can we accept it as accurate and dependable, or must we admit that things could have happened to it in the thirty years which made it in its written form less than accurate? We may be quite sure that the Gospel narrative as we have it is a reliable and trustworthy account of the life and words of Jesus for three reasons.

i. There is a wide difference between the quality of the ancient and the modern memory. It is true that the printed book has ruined the human memory. It is now for the most part not necessary to carry a thing in the memory, for at any time a book may be consulted, and the necessary information obtained; but in the ancient world it was largely true that, if a man wished to possess a thing, he had to remember it. Xenophon (*Symposium* 3. 6) tells us of a cultured Greek called Niceratus. Antisthenes asks Niceratus in what knowledge he takes pride, and Niceratus answers: "My father was anxious to see me develop into a good man, and as a means to this end he compelled me to memorize all Homer; and so even now I can repeat the whole *Iliad* and *Odyssey* by heart." The *Iliad* and the *Odyssey* each contains twenty-four books, and each book contains at least five hundred lines, and yet for a Greek this was no uncommon feat of memory. In commenting on this passage T. R. Glover points out that in Finland there are young people who have learned the whole of the *Kalevala*, the national epic, at school by heart—twenty thousand lines in three years. The retentiveness of the ancient memory was many times greater than the retentiveness of the modern memory; in the ancient world there was much less chance of material being either forgotten or distorted.

ii. It must never be forgotten that all the stories of Jesus' life and all the material of Jesus' teaching were constant preaching material. The repeating of it was not dependent on one man's memory; the memory was a communal memory. The stories were continually being repeated and were constantly being used, and any deviation from them would quite inevitably be noticed and pounced upon. For the material of the life and teaching of

Jesus we are not dependent on single individuals; we are dependent on the memory of the Church.

iii. We may put this in another way. The stories about Jesus and the teaching of Jesus very early became stereotyped. Anyone who has to do with children knows that a favourite story has always to be told in the same way, and any deviation from the known and loved form of the story is at once noted, and correction and retelling are at once demanded. It was thus that the form of the gospel material was very early fixed and finalized.

The "Forms" of the Gospel

The realization of this has produced a recent development in New Testament scholarship. It has produced the science of what is called Form Criticism. The basic contention of this science is that the Gospels are composed of units of teaching material, and that these units fall into certain fixed and unvarying forms. Five of these forms have been identified and distinguished.

i. There are *Paradigms, Apothegms,* or *Pronouncement Stories.* These are stories which are preserved solely for the sake of some notable saying which they contain and to which they lead up. The importance lies entirely in the saying, and the events or the incident simply form a setting for the jewel of the saying. For instance, the story of the plucking of the ears of corn on the Sabbath day exists solely to enshrine the saying: "The Sabbath was made for man, and not man for the Sabbath" (Mark 2: 23–28). The story of the call of Matthew exists solely to preserve the saying: "I came not to call the righteous but sinners to repentance" (Matthew 9: 9–13). The story of the tribute money exists to hand down the saying: "Render to Caesar the things that are Caesar's, and to God the things that are God's" (Mark 12: 13–17). All over the Gospels there are these units of teaching which exist to preserve some important saying of Jesus.

C*

ii. There are *Tales* or *Novellen*. These are stories which depict Jesus exercising a wonderful and miraculous power over nature and over human nature. They exist, not to enshrine some saying, but to retain the memory of some significant event. They almost always follow the same pattern. They give a history of the illness, an account of the cure, and the result of the cure. Such a story is the story of the healing of the lame man at the pool (John 5: 1–9); the opening of the eyes of the man born blind (John 9: 1–7); the stilling of the storm (Mark 4: 35–41); the feeding of the five thousand (Mark 6: 32–44). These stories exist to preserve the story, not of something which Jesus said, but of something which Jesus did.

iii. There are *Sayings*. These are sayings of Jesus which are preserved in isolation, without a context. They are collections of the sayings of Jesus made for teaching purposes. The best example of such a collection of sayings is the Sermon on the Mount. In this case the saying is so epigrammatic and so intrinsically memorable that it needs no context and no story as its setting, and it is preserved by itself or in conjunction with other connected sayings.

The two final groups of sayings are described by two words used in a technical sense, and it is to be noted that the use of these words does not necessarily prejudge the historicity of the incidents which they are used to describe.

iv. There are *Legends*. These are stories written for edification about extraordinary happenings involving a holy man or a holy place. The best examples of these stories are the Birth and Infancy stories of Jesus. In these stories there is always the element of the extraordinary, and there is always an extraordinary person involved.

v. There are *Myths*. The Greek used the word *muthos*, myth, in a quite technical sense. He used it of a story which is an attempt "to state the eternal, the spiritual, and the divine in the language and pictures of time, matter, and humanity". Myths are stories which are attempts to state in human language and human pictures that which is essentially beyond human language

58

to state at all. Such stories are the stories of the Baptism, the Transfiguration, and the Temptations.

Into these forms the stories about Jesus and the record of His teaching became stereotyped. They were all used for preaching and for instruction and for missionary purposes. In all cases there was a *point* to be made and presented in the most vivid and memorable and cogent way possible; and, therefore, it was entirely natural that such stories would become fixed and stereotyped and unalterable in form. Just because of this we can be certain that in the years between, the gospel story and the teaching of Jesus did not suffer distortion or elaboration but were handed down in unvarying form. F. C. Grant in *The Gospels* writes: "This has the most important consequences. It means that the Gospels are in fact the possession of the Church; it means that they embody a social tradition, which was the common property of all the Churches, and which did not rest on the recollections of a few individuals. The significance of this is obvious. The memories of a few individuals might be mistaken—since human recollection is notoriously fallible—but the testimony of a group, even if anonymous, is more likely to have been verified, criticized, supported, culled, and selected during the first generation of early Church evangelism. The possibility of fabrication by one or two individuals is completely ruled out."

The thirty years of apparent silence need trouble no one; the circumstances in which the material of the Gospels was handed down are the best guarantee of its reliability.

How the New Testament Emerged

How, then, did the canon of the New Testament emerge, and how was it built up?

Once a Christian literature began to be written it flourished almost luxuriantly. Luke tells us that many before him had taken in hand to give an account of the gospel events (Luke 1:

1). Jerome in his *Prologues to the Four Gospels* tells us of many Gospels—the Gospel according to the Egyptians, the Gospels according to Thomas and Matthias and Bartholomew, the Gospels of the Twelve Apostles and of Basilides and Apelles and of the rest. It would take too long, he says, to enumerate them all, and many, if not all, of them were dangerous and heretical. Equally, many books of Acts had emerged—the Acts of Thomas and Andrew and Philip and Peter and John, the Acts of Paul and Thecla. There were other Apocalypses beside the one Apocalypse of John which gained a place in the New Testament, such as the Apocalypse of Peter. There were not a few books which in certain Churches were at least for a time accepted as Scripture, although they were never accepted by the whole Church. Such books were *The Teaching of the Twelve Apostles, The First Letter of Clement to Rome, The Letter of Barnabas, The Shepherd oj Hermas.* What in this mass of literature was to be regarded as Scripture, and what was not? What was to be completely banished and discarded, what was to be tolerated, and even encouraged, for private reading? And what was to become part of the actual canon of the New Testament?

There was one thing which gave a book prestige and authority, and which set it well on the way to being fully regarded as Scripture; that was, its reading at the public worship of the Church. Once a book began to be so read, it had acquired a status which lifted it out of the ruck of ordinary literature. For a book to be read at the public worship of the Church and for a book to be canonical came to very nearly the same thing. So, then, its being read at public worship was the first thing to single out a book.

But, who was it who took the decision that a book should be so used, or who decided that a book must not be so used, or that its usage in such a way must cease?

The early Church was characteristically a Church of the Spirit, and this, as Harnack points out, had in two ways much to do with this process of selection.

First, there were men who were men of the Spirit *par excel-*

lence. These were the prophets, the apostles, and the teachers. When they gave a decision that decision had to be obeyed. They were the watchdogs and the sentinels and the guardians of the faith. They would be quick to see anything which would damage the faith, which would distort it, which would deflect the minds and thoughts of men from the true way. They could seal any document with their approval, and equally they could eject it with their disapproval. Beyond a doubt this is a right which such men did exercise. Augustine tells us that it was the decision of *sancti et docti homines*, holy and learned men, which prevented the documents of the Manichaeans from being regarded as Scripture. It was such men who under the guidance of the Spirit decided what should be read, and what should not be read, at the services of the Church.

Second, when a congregation of the Christians was meeting as a community of Christ, and when it was conscious that it was so doing, it was always deeply conscious that it was meeting and acting and deciding under the influence of the Spirit. When Paul gave judgment regarding the disciplining of a certain man, he said: "I have already pronounced judgment in the name of the Lord Jesus" (1 Corinthians 5 : 3, 4). Clement writing to the Corinthians dared to say: "What we have said, God has said through us" (1 Clement 59). "We have spoken or written," he said, "through the Holy Spirit" (1 Clement 63). When the decisions of the Council of Jerusalem were announced, they were announced with the words: "The Holy Spirit and we have decided" (Acts 15 : 28). "The Church," says Harnack, "in solemn assembly was especially an organ of the Spirit." The Church, therefore, could and did decide what books it would use in its own public worship, and what books it would mark with its disapproval, and the approval of any book was its first step on the road to its full and final acceptance as holy Scripture.

A question of the first importance now arises. Granted that men of the Spirit, and Christian assemblies acting under the Spirit, had a very great deal to do with sealing books with approval or ejecting them with disapproval, what was the standard which they used to assess the value of a book? By what yardstick was a book judged? The answer to that is clear and unmistakable. The test which was applied to every book was— Is it, or is it not, apostolic? Was it written by an apostle, or at least by a man who was in direct contact with the circle of the apostles? Apostolicity and canonicity went hand in hand. There were reasons for this.

The Apostolic Authority

i. The older any institution grows, the more it is likely to worship its past, especially if that past has been undeniably great and glorious. So Harnack says: "The more perplexing, troublous, and feeble the present appeared, the more sacred became its own past, the time of creative energy, with all that belonged thereto." "Tradition," he says, "always means the need of the present appealing to the authority of the past." The apostles appeared to be clad with a certain aura of forgotten and unsurpassable greatness simply because they belonged to what was looked back on as the great age of the Church.

ii. But there was more than a mere worship of the past, as, indeed, Harnack is careful to say. In the Church the apostles held a place that no others could ever hold. It is quite true that very soon most of them vanished from history, and our knowledge of any of them is astonishingly meagre. But they were always looked on as the future rulers and judges of the Messianic kingdom, and they were always regarded as men who had been uniquely in the confidence of Jesus. Did not Jesus say: "I appoint unto you a kingdom, as my Father has appointed unto me" (Luke 22:29), "He that receiveth you receiveth me" (Matthew 10:40)? Could not Paul say to the Galatians: "You received me as Christ Jesus" (Galatians 4:14)? Were not the twelve foundation stones of the holy city, the new Jerusalem, inscribed with the names of the twelve apostles (Revelation 21:14)? Serapion, speaking about A.D. 200, could say: "We receive both Peter and the other apostles as Christ."

It was a standard idea of the Jews that he who is sent is in some sense equal to him who sends. The delegate is equal to the person who sends him out as his representative on his task. So without irreverence, when they were thinking of the bringing of the Christian message and the Christian truth, they could say that Jesus equals God, and the apostles equal Jesus. Clement of Rome writes: "The apostles were made evangelists to us by the Lord Christ; Jesus Christ was sent by God. Thus Christ is from God and the apostles from Christ. He and they came into being from the will of God in harmony. The Church is built on them as a foundation" (I Clement 42).

The apostles had a place, and a rightful place, as the supreme representatives of Jesus, and as the supreme bearers of His message and interpreters of His purposes. The Church was not wrong when it made apostolicity its acid test.

iii. But there was something perhaps even more important yet. Any historical religion comes to a time when attestation is of the first importance. Attestation, as Harnack says, can be as important as the revelation which it attests. Christianity is founded on certain historical facts, on an entry of God into the historical situation. And the supreme question is—*Are these facts true?* In the early Church that was of the first importance. Many of the heretical sects, such as the Gnostics, claimed a private revelation. Basilides, for instance, claimed that he had received special information from Glaukias, who, so it was said, was an interpreter of Peter. Valentinus claimed that his version of Christianity came by way of Theodas who was, so it was said, a friend of Paul. Some claimed that their particular brand of teaching was based on a private revelation given by Jesus Himself to a chosen few.

Apart altogether from the claims of the heretics within the Church, there is the fact that the pagan world was full of stories of dying and rising gods. There were such stories in every Mystery Religion. Pagan mythology was full of them. And the obvious question was—Is this Jesus only another of these dying and rising gods? Is He no more than the centre of another myth? Or, is He a real person, and did the things which are told about Him really and truly happen?

Obviously only one thing can settle that question—unimpeachable and undeniable attestation going back to eye-witnesses of the facts. Now that is what the apostles alone could give. "We lay it down," said Tertullian, "that the evangelical instrument has the Apostles as its authors, upon whom this duty of promulgating the gospel was laid by the Lord Himself" (Tertullian, *Against Marcion* 4. 2). The only real attestation was evidence brought and given by eye-witnesses of the facts, and that the apostles alone could supply. What the Church had to have was an unbroken human chain of reliable witness going back to the historical facts of the life, the death, and the Resurrection of Jesus Christ. What troubled John Bunyan in the days of his uncertainty was that the Jews thought their religion the best, and the Mohammedans thought their religion the best; and he was afraid that Christianity might be only a *think so* too. Without this unanswerable attestation Christianity could only be a think so; and therefore the Church was abundantly right in making the apostolic witness the foundation of her faith.

The test of any book was—Is it, or is it not, apostolic?—and it was a good and right test. The weight which was attached to this standard of apostolicity may be seen in Tertullian's account of the Gospels. Matthew and John pass the test of apostolicity without question. But what of the other two Gospels? Tertullian goes on to say: "What Mark edited may be affirmed to be of Peter, whose interpreter Mark was: and as for Luke's account, men are accustomed to ascribe it to Paul." Mark's and Luke's claims to acceptance come from their association with men who were apostles.

We are now in a position to examine in detail the actual process of the building up of the New Testament. Before a book can become canonical it has to undergo certain stages of development. It has to be written; it has to be widely read; it has to be accepted as useful for life and for doctrine; it has to make its way into the public worship of the Church; it has to win acceptance not simply locally but throughout the whole Church; and finally it has to be officially approved by the voice and decision of the Church.

The First Christian Books

The first Christian books to form a collection were the letters of Paul. Even within the New Testament itself there is proof that they existed as a collection and that they were well known; for the writer of 2 Peter refers to them as if they were perfectly familiar to his readers, even if he does say that they have their difficult passages, and that certain heretical thinkers have twisted their teaching for their own ends (2 Peter 3: 16). Clement of Rome writing to the Church at Corinth could say: "Take up the letter of the blessed Apostle Paul" (1 Clement 46: 1) in the certainty that his readers possessed it, and that they were prepared to grant it respect at least, if not authority. Ignatius can write to the Ephesians reminding them that Paul remembers them in every letter (Ignatius, *Ephesians* 12: 2). Polycarp, writing to the Philippians, reminds his readers that Paul in his absence wrote letters to them by the study of which they can build them up in the faith which had been given to them (Polycarp, Philippians 3: 2). It is clear that by A.D. 100 Paul's letters had been collected and were widely known and widely accepted.

There is a sense in which this is very surprising. In almost every case Paul was writing to deal with a local and a temporary situation. Dark and dangerous heresies reared their heads, or threatened to arise; practical problems arose; troubles threatened the peace of some Church; and thereupon Paul, not being able to be everywhere personally present, sat down to write a letter to combat the mistaken thinkers, to give guidance for the practical problem, to seek to preserve the peace and unity of the Church.

Paul's letters were far from being theological treatises composed in the peace of a study or a library. They were meant to deal with an immediate situation in a definite community at a particular time. As Deissmann says: "Paul had no thought of adding a few fresh compositions to the existing Jewish epistles, still less of enriching the sacred literature of his nation . . . He had no presentiment of the place his words would occupy in universal history, not so much that they would be in existence in the next generation, far less that one day people would look on them as Holy Scripture."

At the same time, even when we have said that, it must still be remembered that there is no reason why something produced for an immediate situation should not become a universal possession cherished for all time. Every perfect love poem and love song, such as those of Robert Burns, was written for one person and has yet become a universal possession. The music of Bach was often written for Sunday by Sunday performance by his choir in Leipzig and is yet such that it will be performed so long as men everywhere know what music is. There is nothing unusual in a thing being temporary and local and immediate and yet at the same time having in it the seeds of a universal immortality.

It must be remembered that there are times when Paul goes out of his way to remind his readers that he is speaking as no more than a man. "I speak in a human way," he writes to the Romans (Romans 3: 5). "Concerning the unmarried," he writes to the Corinthians, "I have no command of the Lord, but I give my opinion as one who by the Lord's mercy is trustworthy" (1 Corinthians 7: 25). "What I am saying," he says, "I say not with the Lord's authority but as a fool, in this boastful confidence" (2 Corinthians 11: 17). There were times when Paul made no claim to infallibility and made no claim that the divine voice spoke through him.

Still further, it is an astonishing fact that, if we possessed only the book of Acts, we would never have known that Paul had ever written a letter. Luke was the hero-worshipper of Paul, and from chapter 13 Acts becomes to all intents and purposes the biography of Paul, and yet Luke has nothing to say about Paul the letter-writter. Sometimes Paul was by no means sure that his letters would be read by everyone. "I adjure you," he writes to the Thessalonians, "by the Lord that this letter be read to all the brethren" (1 Thessalonians 5 : 27). So little attention was paid to his letters, that we know that many, and in particular a letter which had to do with Laodicea (Colossians 4 : 16), were lost and vanished from sight.

Collecting Paul's Letters

In view of all this how were Paul's letters collected, and how did they become the universal possession of the Church? There were, of course, ample precedents for the collection and publication of the letters of great men. The letters of Plato, of Cicero had been collected and published. How did Paul's letters attain to the dignity of collection and publication, and how did they in the end gain their place of authority as Holy Scripture? At the moment we shall try to answer only the first half of that question, and the answer to the second half will come later. We have certain pointers to aid us in our investigation.

It is significant that in writings before A.D. 90 there is no mention of the letters of Paul and no reference to them. In writings after A.D. 90 there are abundant references to the letters of Paul and abundant proof of full acquaintance with them. In the Synoptic Gospels, even in Luke, there is no trace of Pauline language or ideas. But in the Fourth Gospel, in James, in 2 Peter, and in the Letters of John there is clear acquaintance with Pauline thought and language. Obviously something must have happened to bring this about.

Further, it is significant that from A.D. 90 onwards there came into the Church what E. J. Goodspeed calls "a shower of Christian letters". Consider the beginning of the Revelation.

The Revelation begins with the letters to the Seven Churches. Why should a book begin with a collection of letters? Why should Pergamum read the letter to Ephesus, and Thyatira read the letter to Laodicea, and Philadelphia read the letter to Smyrna? The very way in which the Revelation begins shows that there must have been a precedent for issuing a collection of letters. It may well have been close to that time that Hebrews and James and Jude were written, as well as the letters of John, and most of these are not so much real letters as treatises cast in epistolary form. There must have been a good precedent for letter writing. It is certainly just shortly after this that Clement wrote his letter to Corinth. And it was not very long after this that Polycarp collected and issued the seven letters of Ignatius. Not long after A.D. 90 there was a veritable epidemic of letter writing and something must have given it its impetus.

The deduction must be that it was just then that the letters of Paul were first collected and issued, and that this collection provided the precedent and the stimulus for this outbreak of letter writing.

But how did this happen? It was for long believed that the growth of the collection of Paul's letters was a long, slow process, a kind of natural growth. The idea was that a Church possessed a letter of Paul of its own; it knew that a neighbouring Church also had a letter; it asked for a copy of its neighbour's letter; and so bit by bit the collection was built up, varying from place to place according to the number of letters each individual Church had been able to obtain, and coming to its completion somewhere towards the end of the century.

But in recent times E. J. Goodspeed and John Knox in America and C. L. Mitton in Britain have produced a quite different, and we think a better, theory. We have to explain why between A.D. 60 and A.D. 90 there is no trace of the letters of Paul. These scholars think that the letters of Paul were forgotten, that they were seldom or never used, that they were laid away in some chest amongst the archives of their Churches, covered in dust and buried in neglect, that there was in fact a generation who knew not Paul.

What was it that changed all that? We have seen that the change must have come not very long before A.D. 90. What happened to affect the situation somewhere between A.D. 80 and A.D. 90? The answer is that it was sometime near the middle of that decade that Acts was written and published at least in its first form. The result was that the half-forgotten figure of Paul suddenly burst upon the Church as the most epic, the most heroic, the most colossal and dominating figure in the early history of the Church. Immediately everything about this extraordinary man became precious. Every relic of him must be rescued from oblivion; everything he wrote must be recovered and studied and reverenced. The publication of Acts suddenly reminded men of the half-forgotten greatness of the incomparable apostle to the Gentiles, and it was that which provided the stimulus to the collection and the publication of the letters of Paul.

Making the Collection

Can we go on to say where the collection was made and issued? There are certain indications which point strongly to Ephesus. It was there that Paul spent three years, longer than in any other place in the days of his freedom. It was there that Revelation with its seven letters was published; it was there that the Johannine letters with their knowledge of Paul were published; it was in Asia Minor that the Ignatian collection was made; and it is there that references to the letters of Paul as a collection appear. Ephesus was in any event what Harnack called "the second fulcrum of Christianity", Antioch being the first. Goodspeed and Mitton both regard Ephesians as a letter produced by a disciple of Paul, who was soaked in the Pauline letters and especially in Colossians, as a preface and introduction to that collection. That may or may not be so; ourselves we very much doubt it; but it is in any event not an essential part of the ory. There is good evidence that it was in Ephesus, about A.D. 90, consequent upon the publication of Acts, that the Pauline letters were collected and published.

One last question arises—Can we say who was the moving figure behind this collection? Once again Goodspeed and Knox have a suggestion to make. True, we are now in the realm of conjecture, if not of imaginative reconstruction, but it is a suggestion of such interest and charm that it is more than worth while to look at it.

There is one letter in Paul's collection which stands out as different from all the others—and that is the letter to Philemon. It is a little personal note, quite different from the others. As long ago as Jerome there were those who were saying that it was so trivial that it was quite out of place. It is certainly true that anyone must wonder how it succeeded in gaining an entry into the New Testament at all, and why it was included in the collection. For its inclusion there must be a reason. John Knox writes: "The more anomalous the presence of Philemon in the collection appears, the more significant it must be. The more grounds which can be cited for its exclusion, the more important must have been the ground upon which it was actually included. The very fact that Philemon seems so out of place is evidence that the original editors had very good reason for including it. We are convinced that if we knew that reason we should know something very important about the publication of the Pauline letters." Can we then discover the reason for the inclusion of this little letter, so different from the others?

The letter is a letter about the sending back to Philemon of the runaway slave Onesimus. Onesimus must have become very dear to Paul. His name means "the useful one" and Paul puns on that name. "Formerly he was *useless* to you, but now indeed he is *useful* to you and to me" (verse 11). Now let us hear what Paul says: "I would have been glad to keep him with me, in order that he might serve me on your behalf during my imprisonment for the gospel, but I preferred to do nothing without your consent in order that your goodness might not be by compulsion

70

but of your own free will" (verses 13, 14). Could there be a clearer indication that Paul would very much like to have Onesimus back again? And could the heart of Philemon have been proof against that gentle and courteous and half-humorous appeal?

Let us, then, assume that Paul received Onesimus back from Philemon as his personal helper and attendant. If that is so, Onesimus would become very much Paul's right-hand man.

And now let us go on rather more than fifty years, when, if Onesimus was still alive, as he might well be, he would be an old man. Ignatius is on his way to Rome to fight with the beasts in the arena. As he goes, he writes to the Church at Ephesus and he speaks of their bishop—"a man of indescribable charity and your bishop here on earth" (Ignatius, *Ephesians* 1:3). And what is the bishop's name? *It is Onesimus.* This is to say that at the very time when the Pauline collection was made at Ephesus the name of the bishop was Onesimus. Can Onesimus the bishop be one and the same as the runaway slave, who had twined himself around the heart of Paul?

No man can say for certain, but it is certainly possible. It may well be that, after the publication of Acts had drawn the full-length picture of Paul to the Church, and had given the stimulus to the collection and preservation of everything connected with this colossal figure, in Ephesus Onesimus took steps to collect and publish the letters of the master whom he had loved and who had loved him. And in that collection he included the little letter to Philemon, because it told of himself as a thieving and runaway slave. He left deliberately the record of his shame, as if to say: "See what I was—and see what Jesus Christ did for me." If that is so, it is one of the loveliest hidden romances of the New Testament, for it is a moving thing to think of the great and good bishop deliberately including the letter which told of what once he was, as if to say: "That is what Christ did for me—and he can do it for you."

In regard to Onesimus we are in the realm of conjecture, and all we can say is that we hope that that story may be true. But we may regard it as all but certain that the letters of Paul were collected in Ephesus in A.D. 90 as a consequence of the publication of Acts.

It is true that they are not yet fully Scripture—that final step is still to come—but C. L. Mitton is not wrong when he writes: "It may very well be that this acceptance of Paul's writings as authoritative was the first clear act in the formation of what later came to be the canon of the New Testament."

The Gospels Win their Place

We can now turn to the story of how the Gospels won their place as sacred Scripture.

Jesus Himself wrote nothing and left no written book. It was not His writing but His words which were always quoted. "Remember," said Paul, "the *words* of the Lord Jesus, how he said, It is more blessed to give than to receive" (Acts 20: 35). "Remember," said Clement, "the *words* of Jesus, which he spoke, when he was teaching gentleness and long-suffering" (1 Clement 13: 1). The gospel began by being a spoken gospel, and for long it remained so. The gospel, as Irenaeus says, was first *proclaimed* by the eye-witnesses of the saving events, and it was only afterwards that it was by the will of God handed down to us in the Scriptures to be the foundation and pillar of our faith (Irenaeus, *Against Heresies* 3. 1. 1).

In the early Church it is persons and not books who dominate the scene. It was not through books but through persons that the gospel went out, and that the work of the Church was done. It was not a letter but Peter and John that the apostles sent to Samaria when the power of Christ began to work there (Acts 8: 14). It was not a letter but Barnabas who was sent to Antioch when the great experiment of taking the gospel to the Gentiles began there (Acts 11: 22). Paul wrote letters, but again and again he used Timothy or Titus or Mark as well as the written word

(1 Corinthians 4: 17; 16: 10, 12; 2 Corinthians 7: 6; 8: 6; Philippians 2: 19; Colossians 4: 10; 1 Thessalonians 3: 2).

The very words used of the spread of the gospel are all speaking words. To receive the gospel and its facts is *paralambanein*, and to pass it on to someone else is *paradidonai* (1 Corinthians 11 : 23; 15 : 3), and these are the Greek words which are characteristic of and special to oral tradition. The gospel itself is *euaggelion* which is *good news, glad tidings,* and which only later came to mean a kind of book. To preach the gospel is expressed by the word *kērussein,* which literally means *to proclaim as a herald.* The supreme function of the Christian is *marturia,* which is personal witness. The gospel itself is *logos akoēs,* which literally means *the word of hearing,* the word which is heard (1 Thessalonians 2: 13; Hebrews 4: 2). Certainly in the beginning it was in terms of speech and not of writing, in terms of persons and not of books that the Church thought—and it still remains true that the best epistle of all is a living epistle known and read of all men (2 Corinthians 3: 2).

It may be that in the early Church the order of teachers has never been given its true importance. The teachers are mentioned in 1 Corinthians 12: 28; Acts 13: 1; Ephesians 4: 11; Hebrews 5: 12. The teachers must have been the men in every Christian community who knew the Christian story and who taught it to those who entered the Church long before there were any Christian books. The teachers must have been the living repositories of the gospel story.

But as we have seen the day came when a written gospel became a necessity. We know that the Gospels as we have them are not first attempts. We know, for instance, that before the Gospels emerged in their completed form there must have existed a kind of source book on the teaching of Jesus on which both Matthew and Luke freely drew. To that source book, which of course does not now exist, scholars give the symbol Q, which stands for the German word *quelle,* which means a source. We know also that it is highly probable that there was a book of *Testimonia,* that is, a collection of Old Testament prophetic

73

passages with their fulfilments in the life of Jesus. We know that there must have been many Gospels in circulation, for Luke tells us that many had set their hands to the task of setting out the Christian story, and Luke's implication is that none of these earlier Gospels was wholly satisfactory. We know that the Gospels of our New Testament must have had their rivals and competitors, for we have already noted that Jerome spoke of those "who have attempted without the Spirit and the grace of God to draw up a story rather than to defend the truth of history." Cyril of Jerusalem says: "The four Gospels alone belong to the New Testament; the rest are pseudepigrapha (that is, written under assumed names and falsely attributed to great apostolic figures) and harmful" (Cyril, *Catecheses* 4. 36). Just what the steps in the process were we do not now know, but it is clear that it was not long before our four Gospels triumphed over all their rivals and became supreme. We may say that from the beginning our four Gospels had a ring of truth and the Spirit of God about them, which was obvious to every honest reader and seeker.

A Written Gospel

The first instances when the word *Gospel, euaggelion,* comes to mean a written gospel come from very early in the second century. The *Didachē,* the book known as the Teaching of the Twelve Apostles introduces the Lord's Prayer with the words: "Do not pray as the hypocrites, but as the Lord commanded in his Gospel" (*Didachē* 8. 2). Ignatius speaks of those who say that if they do not find a thing in the chapters in the Gospel they do not believe (Ignatius, *Philadelphians* 8. 2). Polycarp speaks of the apostles who brought us the Gospel (Polycarp, *Philippians* 6. 3).

When we trace the story, we find that the progress of the four Gospels is triumphant and apparently almost unopposed. Justin

Martyr (A.D. 110-165) quotes copiously, although not accurately, but practically never from anything other than our Gospels. Theophilus of Antioch (c. A.D. 170) is the first to quote the New Testament as a definitely inspired work on a level with the prophets of the Old Testament. He quotes "The Word became flesh and dwelt among us" (John 1 : 14) and says that it is the word of a Spirit-bearing man called John. Origen (A.D. 182–250) speaks of "the four Gospels which alone are undisputed in the Church of God under heaven" (Eusebius, *The Ecclesiastical History* 6. 25. 3). Eusebius speaks of "the holy quaternion of the Gospels" (*The Ecclesiastical History* 3. 25). And Athanasius in his Easter Letter in A.D. 367 mentions no other Gospel but our four. It may be said that our four Gospels held undisputed sway long before A.D. 200. Very occasionally we come across quotations from or references to other Gospels, but, as far back as we can go, our four Gospels are the fundamental documents of the Christian Church.

One final point emerges. Did the Church always intend to have four Gospels, or did it ever have the intention of reducing or unifying them into one? The existence of four different Gospels obviously presents difficulties. For instance, the genealogies of Jesus in Matthew and Luke are different; John places the cleansing of the Temple at the beginning of the ministry of Jesus, the other three Gospels at the end; the first three Gospels declare that Jesus was crucified after the Passover, and John that He was crucified before the Passover; there are undoubted differences in the Resurrection narratives in the different Gospels. Did the Church ever have any intention of somehow making the four Gospels into one? There was in fact a deliberate attempt to do so. Sometime about A.D. 180 Tatian produced the *Diatessaron*— *dia* means *through* and *tessaron* means *four*—which was the first harmony of the four Gospels. For a time it was a very influential book, and it seemed possible that it might even supplant the four Gospels. But in the end it utterly failed to do so; it failed so completely that for many years it went completely lost.

In fact the swing away from any idea of one composite Gospel was so complete that we find Irenaeus (A.D. 125–200) insisting that the fourfold Gospel is in the very nature of things: "As there are four quarters of the world in which we live, as there are four universal winds, and as the Church is scattered over all the earth, and the Gospel is the pillar and base of the Church and the breath of life, it is likely that it should have four pillars breathing immortality on every side and kindling afresh the life of men. Whence it is evident that the Word, the architect of all things, who sitteth upon the cherubim and holdeth all things together, having been made manifest unto men, gave to us the Gospel in a fourfold shape, but held together by one Spirit" (Irenaeus, *Against Heresies* 3. 11. 8). Later Jerome was to take the four corners and four rings by which the ark of the Covenant was carried as a symbol of the four Gospels (*Prologue to the Four Gospels* in the commentary on Matthew). The Church unhesitatingly retained the four Gospels and unhesitatingly turned away from any attempt to turn them into one, in spite of the undoubted problems that the fourfold Gospel raised. Why should that have been? It was due to the dominating importance of apostolic witness and apostolic testimony. No document which bore the name of Matthew or of John, no document which was held to go back to Peter or to Paul could possibly be discarded. The Gospels were apostolic, and were, therefore, the essential documents of the Christian faith.

We have still to reach the position when the Gospels are sacred and holy Scripture, but we can already say that midway through the second century our four Gospels held a place of undoubted and unquestioned authority within the Church.

Authoritative and Sacred

As we have seen, the Pauline Epistles and the Gospels came to be regarded as authoritative Christian books as groups, and along with them the book of Acts gained full acceptance. The other books of the New Testament gained authority in a much more piecemeal way, just as the Old Testament Writings did; and we must postpone the story of their acceptance and entry into the canon in order to look at a very important question and a very important development.

The question we are now bound to ask is—How did these books come to be regarded and set apart as *Scripture*? How and when did they cross the line between being books which were regarded as important and even authoritative, and books which were regarded as holy and sacred and inspired and the word of God? How, to put it in one word, did they become canonical? There is more than one answer to this question.

i. Without question the books which are Scripture and which are truly the word of God have about them a self-evidencing quality. They carry their uniqueness on their face. To read them is to be conscious of being brought into the presence of God and truth and Jesus Christ in a unique way. They have always exercised, and still exercise, a quite unparalleled power upon the lives of men. In *The Bible in World Evangelism* A. M. Chirgwin cites a whole series of stories to illustrate this unique power of Scripture. In Brazil there was a certain Signor Antonio of Minas. A friend urged him to consider the claims of Christ and again and again tried to make him accept a Bible. Finally he took the Bible—with the sole idea of taking it home to burn it. When he arrived home, the fire was out, but such was his determination to burn this book that he rekindled it. He opened the Bible so that it would burn more easily and he was just about to throw it into the fire. It opened at the Sermon on the Mount, and he glanced at the words. "The words had in them something that held him. He read on, forgetful of time, through the hours of the night, and, just as the dawn was breaking, he stood up and declared, 'I believe.'"

In New York there was a gangster, recently released from prison after serving a sentence for robbery and violence. He was on his way to join his old associates to plan another exploit in crime. As he went along Fifth Avenue in New York, he picked a man's pocket. He slipped into Central Park to see of what his haul consisted, and he found himself in possession of a New Testament. Since he was too early for his appointment with his fellow-criminals, he sat down and idly began to read the book. "Soon he was deep in the book, and he read to such effect that a few hours later he went to his comrades, and told them bluntly what he had been doing, and broke with them for good." Here is the unique effect of the Bible. Its power is self-evidencing. When Coleridge was asked what he meant by the inspiration of the Bible, he said that he could give no other answer than to say: "It finds me." It is the simple truth to say that the New Testament books became canonical because no one could stop them doing so. There were other books circulating; and there were even other books which in certain Churches enjoyed for a brief time a position in which they might possibly have entered the canon. Many of these books we still possess; and we can say that to read them and then to read the New Testament is to enter into a different world.

ii. Certain books began to be read at the public worship of the Church. We have seen that as early as Justin Martyr (A.D. 150) what Justin called *The Memoirs of the Apostles*, which was the title by which he described the Gospels, were an essential part of the Christian service (Justin Martyr, *First Apology* 1. 67). Clement of Rome wrote a letter to the Church at Corinth, and Eusebius tells us of a letter of Dionysius of Corinth, written about A.D. 175, in which Dionysius says that it was still the custom in his day to read Clement's letter at public worship (Eusebius, *The Ecclesiastical History* 4. 23. 10). And, as Harnack pertinently asks, if the letter of Clement was read, how much more would the much greater letters of Paul be read in the Churches to which they were sent, and in other Churches which knew of them? Books which were read at the worship of the Church had a special position, and had at least begun on the road that lead to their full entry into the canon of Scripture.

iii. But something happened which forced the hand of the Church. About A.D. 140 there came to the Church in Rome a man called Marcion. Marcion was a wealthy and much-travelled ship-owner from Sinope, and he was generous with his money to the Church at Rome. Marcion was a Gnostic, and a knowledge of the broad principles of Gnosticism is necessary to understand Marcion's position and the Church's reaction to him. The Gnostics believed that they possessed a special and an inner knowledge which had come to them direct from the secret teaching of the apostles, or even from the secret teaching of Jesus Himself. It was an essential principle of the Gnostics that the whole universe was founded on a dualism. They believed that spirit and matter were both eternal. God is pure spirit, and altogether good. Matter is essentially flawed and evil. Since matter is eternal, the world was not created out of nothing; it was created out of this essentially flawed matter. God being altogether good could never directly touch or handle this flawed matter. So God put out a series of emanations called aeons. As each aeon was further from God, so each aeon was more and more ignorant of God. As the aeons proceeded down this scale, they became not only ignorant of God, but actually hostile to God. At last in the series there emerged an aeon so distant from God that he could touch and handle evil matter and so create the world. This creating aeon was called the Demiurge. From this it can be seen that the Gnostics believed that the God of creation is quite different from and quite hostile to the true God. It was in this way that they explained the sin and sorrow and suffering and evil of the world. This kind of belief had many serious consequences. It had serious consequences on their beliefs about Jesus. If matter is evil, then Jesus never could have had a real body, and was nothing other than a kind of spiritual phantom with only the appearance of a body. If the body is evil, one of two courses follows. Either, the body must be denied, and starved and kept down in a rigid asceticism, or, the body does not matter, and, therefore, its instincts may be sated and glutted in a wild antinomianism.

But in the case of Marcion and in regard to the canon of the New Testament, Gnosticism had very definite consequences. The Gnostics identified the ignorant, hostile God of creation with the God of the Old Testament, who, they said, was a quite different God from the God of the New Testament whom Jesus had revealed. Sometimes this made them, as it were, turn the Old Testament upside down. If the God of the Old Testament is an ignorant and inferior God, hostile to the true God, then the people he punished are the good people, and the people he blessed are the bad people. So there were Gnostics who believed Cain and Korah and Baalam to be the heroes of the Old Testament, and who actually worshipped the serpent as the representative of the true God. In particular most kinds of Gnosticism obviously demanded the complete and total abandonment of the Old Testament and all those that had to do with the Old Testament as the work and the words of the evil God.

In view of this attitude to the Old Testament Marcion very naturally produced his own canon of Scripture. In it the Old Testament was completely discarded. The Old Testament had held three parts—the Law, the Prophets, and the Writings. In place of the Law Marcion put the *Gospel*. He discarded Matthew, Mark and John as being far too much tinged with Judaism, and in place of them substituted an expurgated version of Luke, from which every Old Testament reference had been removed. In place of the Prophets he substituted the *Apostle*, in which he included ten letters of Paul, whom he regarded as the great enemy of the old Law and the great exponent of the new gospel. The ten letters were Galatians, 1 and 2 Corinthians, Romans, 1 and 2 Thessalonians, Laodiceans (arguing from Colossians 4 : 16 he regarded Ephesians as having been written to Laodicea), Colossians, Philippians, and Philemon. For the Writings he substituted a book of his own called the *Antitheses* in which he compiled a list of Old Testament passages with the New Testament contradictions of them.

This presented the Church with a real problem. Here was a heretic who had compiled a canon of Scripture for himself while the Church still officially had none. The greatest problem of all was the position of Paul. Marcion worshipped Paul barely this side of idolatry. As he saw it, Paul was the great enemy of the Law, and the great bringer of the gospel. For Marcion Paul was the supreme figure in the Church. He held that in heaven Paul sits at the right hand of Christ, who sits at the right hand of God. He held that Paul was the promised Paraclete, the Comforter whom Jesus had promised to His followers. Christ, he said, had descended from heaven twice, once to suffer and to die, and once to call Paul and to reveal to Paul the true significance of His death. As Tertullian ironically put it, Paul had become the apostle of the heretics. Of course, Marcion had to misinterpret Paul to make Paul fit his beliefs, but the impression was that Paul had been annexed and appropriated by the heretics. So, then, Marcion, as Tertullian put it, "criticized the Scriptures with a pen-knife," cutting off the parts which did not suit him, and forming his own canon. The Church had to act.

The Church's Decision

The Church had to act; the Church had to say which books it did regard as holy Scripture. And what was to happen to Paul? Was he to be abandoned to the heretics, or was he to be legitimized? It could be argued that Paul was no apostle because he was not one of the original twelve; it could be argued that his letters contained statements which could be used as a basis for heresy; and it was true that the heretics had wellnigh made him their patron saint. Paul's fate was swinging in the balance. But two things rescued Paul. First, his letters were read in all the

Churches, and were mightily effective in the spread and defence of the gospel. Second, there was the book of Acts. In it Paul was set forth in all the glory of his apostleship, and it was proved in it that Christ had called him and that the Twelve had accepted him. *That is why Acts comes where it does in the order of the New Testament books.* Logically Acts should come after Luke, of which it is the second volume, but in point of fact it comes between the Gospels and the letters of Paul, because it is the bridge between them, and it is the document which guarantees that the letters which follow are the letters of an apostle, and of the greatest of the apostles. Acts provides Paul's title to apostolicity, and, therefore, immediately precedes his letters.

So the Church finally legitimized Paul. It further sought out such additional apostolic materials as it possessed and it finally arrived at a list. That list, it is fairly certain, is embodied in a document called the Muratorian Canon, which takes its name from its discoverer L. A. Muratori, who first published it in 1740. The Muratorian Canon is damaged at the beginning, and actually begins with Luke, but its list of books is as follows—Matthew, Mark, Luke, John, Acts, 1 and 2 Corinthians, Ephesians, Philippians, Colossians, Galatians, 1 and 2 Thessalonians, Romans, Philemon, Titus, 1 and 2 Timothy, Jude, 1 and 2 John, the Apocalypse of John (that is, the Revelation), the Apocalypse of Peter. To this list is added The Wisdom of Solomon.

Here, then, is the first list of the New Testament Canon. The date of the Muratorian Canon is about A.D. 170, and these are the books which at that time the Church accepted as sacred Scripture. The only startling omission is the omission of 1 Peter, and, although it is absent from this list, it may be regarded as certain that the Church even then did accept it.

Already the Canon is taking shape. The omitted books—James, 2 Peter, 3 John, Hebrews—are precisely the books which took longest and had the hardest struggle to enter the canon, and to their history we shall later return. The New Testament is well on the way to being finalized—and the strange thing is that the stimulus to this first step was the work and influence of Marcion the heretic, and the enemy of true Christianity.

Closing of the Books

iv. The process of canonization was, therefore, begun by a heretic, and it is a curious fact that it was also completed by a heretic, or at least completed in principle. How did it come about that the canon of the New Testament was closed? Christianity has always been a religion of the Spirit; according to the Fourth Gospel Jesus had promised to His people ever greater and greater revelations and insights into the truth (John 16: 12). How then did there ever come a time when the Church declared that all the inspired books that could be written had been written, and that nothing more could ever be added to the written word of God? How did it come about that, as Tertullian bitterly put it, "the Holy Spirit was chased into a book"?

In the second half of the second century a change was coming over the Church. The days of enthusiasm were passing and the days of ecclesiasticism were arriving. No more was the Church a place in which the spirit of prophecy was a commonplace. People were flooding into the Church. No more was there the sharp distinction between Church and world. The Church was becoming secularized; it was coming to terms with heathen thought and culture and philosophy. The Christian ethic was tending to become less lofty, and the Christian demand less absolute. Into this situation somewhere between A.D. 156 and 172 there burst a man called Montanus. He had once been a priest of Cybele, and had been converted to Christianity, and he emerged in Asia Minor. He came with a demand for a higher standard and a greater discipline and sharper separation of the Church from the world. Had he halted there, he could have done little but good, and, when Montanism did settle down and purge itself of its extravagances, in the days when Tertullian became a Montanist in A.D. 202, that was the emphasis of Montanist teaching. But Montanus himself went much further. He and his two prophetesses Prisca and Maximilla went about prophesying in the name of the Spirit, and foretelling the speedy second coming of Christ. More, Montanus claimed to be the promised Paraclete, come with a new vision and a new message for the Church. He was convinced that he and his prophetesses were the God-given instruments of revelation, the lyres across which the Spirit swept to draw new music. But this can be a dangerous tendency. As W. D. Niven writes in *The Conflicts of the Early Church*: "When Montanus said, 'I am the Father and the Son and the Paraclete,' he had manifestly crossed the line which separates fervour from extravagance. When one prophetess declared that Christ, in the form of a woman, slept with her, she was on the verge of something more repulsive."

Clearly this was a situation in which the Church had to act. Montanus as a herald of a new spiritual vitality and a new challenge to holiness was one thing; Montanus as the claimant to divine revelation was quite another. It was in face of this new situation that the Church decided that Scripture was closed, that the book of the new covenant was signed and sealed, that the basic Christian documents were written. The result of Montanism was the decision in principle that the canon of Scripture was completed and closed.

So, then, by the end of the second century the Church had reached a position in which the Canon of the New Testament was well on the way to being defined, and in which in principle it was agreed that the production of sacred Scripture had come to an end.

The Final Completion

We must now move on to the final step in the completion of the canon of the New Testament. In this we are fortunate enough to have excellent evidence, for two of the greatest scholars of the early Church made deliberate investigations into the status of the various New Testament books in their day, and the results of these investigations have come down to us.

Origen (A.D. 182–251), who was the greatest scholar the early Church ever had, investigated the matter, and his conclusions are passed down to us by Eusebius (*The Ecclesiastical History* 6. 25. 7–14). The following books he regards as beyond question part of the New Testament—the four Gospels, the letters of Paul, including Hebrews, 1 Peter, 1 John, the Apocalypse. He says that Peter may have left a second letter, "but this is doubtful." Of 2 and 3 John he says that "not all consider them genuine". Acts he does not actually mention in his catalogue but he certainly accepted it. James and Jude he does not list at all. He thinks that Hebrews has some connection with Paul, and he never doubts the excellence of its thought and its right to a place in the New Testament. He may well have known the opinion of Clement of Alexandria that Paul wrote it in Hebrew and that Luke translated it into Greek; he hands down the opinion of some that Clement of Rome wrote it. But his own verdict is: "Who wrote the letter, God alone knows."

Eusebius of Caesarea (A.D 270–340) made a similar investigation. He divided the books into three classes—the *homologoumena*, which are accepted by everyone; the *antilegomena*, which are disputed; and the *notha*—the word means bastard—which are spurious and to be definitely rejected (*The Ecclesiastical History* 3. 25). The *universally accepted* books are the four Gospels, Acts, the letters of Paul including Hebrews, 1 John, and 1 Peter. The Revelation is in an intermediate position. Eusebius lists it with the accepted books, with the comment, "If it really seems proper," and notes that some reject it. The *disputed books* are "the so-called" letter of James, Jude, 2 Peter, "those that are called 2 and 3 John, whether they belong to the evangelist or another person of the same name." Elsewhere he is more definite about 2 Peter (*The Ecclesiastical History* 3. 3), for he says: "We have learned that Peter's extant second letter does not belong to the canon;

yet, as it has appeared profitable to many, it has been used with the other Scriptures." He is also elsewhere (*The Ecclesiastical History* 2. 23. 25) more definite about James. In his notice on the life of James he says: "James is said to be the author of the first of the so-called Catholic Epistles; but it is to be observed that it is regarded as spurious, at least not many of the ancients have mentioned it," and then he goes on to include Jude under the same verdict.

So, then, by A.D. 300 it is quite certain that the New Testament contained the following indisputable books—the four Gospels, Acts, fourteen letters of Paul including Hebrews, 1 Peter, 1 John, and the Revelation with just a tinge of doubt. Still on the fringe of the New Testament were James, 2 Peter, 2 and 3 John, Jude, although Jude was included as early as the Muratorian Canon. We must be quite clear about these books against which there was a question mark. Their usefulness for life and doctrine is not in question; they were freely used and freely quoted; there is no question of their rejection. Eusebius supplies a list of books which were definitely rejected—the Shepherd of Hermas, the Apocalypse of Peter, the Letter of Barnabas, the so-called Teaching of the Apostles. Although Eusebius and Origen list these books as disputed, they never suggest discarding them.

What, then, was the real trouble about these books? The real trouble was that the test of the Church for any book, as we have seen, was apostolicity, and no one was quite sure who had written these books. No one, for instance, questioned the value of Hebrews, but the trouble was that no one knew who had written it, although Tertullian states as a fact that it is the work of Barnabas (Tertullian, *Concerning Modesty* 20). That is why in the end Hebrews was attributed to Paul, although it was clear enough that Paul did not write it, why James was attributed to the brother of our Lord, Jude to another of Jesus' brothers, 2 Peter to Peter, 2 and 3 John to John. These were of a value which no one disputed, and the only way to bring them fully into the canon of Scripture was to shelter them under the wing of an apostle. And it is certainly true that, even if they are not the work of the apostles whose name they came to bear, they are certainly apostolic.

We have very nearly come to the full-grown New Testament. There are still two steps. Cyril of Jerusalem (A.D. 315–386) in his lectures to those being prepared for membership of the Church lists the books of the New Testament—the four Gospels, the Acts of the Twelve Apostles, the seven catholic epistles, one of James, two of Peter, three of John, one of Jude, and lastly "as the seal of all" the fourteen letters of Paul (*Catechetical Lectures* 4. 36). Here the list is complete save only for the Revelation.

And so we come to the final step. In his Easter Letter of A.D. 367 Athanasius finally lists the full New Testament. His letter is such a landmark that the relevant passage of it must be quoted in full:

> There must be no hesitation to state again the books of the New Testament, for they are these: Four Gospels, according to Matthew, according to Mark, according to Luke, and according to John. Further, after these also, The Acts of the Apostles, and the seven so-called Catholic Epistles of the Apostles, as follows: one of James, but two of Peter, then three of John, and after these one of Jude. In addition to these there are fourteen Epistles of the Apostle Paul put down in the following order: the first to the Romans, then two to the Corinthians, and after these the Epistles to the Galatians and then to the Ephesians: further, the Epistles to the Philippians and to the Colossians and two to the Thessalonians, and the Epistle to the Hebrews. And next two letters to Timothy, but one to Titus, and the last the one to Philemon. Moreover also, the Apocalypse of John.

There stands our New Testament, and, apart from the fact that the Catholic Epistles are placed after Acts, as they are in all early manuscripts, not only the list but the order of the books is the order we possess to-day. The Canon of the New Testament is complete.

FOR FURTHER GUIDANCE

E. J. Goodspeed: *An Introduction to the New Testament*, 1937.

F. C. Grant: *The Gospels, their Origin and Growth*, 1957.

A. von Harnack: *The Origin of the New Testament*, 1925. *Bible Reading in the Early Church*, 1912.

J. Knox: *Philemon among the Letters of Paul*, 1959.

C. Leslie Mitton: *The Formation of the Pauline Corpus of Letters*, 1955.

E. Basil Redlich: *The Students' Introduction to the Synoptic Gospels*, 1936. *Form Criticism, its Value and Limitations*, 1939.

A. Souter, revised by C. S. C. Williams: *The Text and Canon of the New Testament*, 1954.

THE FINAL TEST

THERE IS ONE last question to ask—What is it that makes a book sacred and holy Scripture? What is it that makes a book part of the word of God? What is it that entitles a book to a place among the canonical books of the Church? More than one answer has been and still is given to that question.

Authority of the Books

i. The answer of the Roman Catholic Church is clear and unequivocal. A book becomes a canonical book by the tradition, the authority and the decision of the Church. In 1546 the Council of Trent listed the books which for the Roman Catholic Church form the Old and the New Testaments, and then said that if any man did not accept the list whole and entire, each book whole and entire, he was anathema. In the Roman Catholic Church there is nothing more to be said; these books are canonical, and there can be no demur and no dispute.

ii. For the Reformers the case was different. To base anything on the tradition and the authority of the Church was precisely and exactly what they could not do. It has often been said that the Protestant Church did no more than substitute an infallible book for an infallible Church; but it must be remembered that the Reformers were well aware of the critical history of the books of the New Testament, and were fully prepared to give that critical history its full place in the evaluation of a book. When Oecolampadius the Swiss reformer was consulted by the Waldensians about the constitution of the canon of the New Testament, he named the twenty-seven of them, but at the same time he pointed out that six of them—he did not include Hebrews—were *antilegomena,* disputed books, and that they held inferior rank within the New Testament. "The Apocalypse together with the letters of James and Jude and the second letter of Peter and the two letters of John we do not compare with the rest of the books." The Reformers were not in the least fundamentalists, if that word be taken to describe those who insist that every word of Scripture is equally inspired, equally sacred, and equally infallible.

iii. Curiously enough, the one reformer who wrote on the canon in particular took up a position which is very closely connected with the Roman Catholic position. That reformer was Andreas Bodenstein of Karlstadt. He applied one test—the test of attestation. The earlier and the greater the attestation to any book, the higher the rank he gave that book within the canon. On this basis he divided all the biblical books into three classes. The first class contained the five books of Moses and the four Gospels, which are in a class by themselves and which are "the most brilliant lamps of divine truth" (*totius veritatis divinae clarissima lumina*). The second class contained the Prophets—Joshua, Judges, Ruth, Samuel, Kings, Isaiah, Jeremiah with Lamentations, Ezekiel and the Twelve, together with the fifteen undoubted New Testament letters—thirteen of Paul, one of Peter, and one of John. The third class contained the Writings of the Old Testament, and the seven disputed books of the New Testament—he included Hebrews—which occupy the very lowest rank in the canon. If we apply this test, then the Revelation and Hebrews rank below James, Jude, and John, because they were later in gaining a settled and secure and final place in the canon. The one test is—How early did a book gain admission to the canon, and how fully is it attested? The odd fact about this is that to all intents and purposes it settles canonicity by the tradition of the Church, which is precisely what the Roman Catholic Church does.

iv. There is the test of Calvin. Calvin's test may be defined as

witness of the Spirit

the witness of the Holy Spirit within a man answering to the witness of the Holy Spirit within the book. Calvin was no obscurantist. He is quite certain that Hebrews is not the work of Paul, yet he has no hesitation in using Hebrews magnificently for commenting on, for preaching on, and for doctrine. He declares that it is by no means clear who wrote James, and that the author may well not have been the Apostle, but he gladly and willingly accepts the book as Scripture. In regard to 2 Peter Calvin is critically ready to agree that it is not the work of Peter, but that position does not in the least detract for him from the religious value of the letter. He does not comment at all on the Revelation, but that does not mean that he gave it an inferior place. For Calvin the test of canonicity is certainly not ecclesiastical tradition; it is equally certainly not apostolic authorship; it is in the last analysis "religious intuition". For Calvin the ultimate test of canonicity was nothing other than the witness of the Spirit.

Does the Book Speak of Christ?

v. Of all the Reformers Luther had the best defined and in many ways the most logical position. Luther's one test was—Does a book speak of Christ? It is that test which enables Luther to treat Scripture with an amazing freedom. In the concluding paragraph of his *Preface to the New Testament* he writes: "In sum: the Gospel and the First Epistle of John, St. Paul's Epistles, especially those to the Romans, Galatians, and Ephesians, and St. Peter's First Epistle are the books which show Christ to you. They teach everything you need to know for your salvation, even if you were never to see or hear any other book, or hear any other teaching. In comparison with these the Epistle of James is an Epistle full of straw, because it contains nothing evangelical." Here is the touchstone, and then there comes the startling passage: "That which does not teach Christ is not apostolic, though Peter or Paul should have said it; on the contrary, that which does preach Christ is apostolic, even if it should come from Judas, Annas, Herod, or Pilate."

It is for this reason that Luther felt able to make an actual division in his New Testament as it was printed. There were four books to which Luther gave an inferior place. James derives justification from works; it contradicts Paul; it has nothing to say about the life, death, resurrection or Spirit of Jesus. Hebrews in three places (chapters 6, 10, 12) refuses repentance to sinners after baptism, contrary to all the Gospels and all Paul's Epistles. Jude is useless because it has nothing fundamental to the Christian faith, and is only an extract from 2 Peter. In the Apocalypse there are unintelligible and unbiblical images and visions, and the author had the audacity to add promises and threats about obeying and disobeying his words, when no one knows what his words mean. So, then, on the title page of his New Testament Luther printed these four books in a group by themselves with a space between them and the other twenty-three. Further, he numbered the other twenty-three but left these unnumbered. He quite definitely relegated them to a lesser position. He can admire them; he can admire the austerity of James and eulogize the doctrine of Christ as High Priest in Hebrews, but these books do not manifest Christ, and, therefore, they were not for Luther. There was no point in quoting proof texts to Luther. "If," he said, "in the debates in which exegesis brings no decisive victories, our adversaries press the letter against Christ, we shall insist on Christ against the letter."

He is equally severe on the Old Testament. Of Ecclesiastes he said: "This book ought to be more complete; it wants many things; it has neither boots nor spurs, and rides in simple sandals as I used to do when I was still in the convent. Solomon is not its author." The books of Kings and Chronicles are only the calendars of the Jews, containing the list of their kings and their kind of government. "As for the second book of Maccabees and that of Esther," he writes, "I dislike them so much that I wish they did not exist; for they are too Jewish and have many bad pagan elements."

One thing is to be remembered. Luther granted to others the freedom which he demanded himself. He did not wish to impose his own views on anyone. In the Preface to James he writes: "I cannot place it among the right canonical works, but I do not wish thereby to prevent anyone from so placing it and extolling it as seems good to him." In the Preface to Revelation he writes: "In this book I leave it to every man to make out his own meaning; I wish no one to be bound to my views or opinion . . . Let every man hold what his spirit gives him." Of Hebrews he says that it does not lay the foundation of the faith, but nevertheless the writer does build gold, silver, precious stones (1 Corinthians 3 : 12), even if there is wood, straw, and hay intermingled. "We should receive such fine doctrine with all honour." Luther gave to others the rights he claimed himself.

Faith in a Living Saviour

In the last analysis Luther is right. The great test of any book of Scripture is—In it do we find Jesus Christ? For in the last analysis it is not upon any book that our faith is built but on a living Saviour.

The story of the making of the Bible is a story which enables us to see the supreme value of the books of the Bible as nothing else can or does. It enables us to see that these books did not become Scripture by the decision of any Church or any man; they became Scripture because out of them men in their sorrow found comfort, in their despair hope, in their weakness strength, in their temptations power, in their darkness light, in their uncertainty faith, and in their sin a Saviour. That is why the Bible is the word of God. When the Church did make its canonical lists, it was not choosing and selecting these books; it was only affirming and attesting that these already were the books on which men had stayed their hearts and fed their souls. And that is why there never can be a time when the Church or the Christian can do without this Bible which has always been the word of God to His people, and the place where men find Jesus Christ.

FOR FURTHER GUIDANCE

Edward Reuss: *The History of the Canon of the Holy Scriptures in the Christian Church*, 1891.

BIBLIOGRAPHY

This list is not intended to be exhaustive. It includes only books written in English, and only books specially used in the preparation of this study.

Bewer, J. A.: *The Literature of the Old Testament*, New York 1947.

Buhl, F.: *Canon and Text of the Old Testament*, English translation by J. Macpherson, Edinburgh 1892.

Charteris, A. H.: *Canonicity: early Testimonies to the canonical Books of the New Testament*, Edinburgh 1880.

Cornill, C.: *Introduction to the Canonical Books of the Old Testament*, English translation by G. H. Box, London 1907.

Driver, S. R.: *Introduction to the Literature of the Old Testament*, Edinburgh, 9th Edition 1913.

Filson, F. V.: *Which Books belong in the Bible?* Philadelphia 1957.

Goodspeed, E. J.: *Introduction to the New Testament*, Chicago 1937. *The Formation of the New Testament*, Chicago 1926.

Grant, F. C.: *The Gospels, their Origin and Growth*, 1957.

Gregory, C. R.: *Canon and Text of the New Testament*, Edinburgh 1907.

Harnack, A. von: *Bible Reading in the Early Church*, English translation by J. R. Wilkinson, London 1912. *The Origin of the New Testament*, English translation by J. R. Wilkinson, London 1925.

McNeile, A. H.: *An Introduction to the Study of the New Testament*, revised by C. S. C. Williams, Oxford 1952.

Mitton, C. L.: *The Formation of the Pauline Corpus*, London 1955.

Moore, G. F.: *Judaism in the first Centuries of the Christian Era*, 3 volumes, Harvard and Cambridge 1932. *The Literature of the Old Testament*, revised by L. H. Brockington, Oxford 1948.

Niven, W. D.: *The Conflicts of the Early Church*, London 1930.

Moffatt, J.: *An Introduction to the Literature of the New Testament*, Edinburgh, 3rd Edition 1918.

Pfeiffer, R. H.: *Introduction to the Old Testament*, New York 1941. *History of New Testament Times with an Introduction to the Apocrypha*, New York 1949.

Redlich, E. B.: *The Student's Introduction to the Synoptic Gospels*, London 1936. *Form Criticism*, London 1939.

Reuss, E.: *History of the Canon of the Holy Scriptures*, English translation by D. Hunter, Edinburgh 1891.

Ryle, H. E.: *The Canon of the Old Testament*, Cambridge 1892.

Smith, W. R.: *The Old Testament in the Jewish Church*, 2nd Edition Edinburgh 1892.

Souter, A: *The Text and Canon of the New Testament*, revised by C. S. C. Williams, London 1954.

Theron, D. J.: *The Evidence of Tradition*, London 1959.

Westcott, B. F.: *General Survey of the History of the Canon of the New Testament*, 7th Edition, London 1896.

Wildeboer, G.: *The Origin of the Canon of the Old Testament*, English translation by B. W. Bacon, London 1895.